THE GATHERING MURDERS

The mysterious drowning of Ranald Buchanan, an acclaimed Gaelic fisherman-poet, on the first night of the literary festival hardly sets the right tone for the celebrations. For one thing, it rekindles age-old fears about the Selkie, the seal-folk who claim their victims and drag them beneath the waves . . . Torquil McKinnon, Inspector in the Hebridean Constabulary, soon has his hands full. Not only has his old flame, crime writer Fiona Cullen, returned to the island for the festival, but it also appears there is a serial killer on the loose. And dead writers tell no tales . . .

SPECIAL MESSAGE TO READERS

This book is published under the auspices of

THE ULVERSCROFT FOUNDATION

(registered charity No. 264873 UK)

Established in 1972 to provide funds for research, diagnosis and treatment of eye diseases. Examples of contributions made are: —

A Children's Assessment Unit at Moorfield's Hospital, London.

•

Twin operating theatres at the Western Ophthalmic Hospital, London.

•

A Chair of Ophthalmology at the Royal Australian College of Ophthalmologists.

•

The Ulverscroft Children's Eye Unit at the Great Ormond Street Hospital For Sick Children, London.

You can help further the work of the Foundation by making a donation or leaving a legacy. Every contribution, no matter how small, is received with gratitude. Please write for details to:

THE ULVERSCROFT FOUNDATION,
The Green, Bradgate Road, Anstey,
Leicester LE7 7FU, England.
Telephone: (0116) 236 4325

In Australia write to:

THE ULVERSCROFT FOUNDATION,
c/o The Royal Australian and New Zealand College of Ophthalmologists,
94-98 Chalmers Street, Surry Hills,
N.S.W. 2010, Australia

Keith Moray lives in Wakefield, West Yorkshire.

KEITH MORAY

THE GATHERING MURDERS

Complete and Unabridged

ULVERSCROFT
Leicester

First published in Great Britain in 2006 by
Robert Hale Limited
London

First Large Print Edition
published 2007
by arrangement with
Robert Hale Limited
London

British Library CIP Data

Moray, Keith
The gathering murders.—Large print ed.—
Ulverscroft large print series: mystery
1. Drowning—Scotland—Hebrides—Fiction
2. Police—Scotland—Hebrides—Fiction 3. Hebrides
(Scotland)—Fiction 4. Detective and mystery stories
5. Large type books
I. Title
823.9′2 [F]

ISBN 978–1–84617–594–7

To Rachel
Thank you for everything

PART ONE

The Gathering

Prologue

Howard McIvor, the junior partner of McIvor and Son, Funeral Directors, stood in the large dank hallway of the Poplars, wrinkling his nose distastefully at the faintly putrescent odour that seemed to have permeated into the very fabric of the house. He was used to the many smells of death, yet despite himself he always felt ineffably sad when the deceased had died on their own, without anyone present to help or comfort them, or just to watch their passing. Although he himself had never witnessed a death he had a fond belief that there must be something mystical about the moment of transition, when life became extinct and the body turned into the cold lifeless husk that he had to tend.

And this had been a sad case, he reflected. Despite her obvious wealth, the woman had died on her own and the body had started to decay in the Glasgow heatwave. It had been five days before neighbours had been alerted by the rank smell.

He looked down at the blue ceramic urn that he cradled deferentially in his arms, its bottom ever so slightly resting on his developing paunch. Now of course there was no smell, no decay, just a few pounds of off-white ashes.

He felt rather awkward about letting himself in, but those had been his instructions. He cast an eye round the hall that he had seen only once before, on the morning that he and Jock Galbraith, the company's oncall assistant mortician, had taken the woman's body away in the body bag. Now as he waited he focused on the paintings and photographs on the wall. They seemed to be family pictures of grander days and shooting parties at country houses, portraits of lochs, stags on heather moors and highland gatherings.

He turned at the sound of footsteps descending the stairs and saw the tartan-kilted figure appear.

'I'm sorry, I was expecting . . . ' he began; trying to suppress the look of surprise that he was aware had flickered across his face.

'You were expecting me, I think,' came the smiling reply. 'I'm her next of kin. We talked on the phone.'

'Of course.' He nodded at the kilt. 'Macbeth tartan, isn't it?'

A nod of assent. 'I'm wearing it as a token of — respect.'

'I didn't realize that she was a highland lady.'

This time a slight shake of the head. 'She wasn't. She was a Hebridean, from West Uist. The family had lived there since before the days of Bonnie Prince Charlie.'

Howard McIvor smiled wanly like the professional mourner that he was. Then, in his well-practised funeral director's mode of condolence: 'It was a nice, quiet service as you instructed. Just myself and the minister.'

'She wouldn't have wanted mourning. I'm only sorry that I couldn't get back in time.'

'I understand.' He bobbed his head respectfully, belying the train of thought that was actually running through his mind. I understand only too well, he thought. No mourners, keep the expense down, fumigate the house and sell up as quickly as you can. Forget the old dear ever existed. No wonder undertakers ended up as cynical as his father. Or as cynical as he himself was becoming.

He reverently handed over the urn and took his leave, his part now done. No need to worry about the fee; that was one good thing about being a funeral director. The first cheque paid out of the deceased's estate, no matter how small that estate, was the undertaker's fee. Regular income, easy money in a way. Dust to dust, ashes to ashes, a life reduced to detritus that would soon be blown by some wind to ephemeral nothingness.

Just as the breeze was now blowing away the putrescent odour that had so recently assailed his nostrils. His stomach rumbled and he realized that it was almost lunch time. He smiled at the thought, food being close to his heart. He climbed into his car, all sadness for the old woman left behind with her urn.

He was unaware that he was being watched through the net curtains. A smile spread across thin lips as the black BMW funeral wagon drove away.

'So, just you and me now. Shall we have a cup of tea before we go?'

And a few moments later, with a pot of tea, jug of milk and the best china on a tray, the relative sat and read the letter again. 'I remember you said that you used to like the Gatherings, didn't you? And just look at this letter from the Reverend Lachlan McKinnon. An invitation to the Gathering and the West Uist Literary Festival. He's even put in a list of all the invited guests, all the finest Scottish writers from the west coast and the islands. The bastards will be there!'

The relative finished the cup of tea, and then threw it forcefully into the empty fireplace where it shattered into myriads of jagged pieces. Then, picking up the blue urn and unscrewing the lid: 'Who'd have thought that a thirteen-stone woman like you could fit into a little jar like this.'

Slowly, as if enjoying the deliberateness of the action, the urn was tilted over the hearth. 'All you needed was a little help, wasn't it?'

And the recollection of the simplicity of it all brought the smile back to those cold lips. A large dose of insulin on that last evening, then nature just took its course. The Procurator Fiscal hadn't even challenged the GP's diagnosis of death through diabetic complications. The inference being that it could have happened at any time.

'You deserved it! You know that, don't you? Just like that rat of a husband of yours deserved it. He never heard me behind him at the top of the stairs. A quick shove, a tumble and a broken neck. Now you've both paid for what you did. And soon it will all be over.'

The first of the ashes began to fall into the hearth. 'Out with the ashes. Remember how you used to make me clean out the hearth!'

But the photograph on top of the mantelpiece halted the action. The sea and sand of West Uist seemed to beckon.

'But that's perfect! You can be really useful after all. I should have thought of it before.'

The sound of laughter echoed round the room. The first laughter for many a month.

'We're going to go to West Uist. Home — and then the reckoning!'

1

Inspector Torquil McKinnon, 'Piper' to most people on West Uist, opened up the throttle on his classic Royal Enfield Bullet 500 and accelerated along the snaking headland road past Loch Hynish with its famous crannog and ancient ruin, then along the edge of the machair, the sand on peat meadow that intervened between the heather-covered Corlin Hills and the seaweed-strewn beach below. As the engine responded and the exhaust gunned noisily, innumerable rabbits scuttled for their sandy burrows and flocks of herring gulls rose from the dunes to fly screeching and squawking protestingly seawards, towards the stacks and skerries that typified the coastland of West Uist.

It was a glorious summer morning and he was anxious to get to St Ninian's Cave for a practice before he turned in for work. With the Gathering just a couple of days away the policing of the event was bound to stretch the West Uist Division of the Hebridean Constabulary to its limits. That is, all three of them were going to have to work like the devil, especially as two of them would be competing as well.

He adjusted his Mark Nine goggles and grinned to himself at the thought of how peeved the Padre would be this morning. He had two pastoral visits booked, then a myriad of tasks related to the Gathering, or rather to the Literary Festival that was his part in the event. All in all it would mean that the old boy would have to forgo his early nine holes of golf. And that meant he'd likely be in an ill humour for the rest of the day.

He changed down gear with a couple of flicks of his right foot, relishing the gun-like exhaust that made the machine's Bullet name seem so apt, then coasted into the lay-by. He switched off the ignition, dismounted and hauled the bike onto its central stand. Then he stripped off his leather jacket, tartan scarf and Cromwell helmet and removed his pipes from the pannier. He was a well-built young man of twenty-eight with raven-black hair and a handsome if slightly hawk-like face. Crunching down the machair sand to the shade of the cliffs and St Ninian's Cave he was grateful for his thick navy blue Arran jumper, the semi-official West Uist Division police uniform.

The Gathering! The whole life of West Uist had become focused on it of late. The population of six hundred could expect to double, if not treble, during the Gathering as visitors, guests and competitors at the various events streamed onto the island. The Padre and his cronies on the Literary Festival Committee were busy arranging lecture venues; the police — that is, PC Ewan McPhee, Sergeant Morag Driscoll and himself, the newly appointed inspector — were embroiled in car parking arrangements and 'security'; and virtually every other family would be involved in one or other of the events, be it field or track sport, music or dance competition or some type of craft show. And of course, with the kudos of winning an event firing pride and ambition, many an islander could be found practising his or her skill at odd private moments, just as Torquil was about to do with his pipes.

He had timed it just right. The sea had receded down the beach, leaving a fresh crop of multi-hued kelp that sizzled in the early morning sun, filling the air with the fresh tang of brine and iodine. Torquil scrunched across the shingle in his heavy buckled Ashman boots and stood at the entrance to St Ninian's Cave and sighed.

'*Latha math*! Good Morning!' he called in both Gaelic and English, as he always did when he came to practise in the great basalt-columned St Ninian's Cave, just as so many island pipers had done before him. His uncle, Lachlan McKinnon himself — known locally as the Padre — had practised there in his younger days and had introduced Torquil to its special magic when he was a wee boy. 'Show respect, Torquil. St Ninian's Cave is the best teacher a piper could ever have.'

And as Torquil's echoing voice died away in an instant he smiled. Nature had carved this sea cave beautifully, so that it seemed to hold a sound perfectly for a moment and the piper was able to actually hear the correct pitch of his playing. A natural tape recorder for a musician. He walked into the centre of the great cave, which was as large as a church hall, and hoisted his pipes over his shoulder. He blew up the bag and the inevitable tuneless start-up sounded as uncontrolled air passed through the large bass and two tenor drones before he began to play. His fingers moved over the chanter holes as his left elbow moved bellow-like on the bag to produce a continuous flow of air through the chanter and the three drone pipes.

Torquil ran through his repertoire of warm-up exercises, to get his finger movements right. He played a string of ever more complex movements — *leumluaths, taorluaths, grace notes* and *birls*. Then he played a strathspey and reel, then a hornpipe and jig, before concentrating on the one that he found the hardest, the *piobaireachd*, the pibroch. At the last three Gatherings Torquil had won cups for the strathspey and the jig, but the pibroch had eluded him. And he needed that if he was to claim the title of Supreme Champion of the Outer Isles, awarded to the winner in all three categories. The trouble was that the pibroch was so difficult to execute well, and Hamish Munro, Pipe Major of the South Uist Pipe Band, had nipped the pibroch prize away from him on those past occasions, thereby depriving him of the chance of gaining the Silver Quaich, that most revered of piping prizes. It had not been won for many years.

Yet one Silver Quaich already rested permanently atop the mantelpiece at the manse, inscribed with the winner's name — Lachlan McKinnon, 1967 Supreme Champion of the Outer Isles.

A sour note from a faulty fingering grated around the cave as Torquil thought with a tinge of envy about his uncle's, the Padre's, skill. The old boy had magic in his fingers, even now when he rarely played, since golf had taken over as his number one passion — after motorcycles, literature and his faith, of course. Yet sometimes it helped Torquil to conjure up an image of the Padre standing beside him as he used to do when he gave him piping lessons in the past.

'Play smoothly, laddie. Stroke the holes, don't dab at them. You sound like a constipated crow!' Then he would sing out a series of vocables, the system of oral teaching devised hundreds of years ago by the great MacCrimmons, the hereditary pipers to the clan MacLeod. And putting his *feadan*, his practice chanter, to his lips he would play sublimely, to emphasize the technique and the sound of how the pipes should be played: '*hiodroho, hodroho, haninen, hieachin*!'

'I'm going to win that damned pibroch this year,' Torquil promised himself. And he began to play one of the three pibrochs that he had chosen to put before the judges at the Gathering. Each piece ran to fifteen minutes and had to be played entirely from memory, the judges deciding which of the three they would hear. This morning he was practising '*Cha till MacCruimean*' — 'No more MacCrimmon,' a piece composed by Donald Ban MacCrimmon himself, after a vision of his own death, which was to prove true during the 1745 Rebellion.

The three parts of the pibroch built one upon the other, the salute, the lament and then the gathering, each interspersed with the theme, the *urlar*. Torquil played each movement: *siubhal, taorluath* and *crunluath*, finishing of with the *urlar* again, all the while looking out to sea, where South Uist could be dimly seen as a low blue shadow on the horizon. And as he looked and played, the words of the chorus ran through his mind:

The breeze of the bens is gently blowing,
The brooks in the glens are softly flowing;
Where boughs their darkest shades are throwing,
Birds mourn for thee who ne'er returnest!

Good, he thought. Not so much like a constipated crow today, Torquil. That was more like it.

And out of the distant haze, coming round far off South Uist and Bara he saw a shimmering speck on the horizon. He let the mouthpiece drop from his lips as the last note of the pibroch reverberated around the cave. 'The ferry,' he mused. He nodded as he walked out of the cave into the sun. 'Time for work then. I best be in the office when the ferry gets in.'

* * *

Fiona Cullen stood on the upper viewing platform of the Macbeth ferry, *Laird o' the Isles*. She had stood there smoking a cigarette, watching the hazy blue silhouette of West Uist slowly grow in size as the ferry ploughed through the waves towards it. She was an elegant, slim woman dressed in black motorcycle leathers. Strikingly attractive by any measure, the contrast of her black garb with her short-cut platinum-blonde hair made her stand out.

But to stand out at that moment was the last thing that Fiona wanted. Especially when her writing had thrust her into the limelight of celebrity. Newspaper, magazine and chat-show interviews had done well for her, had boosted her sales into a comfort zone and had opened doors into several areas of society. She had loved it all; revelled in each new experience that came along, the parties, the affairs, the betrayals and the deceits. All good plot material for a writer. Then things just seemed to get too complicated. There seemed to be so many things going on in her life, so many complex threads that had somehow merged together to make the tangled skein that she was now living through. She needed to get away, to sort out her head, to immerse herself in her writing. And that was why the Gathering and Literary

Festival had seemed such a godsend. To give a lecture, do a bit of plotting on the already overdue crime novel, and maybe even to see a few old friends — perhaps even one in particular. It had all seemed serendipitous, so right.

Catching the overnight ferry from Oban to Lochboisdale in South Uist had been the first part of her plan. She had powered up the west coast roads on her scarlet Honda Fireblade, boarding the ferry at the very last minute. She had avoided the crowded restaurant and bar to take a solitary supper of cheese sandwiches and coffee in her cabin. Upon arrival at Lochboisdale she had showered, drunk a cup of boiled water, and then found her way up to the viewing platform. It had all gone well until Genevieve Cooper spotted her from the lower deck.

Damn! This is going to be awkward, she thought to herself. How do I tell my agent it's time to part company?

Genevieve arrived slightly breathless a few moments later, but not alone. She had a group of eager beavers with her. A coterie of literary groupies that she had undoubtedly ensnared over breakfast. Genevieve was good at that. A big woman in every sense of the word. Rubinesque and overbearing.

'Fiona! Where have you been hiding from

your Genevieve?' she cried, advancing along the platform at the head of her troop. She engulfed Fiona in her arms and squashed her against her ample chest. Then before Fiona could get a word out in return, she had turned to the group, hands outstretched like a circus master. Her cheeks bunched up into natural chuckle pouches of gleeful ownership. 'Ladies and Gentlemen, I'm sure you will all have read some of the works of Fiona Cullen — *the Queen of Scottish Crime* — my most celebrated client!'

Then followed a cacophony of banter, adulation for Fiona's books and a scrabbling for concealed paperbacks and autograph books. Fiona went into smiling autopilot: pure literary cocktail chatter and well-practised looped copperplate autograph signatures that she could do in her sleep.

Inevitably, after a flurry of question and answering, the troop dispersed as another writer was spotted and targeted for assault. Fiona waved as they went, all mumbling promises to attend her lecture at the Festival, and to buy drinks, books or to wish her well. A few, as usual, had managed to inveigle her into agreeing to cast an eye over their own amateurish scribblings.

Genevieve lit a Gauloise and held out the packet to Fiona. 'Darling, did you see how well the 'Queen of Scottish Crime' thing went down?' she asked in her usual staccato voice. 'They loved it. I have such plans for the new book. What did you say it was called again?'

Fiona suppressed a sigh. '*Dead Writers Tell No Tales*. It's a word play on E. W. Hornung's book, *Dead Men Tell No Tales*. Genevieve I — '

'Hornung! He was Arthur Conan Doyle's brother-in-law, wasn't he? Raffles the gentleman thief and all that. That's good Fiona, that's really good. I like the title, it implies — '

'Genevieve, we need to talk.'

But the agent was smoking furiously, like some sort of engine working up steam. 'I know, I know, Fiona. We need to get together on this one before the Festival gets going. So that we can have a united front. Allegra McCall, your editor from Castlefront, will be about and I need to give her some ideas I'm working on.'

'That's what we need to talk about, Genevieve. About Allegra and about — '

'About Allegra? Oh she's all right. A bit stand-offish, I know, but with a bit of pushing here and there,' she said, with a grin as she jokingly prodded Fiona in the side, 'I think we can get her to go for a bigger print-run this time. I've had a boxload of photographed bookmarks made up for the Festival. You know, the photograph with you at that Japanese Festival in Osaka. It looks — '

'You've what?' Fiona suddenly demanded, clasping Genevieve's wrist and preventing her from raising the Gauloise to her full scarlet lips. 'You've had bookmarks made up with my photograph? Genevieve, how could you. That's so — so tacky!'

Genevieve was momentarily nonplussed. Then she smiled beneficently and shook her head reassuringly. 'No, they're not tacky, darling. They're good, very good, very flattering.' She smiled as she pursed her lips coquettishly and added: 'Smouldering, exotic.'

'You should have asked me first, Genevieve. And that's been half the trouble lately. You just never consult me. That's why I'm leaving.'

Genevieve stared at her uncomprehendingly. 'Leaving? You mean you're cross? Have I upset you, darling? I'm sorry and I'll make it up, I promise.'

But Fiona had picked up her helmet as the ferry's horn blast was followed by the tannoy message advising all passengers to make their way to their vehicles as the ferry would be imminently arriving at Kyleshiffin. She pulled on the helmet and strapped up. 'It's just one thing after another, Genevieve. I think it's time that we parted company. I'm going to look after my own affairs from now on.' And snapping the visor closed she made for the stairs.

The colour drained from Genevieve's face as she stared at Fiona's retreating back. 'But you can't leave now,' she mouthed, her jaw muscles tightening. 'You can't possibly leave me now. I won't let you.'

* * *

The crescent-shaped harbour of Kyleshiffin thrummed with activity as a couple of hundred passengers in their cars, minibuses and bicycles rolled off the *Laird o' the Isles* ferry. The main street, a half moon of multi-coloured shop fronts and businesses that had passed down through the generations, resembled an island kasbah. Flags and bunting hung from the lamp posts proclaiming a welcome in both English and Gaelic for the West Uist Gathering and Literary Festival. Locals and holiday makers ambled around market stalls clustered along the harbour wall, inspecting lobsters, crabs, local crafts and second-hand ephemera. Beyond the wall a flotilla of assorted fishing boats, yachts and launches bobbed up and down in the water, attesting to the fact that Kyleshiffin was both a working and a pleasure harbour.

Fiona Cullen's Honda Fireblade roared along the crescent as she made her way to the Bonnie Prince Charlie Tavern, where she had booked a back room without the distraction of a seaview. She planned to do some serious work on her novel.

A slim leather-clad woman on a powerful machine, she attracted many appraising and admiring looks as she rode by.

One such observer was Ranald Buchanan, the proprietor of the Kyleshiffin Antique Bookshop, Tobacconist and Fishing Tackle Emporium. As he looked over the shoulder of the customer he was serving he saw the Fireblade zip along the road, the svelte rider conjuring up the pleasing image of a Peter Pan on wheels in his artistic mind. Then he turned his attention back to the important matter in hand. Money — the making of!

'You will be liking this Dragon-fly model, made with these old hands of mine, I am thinking,' he said with a grin, as he handed the package over.

The American in the Chicago Bears baseball hat beamed, his unlit cigar clenched between perfectly capped teeth. 'Looking forward to it. I've fished all over Scotland, but this is my first time in the Hebrides. I hear tell that the fish give you good sport round here.'

Ranald Buchanan ran his fingers through his unkempt pepper-and-salt beard that hung like a curtain to cover his scrawny neck with its prominent Adam's apple. He was a small thin man with shifty grey eyes that had about them a permanent rheumy look. People who had heard of him attributed that look to his poetic vision, as if he were able to see things beyond the sense of most. Those who really knew him, however, put the look down to a surfeit of peatreek, the illicit whisky that he manufactured himself at his croft and stored in his shed on the Machair Skerry to the North of Kyleshiffin, and which he sold illicitly to the cognoscenti throughout the Western Isles.

'*Am fear a thèid a ghnàth a-mach le lìon, gheibh e iasg uraireigin,*' Ranald rattled off in melodic Gaelic. Then, as the American raised his eyes in bewilderment, he translated with a grin: 'If you go fishing a lot, sometimes you'll catch fish. That is to say, you will be finding that most of the creatures of the Isles are singularly intelligent.'

The American departed with a laugh after having left a substantial tip alongside his payment for a 'cut-price' telescopic rod and three over-priced handmade flies, prepared by Ranald Buchanan, the celebrated Gaelic Bard, himself.

Ranald grinned to himself as he surveyed his emporium, half antiquarian bookshop, half angler's paradise-cum tobacconist. There were about half a dozen browsers scanning the bookcases and piles of books while the melodic lilt of the Gaelic filled the room. Bloody brilliant is what I am, he thought to himself. A brainwave to tape-record my own poems, first in Gaelic, then in English, and have them on a permanent play-loop to the customers.

A look of pleasure flashed across a young man's face and he elbowed his companion, a young woman dressed in the modern 'bag-head' style. Ranald grinned at them, as they approached with copies of his latest volume of poems, *Songs of the Selkie*, with both Gaelic and English versions printed alongside each other.

'I can't believe it! Served by Ranald Buchanan, the Gaelic Bard himself,' the young man enthused. 'Would you sign these for us?'

Ranald took the books and scrawled his name in biro on the flyleafs. '*Is ann a tha 'n sgoileam air an sgoilear*,' he said. ' 'It's the scholar that's the talker', as we say in the Gaelic. You must be reading them aloud to get the real meaning.'

The girl flushed. 'God, that Gaelic is so sexy.'

The fisherman-poet shrugged his shoulders modestly, allowing himself to take a lingering stare at her apple-shaped breasts. He smiled as she flushed in response. Sixty-eight years of age, yet with the loins of a lecher half his age, Ranald Buchanan flirted outrageously whenever the opportunity arose. He loved the advantage that his new-found celebrity had given him.

'Are you here for the Gathering or the Literary Festival?'

'Both,' replied the man. 'We're sort of honeymooning. We graduated this year. We both did Scottish Studies at Dundee, and we're having a fling before we have to find jobs.'

'*Is fheàrr sìor-obair na sàr-obair*,' Ranald mused. 'Better get steady work, rather than hard work. Don't be killing yourselves.'

The couple paid and made their way with their purchases. The girl looked back as they reached the door and Ranald pouted suggestively, bringing another instantaneous flush to her cheeks.

That one would fall like a ripe peach given the opportunity, he thought lasciviously. He sighed at the image of having her in the heather, of cuckolding her new husband. Someone will do it soon, he thought with a malicious grin.

The Kyleshiffin town clock struck ten o'clock and Ranald inwardly cursed, dragged back as he was from his reverie. The letter had said to meet at the Machair Skerry at half past ten. 'It will be to your great profit,' the letter had informed him. 'Destroy this letter and tell no one or you will be unmasked!'

He did not know exactly what to make of it, since his life had been full of so many peccadilloes that it was entirely possible that someone knew something Ranald would rather remained secret. Yet the fact that the writer mentioned profit made him feel more excited than fearful of some sort of blackmail. Profit was always close to his heart.

Fighting back the urge to telephone the only person he ever called for advice, his mentor, he noisily set too and announced the presence of the 'honesty box' in the middle of the room, strategically placed beside a pile of his volumes and a small selection of works by other authors who were scheduled to attend the Festival, then he let himself out.

He crossed the road and climbed down the steps leading to his little boat. He struck a light to a roll-up, started up the little outboard motor and chugged his way out of the harbour. As he did so a red Enstrom Shark helicopter roared overhead zooming towards distant South Uist. Ranald snorted. That will be the laird himself, off to bring home his guests in style, he thought.

It took him twenty minutes to round the coast and tie up on the iron spike that was the only mooring point on the crude stone jetty of the Machair Skerry, the little sandy islet which he owned and where he came to be alone to write. It was only about a hundred yards or so across the water from his croft, which he had christened *Tigh nam Bàrd*, the House of the Bard. Behind the cottage were three corrugated outhouses in which he distilled his peatreek and kept a goodly quantity of cases until they were ready to be moved out to the Machair Skerry for final 'distribution'.

The sign at the edge of the skerry proclaimed: PRIVATE PROPERTY — POET AT WORK.

And that seemed to do the job. It kept all and sundry away, even the police, although in their case he knew perfectly well that they knew all about his still and turned a blind eye. Being one of the Padre's oldest friends helped, of that he had no doubt.

But now the inevitable question was on his mind. Who was this mysterious letter writer who wanted to meet him on his own Machair Skerry at half-past ten? There was no one about, and as he approached from the sea, he knew well enough that there was no one approaching from the water.

'*Latha matha*,' he called out. 'A good day to you.'

No reply. He climbed out of the boat and approached the old wooden shed that smelled strongly of the creosote coating that he had given it the week before. He noted that the lock hung untouched from the latch, so no one had forced an entry.

A hoax! Who would go to all that trouble? And the letter had said he'd be unmasked if he didn't go. And what was that about profit? The bastard!

He unlocked the door and carefully peered inside, relieved to see nothing but his lobster creels and the assortment of spare rods and tackle that he kept there whenever he took expensive paying customers out for a day's fishing. And they were all in order, so no one had gotten into his secret press behind, where he kept a subsidiary pot and copper coil, and where every fortnight he ran it for a couple of days to make three quarts of peatreek. Strangely, it actually produced a slightly richer distillate than his big still. This he sold as the *crème de la crème*, a particular favourite of the local fishermen. No one worried about the smoke that rose when the Gaelic Bard was 'in residence', working on a masterpiece they said, and no one noticed the smell for the skerry winds dispersed it continuously.

He suddenly realized that his heart was racing and that his brow was moist. Then it came — the spasm in the chest, followed by the inevitable fear that this would be followed by the big one.

'Bugger, this angina!' he cursed, reaching for the glyceryl trinitrate spray that Dr McLelland insisted he carry with him at all times. But as his hand dipped into his pocket and touched his hipflask, he grinned despite the pain and shook his head. '*Uisge-beath' a' bhalaich mhòir,òlamaid gun taing e*,' he whispered, unscrewing the top. 'The water of life, I'll drink it and spit in the devil's eye.'

There was a splash from outside, as if a fish had broken water. He whirled round and saw the black shape emerge from the sea. At first he thought it was a seal. Then head and shoulders rose from the water and he saw a facemask, snorkel and wetsuit.

'*Co tha'n sud*? Who is there?' He spluttered as the fiery peatreek hit his stomach and he took a step backwards, tripped and felt himself flailing for a moment to land on his back on the dirt floor of the shed.

The figure was out of the water by the time he had sat up. He watched with eyes agog as mouthpiece and facemask were removed to reveal staring eyes that seemed to burn into him.

'Still poisoning yourself with that moonshine?'

Ranald Buchanan blinked at the face in disbelief. 'It cannot be you!' he exclaimed. 'You look just like — '

'That's to be expected, isn't it?'

'Aye, but now you're — different! I was expecting — '

'You were expecting what? A Selkie? Strange isn't it that you should have chosen that subject for your latest volume of doggerel.'

Ranald ignored the heavy sarcasm in the voice. 'It was you who sent the letter?'

'Yes me — your nemesis.'

The Gaelic Bard fumbled for a roll-up and struck a light with his battered old lighter, hungrily drawing on the smoke, like a man trying to suck life into his body. As the nicotine reached his brain, adding to the effect of the peatreek, he felt his nerves calm a little. Enough to ask without his voice quaking, 'Nemesis, eh? Does that mean that you are here to threaten me?'

But despite his bravado he felt the beginning of another spasm in his chest. There was a momentary silence while the Gaelic Bard felt the eyes bore into him, as if discerning that he was in some discomfort, in a state of near panic.

A hollow laugh was followed by words that soothed the poet's nerves. 'Or maybe I'm here to let you profit from your — fame.'

A cunning smile crossed Ranald Buchanan's lips. 'You know about me then? Aye, it's good having friends in high places. They've made me a bit of a celebrity.' He took another swig of his peatreek. 'Ye've nae hard feelings, then? You ken that I only did what I thought was for the best.'

The figure turned and looked out to sea. 'Oh I have very hard feelings actually.' And then nonchalantly: 'Is that where it 'happened'? Or rather, where it didn't . . . '

Ranald heaved a sigh. 'Aye! The boats were out for two days but they didn't find anything.'

'Except for a scarf.'

Ranald inhaled deeply on his roll-up. 'It was done properly.'

'But you ruined her life. Several lives as it happened. I assume she's in the family plot.'

'Aye, in the cemetery.' He ground his

roll-up under his heel and looked up, fear beginning to resurface. 'You've got revenge in your heart, then?'

The eyes bored into him again, and then a hand shot out, grabbing his shirt and pulling him forward to within a few inches of the cruel mouth. The lips softened for a moment as a smile played across them. 'Let's call it — *poetic justice*!'

2

The Kyleshiffin police station was a converted bungalow off Lady's Wynd, which ran parallel to Harbour Street. Torquil was at work in his office poring over a map of the island, as he sought to ensure that there would be enough parking facilities. The influx of tourists and visitors from the ferry for the Gathering and Literary Festival had worried him since it had brought an unprecedented number of cars to the island. West Uist's road system simply would not cope. He began to curse his uncle's idea about the Literary Festival.

The commotion from the duty desk was not helping him concentrate. For five minutes he had worked on, hoping that PC Ewan McPhee would calm the situation, but instead, the latter's voice seemed to be getting louder and louder and less controlled. With a sigh he laid down his pen, opened the door and walked into World War III.

It seemed as if a crowd of belligerent faces was haranguing Ewan, Torquil's six-foot-four, red-maned constable. A champion hammer-thrower and Western Isles wrestling runner-up at the last Outer Hebrides Games, he was underneath it all a sensitive and self-effacing twenty-three-year-old. And indeed, although his voice was getting louder it seemed that it was desperation rather than anger that was behind the rise in decibels.

'Ah, Inspector McKinnon!' cried a stout, lank-haired individual in a mustard-coloured anorak. 'Now we'll maybe get some sense, instead of this great lummox's police officiousness.'

'We'll be having less of your lip Calum Steele,' said PC McPhee. 'I've told you already that parking permits will be required for all vehicles during the Gathering.'

'But the Press need to be exempt, don't they, Torquil? How can I cover all the events if I can't get between them without having to park in your 'official' car parks?'

Torquil suppressed a grin. Calum Steele, the editor and chief reporter, meaning the only reporter, of the *West Uist Chronicle*, had been a pain in the backside ever since they had been in Miss Melville's class at the Kyleshiffin School together. He saw himself as an investigative journalist and man of letters, rather than the custodian of the local rag.

'Perhaps we could issue a special permit for Calum's Lambretta, Ewan?' Torquil suggested.

Calum beamed. 'Good lad, Piper. That's just what I've been trying to tell this hammer-throwing hammer-chewer.'

And while Ewan good-naturedly filled out the appropriate docket, Torquil turned and smiled at Annie McConville, a chirpy old lady who had been standing beside the newspaper editor drumming her fingers on the desk, a large Alsatian dog and a small West Highlander sitting obediently at her feet. She was famed throughout the island for running a dog sanctuary; taking in all waives and strays from across the Outer Hebrides. 'This by-law is stupidity itself, Piper McKinnon,' she protested with an indignant shake of the head.

'And which by-law is that, Annie?'

'These pooper-scooper bins! You're discriminating against us doggie-owners. I'm going to be up to my armpits in pooper bags.'

'It will be necessary during the Gathering, Annie,' Torquil explained. 'As a responsible dog-owner you'll be aware of the threat of toxoplasmosis.'

Annie pursed her lips tightly together. 'So that's it! The taxman again. It's nothing but tax this and tax that. Well let me tell you, the taxman will be getting no more out of me.'

'I said *toxoplasmosis,* Annie,' Torquil began. But it was in vain for Annie had turned and begun pushing her way towards the door. People immediately made way for the Alsatian. 'Not a penny!' she cried with contempt.

Together Ewan and Torquil worked their way through the crowd of complainers, enquirers and general busybodies who had nothing better to do than to join a crowd in case they missed something. They were thankful when Sergeant Morag Driscoll came in from her round of the town to lend a hand. She was only a few years older than Torquil, but had seen life. Pretty, despite a slight weight problem, she had been widowed at twenty-six and left to bring up three lusty youngsters on her own. She was efficiency personified, a multitasker who juggled work, home and children with an effortless no-nonsense approach.

'Gosh Morag,' said Ewan half an hour later as the three were sitting sipping mugs of his well-stewed tea. 'Glad I am that the Gathering and this Literary Festival of the Padre's isn't going to be every week.'

Morag beamed. 'Och, you just have to be more organized Ewan. What you need is a lassie and a brood of bairns to make you realize how to keep order.'

Ewan put his mug down and frowned. 'But I'm fed up with half the enquiries we're getting the now. Bed and breakfast lists, places to eat. It's an information centre they think we are, rather than a police station. And as for putting up all these signs, isn't that a job for those two lazy special constables to be doing?'

Torquil laughed. 'Now you know very well that the Drummond twins will still be out with their fishing boat until later this morning. They'll pull their weight right enough once the Gathering gets in full swing.' He winked at Morag. 'What you really mean is that you're not getting enough time to practise the hammer.'

Ewan failed to detect the humour in Torquil's voice. 'Not a bit of it. I'm out at cockcrow every morning, tossing my practice hammer over the roof of the back shed. I . . . '

He hesitated and looked suspiciously at his friends and senior officers, both of whom had burst into laughter. 'You've been spying on me, haven't you, you pair of scunners!'

Torquil leaned over and clapped the big PC on the shoulder. 'Well Ewan, I see the holes in the shed roof when I go past in the mornings. There seems to be an extra one every day. And I saw Jessie, your mother, scowling at a big one in the shed door before I came in this very morning. She said she was thinking of reporting you for criminal damage.'

Morag almost choked on a mouthful of tea and a slow grin spread across Ewan's face. 'Aye, that's the sort of thing my maw would say.' Then standing up and whirling his arms in a two-handed circular movement, he explained. 'I'm experimenting with the angle of trajectory, you see. If I can just — '

He was interrupted by the door squeaking open. A motorcyclist came in, clad in black leathers and matching black helmet with its black opaque visor down. A fraction of a moment later a tall silver-haired lady of about seventy, dressed in a tweed suit, swathed in a russet-coloured silk shawl entered then deftly bypassed the motorcyclist to reach the desk first.

'Ah Torquil, thank goodness,' she said. Then her words just tumbled out. 'You're my last hope. I really must find Ranald Buchanan to organize him properly for his poetry reading. It's too bad that I have to do all these things myself, but some of the other members of the committee just aren't doing what they said they'd be doing. And now Ranald has done a runner. His shop is open, but he has that honesty box thing of his out, so goodness knows where he is.'

Torquil had risen and approached the desk,

his heart having sunk at the sight of Miss Bella Melville, one of the Padre's fellow Literary Festival Committee members, and also the Kyleshiffin schoolteacher until her retirement some six years previously. Having taught half of the island's population she was used to being listened to and obeyed. And Torquil's erstwhile teacher's scarce-concealed dig at his uncle did not go unnoticed. 'So — er — what exactly do you want me to do, Miss Melville?'

Over his shoulder he heard Morag begin to deal with the motorcyclist, with a friendly greeting, then: 'Is it a parking permit that you'll be wanting?'

Miss Melville's curt retort brought his attention back to heel. 'You must get your uncle to have words with him. Track him down. He's the only one the old fool listens to.'

'But Miss Melville, I'm rather busy at the moment.'

'Really? You seem quite quiet to me, Torquil. Now come on, we need some action. I'm depending on you, laddie.'

She left as she had entered, in a hurry. Torquil heaved a sigh of relief then turned to see Morag and Ewan grinning at him. 'Look who's here, Torquil,' said Morag, nodding at the motorcyclist who had removed her helmet and was holding it under her arm like a knight's helm.

'Hello Torquil,' said Fiona Cullen. 'Old Miss Melville hasn't changed a jot, has she?' Then when he just stood staring at her, Morag took a hand. 'Maybe the two of you would like a cup of tea,' she said, raising the flap on the desk and pushing Torquil towards his office. 'Ewan, how about a fresh pot of tea — and try not to stew it this time.'

* * *

Torquil watched Fiona stroll round his small office inspecting his framed degree, citations and press cuttings. 'So, quite the high-flyer, aren't you — *Inspector McKinnon*,' she said, whirling round and sitting on the corner of his desk with a coquettish smile. 'Last time I was here you were just a wee PC, like big Ewan out there.'

Torquil clicked his tongue. 'And when you left me you were just a reporter on the *West Uist Chronicle*. Calum Steele's side-kick. And look at you now. A famous crime writer.' He pointed at her expensive leathers. 'And you're obviously doing well.'

Fiona folded her arms and gave him a mock interrogatory look. 'So tell me, Inspector McKinnon, how many of my books have you read? All seven of them? Two? One even?'

Then, before he could reply, she wrinkled her nose in that delightful way that used to send shivers up his spine, and stabbed her finger at him with a laugh. 'I'll bet it's none! And why's that, Torquil? Because unless you've changed I bet that *Zen and the Art of Motorcycle Maintenance* still has pride of place by your bedside.'

'You bought that book for me, Fiona.'

'That's true, Torquil. And I left it by your bedside so that you could think of me. Just like I sent you a copy of each book as it came out.'

'I still have them, Fiona.'

'Unread! You never even wrote to tell me — ' she paused for a moment then went on in a mock piqued tone, 'you never even wrote and pretended that you'd read them.'

Torquil made a point of drinking his tea. 'You left me, Fiona. Don't make out it was the other way round.'

Fiona pushed herself off the desk and slumped down in the chair opposite him. She pouted. 'Oh Torquil, I hoped it wouldn't be like this. Not with us. I want us to be good — '

'What, Fiona? You want us to be what? Good friends?'

Fiona sighed with exasperation. 'I had to get away from this island, Torquil. It wasn't that I wanted to leave you. I always meant to come back.'

'After you made your fortune. So are you back here to stay now? Or is it just for the Festival?'

'I think you know that I have to be here for the Festival, Torquil. I'm sure the Padre told you that I have to present the prizes at the short story competition I've helped him to judge.'

Torquil shook his head in disbelief. Damn it, he thought. So the Padre was in on this, the interfering old buddy! 'I didn't know you were judging anything with the old rogue,' he said. 'In typical fashion he never deigned to tell me. I'll have to have words with him.'

Fiona caught his mood and nodded in agreement. 'And so will I! Why don't we go and berate the old rapscallion together.' She leaned over the desk and smiled. 'But let's go as friends, Torquil. Please!'

He had never been able to resist that smile of hers. He shrugged good-naturedly and handing her the untouched mug of tea, he chinked it with his own. 'As friends, Fiona,' he added with a wink.

And with the ice broken, if not melted and gone, they sat back and chatted about the good times at university, then back on West Uist when they had been a couple. Their idyll was broken by the sound of raised voices from the duty desk outside the office.

'I'm telling you that I saw her come in and I know that is her motorcycle parked outside this police station!' boomed the voice of Calum Steele. 'As the editor of the celebrity page, I demand that you let her know I am here to interview her.'

'God, is he still at the *Chronicle*?' Fiona whispered.

'He is the *Chronicle*,' grinned Torquil. 'This seems like a good point to go and see the Padre.'

'But you heard him, my bike is parked outside.'

Torquil reached for his Cromwell helmet and goggles. 'Come on, Fiona, I've got a *real* bike out the back.'

* * *

True to its name, Torquil's Royal Enfield Bullet sped along the west road from Kyleshiffin around the Devil's Elbow.

'Goes like a dream, not bad for a classic old girl, is she?' Torquil shouted over his shoulder, as the dial hovered on the 65 mph mark.

‘She’s OK if you like wee bikes,’ Fiona called back. ‘I ride a Fireblade. It’s got real Oomph!’

‘Is that so? Well it would be no use on West Uist. Can it do this?’ And so saying he patted her arms about his waist, a signal for Fiona riding pillion to hang on. And as she tightened her grip about him, he felt a surge of adrenaline that coincided with him raising the front wheel from the road then accelerating to dart off the road through a fringe of bracken onto a sheep track leading across the moors that led up towards the Corlin Hills. As the machine skidded, sped and leapt along over the two-foot-wide track he felt Fiona cling on as she laughed behind her visor. It was as if they had climbed on the Bullet and gone back in time five years.

Five minutes later they rejoined the road for half a mile before sweeping into the gravel court of the manse, where Torquil had lived with his uncle ever since the boating accident that killed his parents more than twenty years before. Dismounting and entering the house it was clear that the Padre was not at home.

‘His clubs have gone,’ Torquil announced after poking his head round his uncle’s study door. ‘Looks like he’s skiving from school!’

‘And I see that motorbikes are still high on your mutual agenda,’ Fiona said, laying her helmet down on the hall table and pointing to the assortment of carburettor components, oil filters and gears which lay on spread-out oil-stained newspapers along the length of the hall. 'You can tell that this is a bachelor household. Does the Padre still have his Ariel?'

'Aye, the Red Hunter is his pride and joy and he still coaxes it around the parish. But he's also got a Vincent Black Shadow, and together we're rebuilding an Excelsior Talisman.' He nodded at the various engine parts. 'The carburettor is proving a bit tricky.'

'You two were always thick as thieves,' said Fiona lightly. 'As well as being a hazard to the environment.'

Torquil smiled. It was true; he had acquired many of the Padre's interests. The pipes and classic motorcycles were twin passions that they shared. He shoved her playfully towards the door and then led her through the garden to the wrought-iron gate, then across the road to the style that led directly onto the ten-acre plot of undulating dunes and machair that the Padre and several local worthies had converted and transformed into St Ninian's Golf Course. An honesty box hung from the fence for the two pounds green fee per round. Not exactly St Andrews, but it was not far off being a golfing purist's dream. The fairways were tractor-mown once a week, the greens were sheep-grazed to near billiard table smoothness and the bunkers (in the beginning at least) had been excavated by generations of rabbits. Although it had only six holes, players went round three times, each hole having three different tees to introduce different lines of approach and different hazards for errant balls. Carved through steeply undulating dunes covered with patches of thistles and gorse, it was bounded on one side by the Corlins and on the other by the Northern Atlantic Ocean. Because of the forthcoming Gathering, the course seemed deserted.

Torquil looked at his watch. 'I reckon he'll be coming up the eighth by now.'

And cresting the rise they saw him on the 'eighth' green lining up a putt, a tall good-humoured man of sixty-four years with the ruddy cheeks of the outer islander, a pair of thick horn-rimmed spectacles perched on a hawk-like nose and a veritable mane of silver hair that perpetually defied brush and comb. Most incongruous on a golf course these days, however, was his attire, for he was wearing a clerical dog collar and a white summer jacket. He was puffing furiously on a battered old briar pipe as he concentrated. When the putt fell in he punched the air with enthusiasm and Fiona began to clap.

The Padre spun round, immediately recognizing his nephew and the pretty leather-clad girl with him. 'Fiona! The Lord be praised! You're back on hallowed turf,' he called as he covered the ground between them in a short run, sweeping her into his arms and hugging hard. Then immediately releasing her he held her at arm's length, grinning like a schoolboy. 'Did you see that! That was a birdie. If I can par the ninth I'll have played the front nine in two under par.' He playfully prodded Torquil in the stomach with his putter. 'What d'ye think of that laddie?' With a couple of sharp raps he tapped his pipe out on his putter blade and shoved the old briar into the breast pocket of his jacket.

'Great Uncle, but I need . . . '

'It's so good to see you again Lachlan McKinnon,' said Fiona, circling the Padre's waist with an arm and walking him back to his bag of clubs. 'I've loved reading all those awful stories you sent me, simply because I was looking forward to seeing you and the old place again.' She sighed. 'I had almost forgotten how beautiful it is.'

Lachlan McKinnon looked over his shoulder at his nephew and grinned. 'Is that so, Fiona? I've been kind of looking forward to seeing you back on the island myself. Now come on, watch me get a par at the ninth for my best round ever.'

And he teed up his ball between the blue tee markers, the middle series for the second circuit of six holes. It was a straight shot played over a slight hill to a green in the hollow between the cemetery on the left and the church of St Ninian's on the right. A bunker in front of the green caught shots played short, while both the cemetery and the church grounds were out of bounds. Like all of the holes on the course it was named, its particular sobriquet being *Creideamh*, meaning 'Faith'.

Lachlan took a couple of easy practice swings, then set up and sent the ball on a perfect parabolic flight over the hill.

'Good shot!' enthused Fiona. 'Can I have a go? I haven't swung a club in anger for a few years.'

The Padre beamed and fished out a ball and a tee from his pocket and handed her his five-iron. 'I remember you had a way with you at sport. Just swing it easy lass, and don't try to knock the cover off the ball.'

Fiona imitated the Padre's moves, swinging twice, then set up for her tee-shot. Being quite petite she swung flat and from inside to out, the result being an inevitable hook. The ball started off on target and then curved viciously towards the left, disappearing over the hill in the direction of the St Ninian's cemetery.

'I think it'll be a dead ball,' said the Padre with a grin. 'If you'll excuse the pun.'

No sooner had he said it than there was a howl from the other side of the hill that could have been either pain or rage.

'Lord hae mercy!' whispered the Padre. 'I did not think to shout 'Fore!' ' He shouldered his bag and strode off. 'Let's just hope we didn't do any damage to anyone.'

A few moments later they had mounted the crest and could see Lachlan's ball on the green about a yard from the flag. More alarmingly, however, they saw a man on his elbows and knees beside a gravestone in the middle of the cemetery, his hands clasped around his head, as if he was supplicating before an ancient altar. As they approached they could hear a low moaning, and alarmed lest he be badly injured, they all three broke into a run.

Torquil vaulted the fence and reached him first, relieved to find that he was not badly injured, albeit clearly in pain from a bump on his forehead that was swiftly rising. He was a good-looking, well-built man in his late forties, dressed in an open-necked shirt and corduroy trousers.

'Why Professor Ferguson!' exclaimed Torquil, helping him up and gingerly inspecting the bruise. 'Are you all right?'

Professor Neil Ferguson, head of the Department of Marine Archaeology at the University of the Highlands was well known on West Uist, since he had been visiting the Western Isles to study their unique artificial islets or crannogs ever since he had been a Ph.D. student some twenty years previously. He shook his head. 'I'm just shaken, I think. I wasn't expecting it.'

'We should have shouted 'Fore',' said the Padre. 'I do apologize.'

'Actually, I suppose it's me that should apologize,' said Fiona, slowly approaching along the gravel path. 'Only I'm not sure that I want to.'

Torquil and the Padre looked at her in surprise for a moment. Then the Padre cut in, well versed as he was in dealing with awkward situations. 'I'm glad you could make it to the Festival, Neil. Your latest book on the crannogs is selling well already, I'm told.'

'Thank you, Lachlan. I'm actually going to be taking some friends diving round the Loch Hynish crannog over the next few days. You'll probably see a lot of us during the Gathering.'

The Padre pointed to the graves about him. 'Can I — er — can I help you here?'

The professor shook his head, having caught Fiona's persistent look of disdain. 'No thanks Padre, I was just — er — looking for a grave. But it's fine, it'll keep for another time. I — er — must go.'

And once he had gone Fiona nonchalantly hooked her arm through the Padre's. 'Now come on, Lachlan. Let's see you hole that putt for your new record.'

Torquil fell behind them for a few moments until the Padre turned and signalled for him to catch up. Torquil immediately quickened his pace, shrugging off the fleeting impression that someone had been watching them during their strange encounter in the cemetery.

⋆ ⋆ ⋆

Over a frugal lunch at the manse, where the Padre celebrated his best ever nine with a half bottle of claret, Torquil listened as Fiona and his uncle talked about the short story competition that they were judging together.

'There were three decent ones, I thought,' said Fiona, sipping sparkling water. 'The kidnapping one, followed by the poisoned ice lollies, then by the murderous vicar.'

Lachlan guffawed. 'I agree, although I'd hoped we could maybe ditch the vicar! And I think the order is right as well, so the job's all done. Agreed?'

Torquil coughed. 'Not entirely, Uncle. Miss Melville came into the station this morning and rather suggested that you need to get your finger out and organize Ranald Buchanan. He won't play ball with her about his poetry reading or something. She seems to think you're the only one he'll listen to.'

The Padre quaffed some wine then wiped his mouth with his serviette. 'Och, the woman's havering. The poetry reading is not until the day after tomorrow. Time enough. I'll track him down tomorrow.'

'Your funeral, Uncle.'

'Not yet, laddie! Not yet!' And rising, he dusted crumbs from his jacket. 'Fiona, it's grand to see you. But as I bet you can imagine, I need to complete the eighteen holes now that I'm breaking records, then I'll sort out my parish visits and nip in to help with the Festival organizing.' And plucking his cold pipe from his breast pocket and a dilapidated old tobacco pouch from a side pocket he took his leave.

'He hasn't changed a bit,' Fiona said with a snigger when they were alone. Then she added, 'Come on, Inspector McKinnon, let's wash up and you can take me back. I have to sneak into my room at the Bonnie Prince Charlie so I can prepare my talk for tomorrow without my agent or my publisher seeing me.' She wrinkled her nose and laughed, 'Or Calum the nose!'

The Bullet hurtled along the road round Loch Hynish in glorious sunshine. Fiona tapped Torquil's shoulder and called out, 'Can we stop a while at the 'wee free ferry'?'

Torquil nodded, and coasted in to the side of the road, then waited while Fiona dismounted, before switching off the engine and hauling the machine up onto its stand. He pulled his goggles up and watched Fiona pull off her helmet and then stroll down the brae to the edge of the loch. Further along, moored to a small jetty, the 'wee free ferry', as the rowing boat was called locally, floated invitingly. Fiona pointed across the water to the crannog, the artificial Iron Age islet in the middle of the loch. In the centre of the crannog, rising from a swathe of bracken and surrounded by dwarf rowan trees, was the ruin of the old tower, once thought to have been a three-storey affair, but now a bare six or seven feet at its highest.

Fiona picked up a pebble and skimmed it in the direction of the crannog.

'It's beautiful, isn't it?' she sighed. Then

after a moment with a touch of petulance, 'And that idiot has made a name for himself out of it and all the other crannogs in the Hebrides!'

Torquil had joined her and also selected a skimming stone to send scudding across the surface of the loch. 'You mean Professor Ferguson? He's an expert on them, Fiona. Probably the foremost expert on crannogs in the whole of Scotland. What was all that about on the golf course?'

Skimming another stone and focusing her attention on the ripples, Fiona replied, 'He was responsible for my friend's death and I'm going to expose him.'

'Come again, Fiona?'

She sighed and sat down on the jetty. 'My friend Esme wrote a book, a New Age book about the crannogs. She was into Celtic tradition, runes, that sort of thing. The book did well and she was invited on a programme for Scottish TV. But they also invited high and mighty Professor Neil Ferguson along at the same time and he rubbished her! Humiliated her on television. She went home that evening and slit her wrists.'

'But you can't hold him responsible for that, Fiona.'

'Can't I? He's a fraud, Torquil, and I'm going to expose him.'

'How? In a book?'

She shook her head, as if to dismiss any more talk about the professor. She looked him straight in the eyes for a few moments, then reached up and tousled his hair. Snaking her arms about his neck, she drew him towards her, to her waiting lips. Torquil didn't resist, despite his fear of letting this woman get too close to him again. Once more it seemed as if the years had been blotted out and they were together as they were meant to be.

At last, when they parted, she said, 'Do you remember the last time we used the wee free ferry, Torquil? We made love in the ruin.' She nodded towards the boat. 'Can you still row?'

Torquil smiled wanly. 'It's too soon, Fiona. We need time.'

She bit her lip. 'Does that mean you want there to be time for us?'

'I do.'

The noise of a powerful engine approached from the east and they looked up in time to see an Enstrom Shark helicopter zoom over the tops of the Corlins, heading south. On its side it bore the well-known AME entwined logo of Angus MacLeod Enterprises, superimposed on tartan-patterned doors. 'That's the laird flying back in time for the Gathering,' mused Torquil.

Fiona drew his head back and kissed him with her full lips. 'And talking of the great Angus MacLeod, are you going to his ceilidh tomorrow night?'

'The party before the Gathering? Of course. I'm the only practising piper on the island so I've been given the honour of piping in the haggis. All the rich and influential will be there, as well as the paying punters. The Padre as one of the Festival convenors will be in his element, poking fun at the establishment as usual.'

'I'm glad you'll be there, Torquil. But I'd like you to be my partner.' She squeezed the back of his neck. 'I'd feel safe having my own police protection with me.'

3

The first day of the West Uist Literary Festival, the day before the Gathering itself, was almost in full swing. This was mainly because Miss Bella Melville and her band of faithful helpers, mostly all former pupils, had been whipping round Kyleshiffin organizing venues, workshops, bookstalls and lecture times. The reason it was slightly less than full swing was because the Padre had not quite lived up to his promises.

As Torquil walked along Harbour Street, after being buttonholed by his old teacher, he grinned at the thought of how his uncle was likely to receive an earbashing for failing to pin down Ranald Buchanan. Despite the fact that Torquil had told her the Padre was planning to track the fisherman-poet down today, she was less than impressed.

'He never came back to his shop yesterday and he left it unattended all night.'

'He often does that, Miss Melville,' Torquil protested. 'I think it's the poetic image that he likes to foster. Footloose and fancy-free.'

Miss Melville harrumphed disapprovingly,

just as she used to do during her teaching days. 'Poetic *spirit*, more like. I don't know why the police — that's *you*, Inspector McKinnon — allow him to keep producing that illegal peatreek of his. He'll send himself blind one day.'

Torquil grinned. '*Cha choir gòisinn a chur an rathad an doill*. A trap should not be laid in the way of a blind man,' he said, raising his eyebrows quizzically.

Miss Melville suppressed a smile. 'Oh you always were too clever for your own good, Torquil McKinnon.' She patted his arm. 'You just tell that uncle of yours I'm expecting a result.'

Torquil walked on, passing several posters with pictures of Fiona and the words 'Scotland's Queen of Crime Speaks Out and talks about her latest novel, *Dead Writers Tell No Tales*.'

The carnival atmosphere lifted his spirits, which were already high. Fiona! Had she really walked back into his life? He ambled along between the stalls with his head in the clouds, successfully dodging Miss Melville's helpers who were dishing out flyers about the various literary events.

* * *

PC Ewan McPhee was in a similarly light mood when Torquil entered the station. He was still dressed in his waterproof trousers, having just returned in the police *Seaspray* catamaran from the morning patrol round the Kyleshiffin harbour area. He was whistling as he wrote up his report in the day book.

'I think I've met someone, Torquil,' he confessed. 'A girl as bonnie as a picture.'

Torquil grinned and sat down. 'Give me the facts then. Where, when, how?'

Morag came through with a tea tray and the biscuit tin. 'She's a writer!' she said enthusiastically, indicating that Ewan had already confided in his sergeant.

'I met her last night when I was out for my run. You know, my usual five-miler, down to Loch Hynish, then back through town before going across the school field to home. She was coming out of the Lobster Pot restaurant.'

'So you stopped to chat to her?' Torquil prompted.

'Not exactly. I didn't actually see her. The earphones on my CD-walkman had come out and I was fixing them. I wasn't really looking where I was going and I — well — I bumped into her and sent her flying into the doorpost.' He blushed and grimaced as Torquil and Morag laughed softly. 'I know,

I'm a clumsy bugger, but there you have it.' He sucked air between his lips. 'She was good about it, though. And she's a real good-looker. Long red hair and tea bag eyes.'

'He means hazel, I think,' Morag interjected.

'Aye, hazel would be right. And a figure to die for. Anyway, we got talking and I invited her for a drink at the Bonnie Prince Charlie.' He laughed. 'We got on like a house on fire. I even managed to tell her a few things about West Uist.'

Torquil and Morag exchanged expressions of approval.

'She writes travel books,' Ewan volunteered. 'Izzie Frazer's her name. She's here for the Gathering and Literary Festival. She said this was her first visit to West Uist and she was gathering information. She has a wee jotter and she notes everything down. She said that's how she writes. Just absorbs everything about a place and then bashes it into some sort of readable order. Anyway, she was really interested about Ranald Buchanan and his book, and wanted to know all about the Selkie.'

'What did you tell her, Ewan?' Torquil asked, sipping his mug of tea, relishing Morag's brew instead of Ewan's usual stewed version. 'You need to be sure that you didn't give a version that the island folk wouldn't approve of.'

Ewan puffed his cheeks in mock chagrin. 'I'm a police officer, Piper,' he said sarcastically. 'I give the facts and just that. I told her about the Selkie being a seal man, who turns into a handsome lad when he comes out of the water. He usually chooses the best-looking girl and courts her, then leaves her wi' a bairn before disappearing off to sea. Then years later, he comes back and claims his child.'

'And what did your lady friend say to all that?'

'She laughed and said that the old local legends were important in travel books, they were what gave colour to a place.' He smiled as he recounted his tale. 'Then she said she'd better be careful in case I was a Selkie in disguise.' He took a great slurp of tea, sighed with pleasure, then continued, 'And she's coming to watch me practise my hammer the night.'

'Quite the Don Juan, isn't he?' said Morag, dunking a digestive biscuit in her tea.

Torquil was about to reply when the door opened and a large woman wearing a large, flowing floral shawl swept in. She had large red lips, bright red fingernails and had a smoking Gauloise cigarette clamped between the first two fingers of her right hand. She waved extravagantly at the desk. 'Ah, the local gendarmerie!' she said airily. 'I have an absolute emergency on my hands. I've lost an author.'

Morag greeted her at the desk with a smile. 'Any particular author, madam? We have a Literary Festival on at the moment and there are quite a few of them around.'

'Oh not just any author. *My* author, the Queen of Scottish Crime — Fiona Cullen.' With the legerdemain of a conjurer she produced a blue-and-white bookmark with a photograph of Fiona Cullen set against a painted Japanese screen and laid it down on the counter. 'I'm Genevieve Cooper, her agent. I simply have to see her now, because she has a lecture to give at one o'clock and we have so many things to talk about.' She puffed her cigarette and blew out a thin stream of smoke. 'She's just vanished — like smoke.'

Morag coughed and half-turned to see Torquil give the slightest of headshakes. Then she picked up the bookmark. 'Fiona Cullen,' she said, pensively. 'I've read a couple of her books. She's good. If we see her we'll let her know that you're looking for her shall we.'

Genevieve Cooper nodded. 'I can ask no more. But tell her it's urgent.' She reached for the door handle. 'Oh you couldn't direct me to the nearest turf accountant, could you?'

'Try Henry Henderson's at the end of the harbour,' Ewan suggested.

'I have to place a bet for a friend,' Genevieve volunteered, before sweeping out.

Once she had gone, Morag turned to Piper. 'I wonder if that could be construed as the police withholding information, Inspector McKinnon? So why the silence?'

'I'd say it was more to do with protecting a friend,' Torquil replied with a grin.

⋆ ⋆ ⋆

Twenty minutes later Genevieve left Henry Henderson's Bookmakers and looked up guiltily as she heard her name called. A maroon four × four was parked by the side of the road next to a Lambretta scooter. A smart thirty-something woman dressed in a grey pin-striped trouser suit was leaning against the door of her car talking to a scruffy mustard-anorak-clad individual. He was jotting things down in a small wirebound notepad.

'Allegra! Am I glad to see you,' the agent called, crossing the road and hugging the Castlefront publisher. 'I've just been — looking for Fiona.'

Allegra McCall eyed Genevieve suspiciously through round wire-framed glasses that added a touch of severity to her well-groomed image. She was a good-looking woman with high cheekbones, a well-chiselled nose and tightly pulled back hair tied in a pony tail. 'I didn't know that Fiona gambled,' she said, meaningfully. Then added, 'Genevieve, this is Calum Steele, the editor of the *West Uist Chronicle*. He knows Fiona from years back.'

'Aye, you could say I taught her how to write,' Calum said, shaking hands. 'I was her boss on the *Chronicle*. That's before she left the island and you folk made her famous.'

'But now she's disappeared and I need to run over a few things with her,' said Genevieve. 'I saw her on the ferry, but she seemed a bit — stressed.'

Allegra seemed to stiffen a tad. 'And I need to talk to her myself about the next book. I think it's going to make a bit more of a stir than the last one. We need to get a few things straightened out.' She bit her lower lip and stamped her foot. 'Dammit! Why doesn't she use a mobile like everyone else?'

'Ha! That sounds interesting,' crooned Calum. 'Do I detect author-publisher problems?'

Allegra McCall's lips stretched into a smile

and she shook her head. 'Of course not, Calum. Castlefront is going to take Fiona Cullen to new heights. I'm in talks with an American publisher.'

'You're what?' demanded Genevieve, her eyes wide with amazement. 'I'm her agent, Allegra! I negotiate any deals with foreign publishers.'

Allegra patted the agent's arm. 'Of course, dear. I wasn't meaning to stand on your toes. I think that you and I ought to have a little chat together, once we've seen Fiona.'

Calum Steele grinned. 'Ladies, you're talking to the Press here. I can sniff something going on.' He cocked his head and his eyelids half-closed, giving him a vaguely reptilian appearance. 'I have connections with a lot of national dailies, who are always on the look-out for a scoop. What gives?'

Allegra and Genevieve exchanged glances. 'If there is any scoop to be had we want you to have it,' Allegra said, dropping her voice to a conspiratorial whisper. 'Just bear with us and we'll keep you informed every step of the way.'

Calum tapped the side of his nose. 'Trust me, ladies. I'm a professional.'

'I just wish Fiona would show up,' said Genevieve.

'Oh I know exactly where she is,' Calum

volunteered. 'She's staying at the Bonnie Prince Charlie Tavern.' He grinned and added: 'Maybe the three of us should go and see her?'

The Bonnie Prince Charlie was almost packed. The influx of tourists, writers, publishers, agents and literary fans had brought a welcome increase in trade to the Kyleshiffin public houses and hotels; and particularly to the well-known Bonnie Prince Charlie, with its own brewery specializing in Heather Ale and its complete stock of all of the Hebridean Islay Malts. The aroma of seafood greeted them as they entered.

Mollie McFadden, the doughty landlady of almost sixty years, was serving behind the bar and came over at Calum's request. She blinked at him from behind thick-lensed spectacles perched on the tip of her nose. 'It's Fiona Cullen you'll be after, isn't it, Calum Steele?'

The jaw of the editor of the *West Uist Chronicle* had fallen open. It clamped shut when Mollie pulled out a piece of paper from her apron and handed it across the bar. 'She told me that you or two ladies would be coming and that I was to show any or all of you this message.' She smiled at Allegra and Genevieve. 'She described you both to a tee, ladies.'

The two women looked over Calum's shoulders as he read the note, written in Fiona Cullen's neat handwriting.

Dear All,
Sorry to miss you, but I've been thinking and preparing for my lecture. See you after it, or at AM's ceilidh in the evening.
Regards,
Fiona.

'Now would any of you be wanting a drink?' Mollie asked. 'Our Heather Ale is famous, as Calum will tell you.'

But there were no takers.

'Thanks Mollie,' Fiona whispered from the doorway behind the bar, after the trio had gone.

* * *

Lachlan McKinnon was thirsty as he rolled up on his 1954 Ariel Red Hunter, a machine famous across the whole island, for it had been beautifully maintained by its owner and used to transport the Padre round his parish for about four decades. Stowing his helmet in the pannier he pulled his pipe out of his breast pocket, applied a light, then strode purposefully into the public bar of the Bonnie Prince Charlie.

A few moments later, after some banter with Mollie, he was just raising his personal tankard of foaming ale to his lips when he felt a prod in the back.

'Lachlan McKinnon! Just where have you been? There have been four lectures this morning and you've missed every one of them. That's so rude! And have you sorted Ranald Buchanan out yet? I've sold so many tickets for the Gaelic Bard's reading session that I've had to turn people away.'

'It's in hand, Bella.'

'And the Fiona Cullen lecture starts in twenty minutes. You're supposed to be introducing her. Have you talked to her? Have you prepared your speech? Have you — ?'

'He's done all of those things, Miss Melville,' came Fiona's voice. 'I'm ready whenever you are, Lachlan.'

Miss Melville flashed a cold look at Fiona Cullen, who had appeared, still dressed in her black motorcycle leathers.

'You look and sound just the same, Miss Melville,' said Fiona.

'And so do you, Fiona. I always thought you were — '

'A wee minx,' Fiona cut in, with a mock

falsetto voice. 'That's what you used to call me at school.'

Miss Melville straightened up. 'I was going to say that I always thought you were going to be a star.'

The Padre stared regretfully at his full pint of Heather Ale. 'Well then,' he said, detecting a slight frostiness between them. 'Perhaps I'd better escort the star to her admiring audience.' And linking arms with Fiona he wheeled round and escorted her through the crowded bar.

* * *

Torquil slipped into the back of the packed Duncan Institute just in time for the start of Fiona's lecture. Fiona was sitting on the stage as the Padre stood at the lectern delivering a few words of introduction. As the audience laughed at some of his little asides and light-hearted jokes, Torquil managed to catch Fiona's eye. He raised his hand and she winked at him. He noted that her reaction had not gone unnoticed by the large woman, Genevieve Cooper, who was sitting with Calum Steele and a smartly dressed woman with a pony tail and round wire-framed spectacles a few rows ahead and to the side.

The audience applauded when Fiona took

the lectern. And they sat entranced as she began to talk. At first she gave some background to her early life, mentioning in passing her education at the Kyleshiffin School, then her university days at St Andrews before returning to West Uist and her first job at the *West Uist Chronicle*. She spoke of her passion for cinema, fishing and Heather Ale. Then she talked about her move to Edinburgh and her work on various magazines, then about her first novel, *Raw Deal*. It had passed with some acclaim, but little money. Her second, *Nemesis Comes*, had hit the Scottish bestseller lists and was followed by a succession of crime novels, each bringing further success, culminating in her winning a Gold Dagger from the Crime Writers' Association.

Twenty minutes into her talk, Fiona picked up a rolled-up poster and slowly unfurled it.

'But as you can see, my lecture is advertised with the words 'Scotland's Queen of Crime Speaks Out and talks about her latest novel, *Dead Writers Tell No Tales*'. Well, now that you know a bit about my background as the so-called 'Queen of Scottish Crime', let me give you an inkling of how to do it yourself. And I say that because I know full well that the aspiring authors in the audience want to know exactly what they have to do to get to my stage. Basically, the best advice I can give is to — *tell a story*!'

There was a chorus of mild laughter from around the hall. Fiona smiled as she waited for it to settle, then: 'By 'tell a story' I mean you have to base your plot around real life. And that's what I do. I use real life to give me my plots. I aim at what the French call a *roman-à-clef*, literally a 'novel with a key'.'

She waited, allowing her words to register. 'A lot of you will already know that, of course. You will, I am sure, know exactly who the corrupt health minister was in *Nemesis comes*. To give you a clue, he resigned from the cabinet three weeks after the book hit the bestseller list. And you may know about the coven of Satan worshippers who ran a village council. There was an exposé in the Sunday newspapers of a group in Glasgow about a month after *Village Coven* came out.'

There was by now a murmuring of realization and of approval running round the hall. From his place at the back, Torquil noticed several people in the audience begin to move about, as if uncomfortable with the direction that Fiona's lecture was taking.

'In a way I suppose I have taken my early journalistic experience and adapted it in my new role as a novelist.'

'That's the way, lassie!' called out Calum

Steele, to general merriment from many of the locals. 'Remember your roots — and your first boss!'

'And how could I forget him,' replied Fiona, sardonically. And pointing to Calum Steele: 'Ladies and Gentlemen, be careful of anything you say today because the esteemed editor of the *West Uist Chronicle* is in our midst.'

To his immense delight Calum enjoyed a few moments of good-natured approval and banter, before Fiona went on.

'My last book, *Flesh Trimmers*, caused quite an uproar.'

Torquil saw both Genevieve and the smartly dressed woman shift in their seats.

'I can't say too much about it, because it is *sub judice*. That is, I am being sued by someone who thinks I am talking about them in my book. Guilty conscience perhaps! What I can say is that it relates to certain dubious practices in a branch of the medical profession.

'And that brings me onto my new book, which I am still writing, and which neither my ex-agent nor ex-publisher have seen. It's called *Dead Writers Tell No Tales*. It's about — '

'What did you say, Fiona!' someone cried out. All eyes turned to see a large woman in a floral shawl standing, clutching the top of the chair in front of her. 'What did . . . did you just say?'

Fiona looked up and smiled wanly. 'I said I hadn't shown it to either my ex-agent or my ex-publisher.'

A hush fell over the audience then Fiona went on. 'The advert said that I speak out — which is what I'm doing. Things have been happening in my life and I'm speaking out on them, and I'm writing about them. So, to finish my talk, I simply suggest that my readers buy my new book *Dead Writers Tell No Tales*. It's going to be explosive!'

Allegra McCall had been staring at Fiona all this time without saying a word. Now she grabbed Genevieve Cooper's sleeve, nodded to her and walked out down the aisle. Genevieve, ashen-faced, tears in her eyes, followed. A moment later, Calum Steele pulled on his anorak and made after them. Torquil could not help but notice that his old schoolmate had a slight smile on his lips.

By now, the Padre was on his feet, clapping his hands. He took centre stage and held up his hands for calm. 'And now, Ladies and Gentlemen. We thank Fiona for a stimulating and enlightening lecture. Before we break for the next session by Professor Neil Ferguson on his latest book, *The Iron Age Crannogs of the Hebrides*, we have time for a few quick questions.'

Torquil saw Fiona wink at him from the stage. She was a beautiful woman, no mistake. But she still had a brutal side to her.

⋆ ⋆ ⋆

Torquil signed out the station Ford Escort in order to drive Fiona back to the manse after he finished work. She had changed into a simple black dress that amply emphasized her curves, and wrapped a Japanese silk scarf about her elegant throat. The Padre was just about to set off on his Ariel Red Hunter when they drove into the gravel drive.

'I'm off to get Ranald organized,' he explained. 'I'm betting he's gotten the wind up and is in a peatreek-induced fit of poetic indulgence. The old galoot seems to write his best stuff when he's got a quart of whisky inside him and when he's faced with a deadline. But is that good enough for Miss Bella Melville! Is it thump.'

'Isn't that what poetic spirit really means?' Torquil suggested with a grin.

The Padre smiled at Fiona. 'You look beautiful, my dear.' Then he turned to Torquil, 'You are getting as bad as Miss Melville, laddie!' And pulling down his goggles, he started up the Hunter and rode off. 'Apologize to the laird and the fine folk if I'm late,' he called over his shoulder.

'And now,' said Torquil, 'you've got your lecture out of the way, but tomorrow is my big day. The piping competitions start after the official opening of the Gathering and I'm looking on the ceilidh opening ceremony as a wee bit of final practice.'

Fiona smiled. 'Go on then, get the pipes and put on your glad rags then we'll be off. And I promise not to try peeking up your kilt — not yet anyway!'

* * *

Torquil drove into the courtyard of the floodlit Dunshiffin Castle, the thirteenth-century stronghold of the MacLeod family, the hereditary lairds of West Uist. Hired help, the men in kilts and the women in tartan skirts and plaids, all of whom knew Piper Torquil McKinnon, greeted them with trays of champagne and canapés as they entered the main hall. There was a welcoming old-world aroma about the place, enhanced by glass cases of champion-sized salmon and trout, stag heads, antlers, shields, claymores and pikestaffs crisscrossed on the oak-panelled walls. Local dignitaries, celebrities from Edinburgh and the west coast, authors, sportsmen and -women stood about in groups or meandered in and out of the many opened rooms, mingling and noseying among the throng.

Calum Steele, looking uncomfortable in a crumpled and stained tuxedo, was one of the first to break away and join them. 'Well, well, Piper McKinnon and the great Fiona Cullen,' he said, a slight slur indicating how well the editor had already sampled the luxury of Dunshiffin Castle, courtesy of the laird, Angus MacLeod. 'Torquil, you bastard, you have the body and legs for a kilt — even if it is a McKinnon tartan!' He ducked as Torquil playfully raised his pipes to him, then turning to the pretty girl on Torquil's arm: 'Well, any more bombshells, Fiona? Any little nuggets for the *Chronicle*, for old time's sake?'

Fiona graced him with an indulgent smile. 'Only one,' she replied. 'A piece of advice. Buy a dictionary, Calum. I saw a copy of the *Chronicle* today, and you still can't spell.'

The editor of the local newspaper took it in good stead, tossed his head back and roared with laughter.

'And talking about spelling,' came another slightly slurred voice. 'Do you want me to spell out the meaning of your contract — Fiona, *darling*!' said Genevieve Cooper, stopping long enough to glare slightly cross-eyed at Fiona. 'You try and leave me and I'll sue your ass, my girl.'

Allegra McCall was a pace behind her. The trouser suit had been replaced by a sheath-like green designer dress and her hair had been pulled into a topknot. 'Genevieve this isn't the right time or place,' she said, pushing her spectacles higher on her nose. Then to Fiona, 'We shall talk tomorrow, Fiona, civilly and privately. Perhaps a few home truths will be in order.'

Fiona had already quaffed her first glass of champagne and had just accepted a second from a girl in a MacLeod tartan skirt and sash. 'Whatever, Allegra,' she replied. 'Oh, but by the way, you'll be hearing from my solicitor — and my forensic accountant about some *irregularities*.' She raised her glass and drained half of it.

Allegra bustled Genevieve away and Torquil steered Fiona into the main salon, where The Burns Boys, a Scottish traditional band, were playing with fiddle, accordion and tin whistle while clusters of revellers stood around waiting for food and drink before the dancing began in earnest. At the far end of the room a line of young men in chef uniforms were standing at attention behind tables laden with salvers and bowls of food, also awaiting the beginning of the ceilidh and their part in it.

'I went to one of Angus MacLeod's Edinburgh bashes,' Fiona whispered, accepting a top-up of champagne from a young man in a Campbell kilt. 'I think he's pinched the idea from Jeffrey Archer and is trying to do a Scottish version. Champagne and shepherd's pie suppers have become Champagne, haggis and neeps.' She drained half her glass again and added, 'It's OK I suppose if you don't mind offal.'

A trio of men detached themselves from the great fireplace and homed in on them. A tall, distinguished middle-aged man in full highland dress laughed and held out his hand. 'Fiona Cullen, I believe you have perfected the art of whispering so that everyone in a room can hear you,' said Angus MacLeod, the Laird of Dunshiffin and managing director of Angus MacLeod Enterprises, whose business interests included the local malt distillery, hunting, shooting and fishing rights on several of the islands and the well-known chain of cut-price bookshops strung along the west coast of Scotland. 'I did not pinch this idea from anyone. Haggis and turnips were good enough for Robbie Burns, so I don't see why they shouldn't be good enough for the West Uist Gathering.' He nodded to Torquil. 'Glad to see you, Piper. Allow me to introduce you to Roland Baxter, the Scottish Minister for Culture, and my friend Dr Viroj Wattana.' The two men in tuxedos smiled.

Torquil shook hands with the broad, slightly bovine-looking Roland Baxter, well known on Scottish TV for his views about reducing the use of Gaelic in schools. His widely reported belief was that a united Scotland needed a universal language, and that the Gaelic should no longer be a first language, since it promulgated a sense of exclusivity and fostered the idea that the Hebrides were different from the rest of Scotland. The Padre had often been heard saying that such values were typical of the lowland Scot.

'I love the highland dress, Inspector McKinnon,' Roland Baxter enthused.

'*Suas am pìobaires*,' said Torquil raising his glass, 'Up the pipers.'

Baxter laughed. 'I don't speak the Gaelic myself, as you probably know, but I'm a great fan of the bagpipes.'

'And of course, Inspector McKinnon here is the island's best bagpipe player. Apart from the Padre that is,' said Angus MacLeod with a wry smile, before asking: 'Where is the illustrious convenor of the Literary

Festival, by the way?'

'He'll be along later,' Torquil replied. 'I believe he's tracking Ranald Buchanan down.'

'That old reprobate Buchanan, eh?' the laird mused, it seemed with a touch of irritation. Then he turned to explain to Dr Wattana, a slight crop-headed man with half-moon spectacles. 'You see Viroj we have a . . . '

But the doctor was paying no attention. He had taken Fiona's arm and was trying to guide her along to chat in her ear. After a few words she threw his hand aside, and with a look of disgust shouted, 'Forget it, Wattana. You're a bungler and I won't let you bugger anyone else up. Just let our lawyers deal with it.'

The laird looked horrified. 'Fiona, please,' he said in an urgent hushed tone. 'Dr Wattana is my guest. I flew in with him yesterday and want him to — '

'To what? Give someone a penis stretch!' Fiona gave a shrill laugh and put a hand on Roland Baxter's arm. 'That could be you, eh Roland.' She winked provocatively at him, adding: 'Remember.'

The Scottish Minister for Culture shook his head. 'Fiona, you're drunk. And you're insulting everyone. Don't you think you ought to cut back on the booze before you say something dangerous?'

'And what do you mean by that?' Fiona demanded. 'I'll drink as much as I want, say what I want,' she hesitated for a moment, then smiled, feline-like. 'Or write what I like.'

Torquil was indeed beginning to feel embarrassed. Fiona seemed to be knocking champagne back as if it was water, and as it affected her she seemed intent on offending everyone around her. He grasped her arm and addressed Angus MacLeod. 'Is it about time to get this ceilidh on the road, Angus? Shall I pipe in the haggis?'

Angus MacLeod, Laird of Dunshiffin, nodded gratefully. He raised his hand above his head and signalled to an elderly manservant who had been hovering silently at the side of the hall. 'Good idea, Piper. Jesmond will take you through to the kitchen. The pipes will bring some order to the place,' he said, smiling uncertainly.

Torquil followed the elderly retainer through the crowd and managed to catch hold of Calum Steele on the way. 'Look after Fiona for a few minutes will you, while I do the piping for the haggis,' he whispered. 'I think she's drinking too quickly.'

* * *

The Burns Boys started playing again after Torquil had piped in the haggis and people had begun to form queues to collect plates of food. People patted him on the back and expressed pleasure at his rendition of 'Scotland the Brave'. He was looking round for Fiona when he heard her raised voice again. He saw her berating the laird himself. Calum Steele was standing a few feet away, looking shocked and impotent to interfere. Disappointedly, Torquil noted that her voice sounded even more slurred than before.

'That's right, high and mighty *Mister* Angus MacLeod. I know what you're up to, with your cut-price book stores, robbing authors so that you can pump money into the Labour Party. Fawning on ministers so that you can buy a knighthood.'

Angus MacLeod caught sight of Torquil as he approached. He hissed through gritted teeth. 'Get her out of here, McKinnon. She's drunk and she's making a spectacle of herself. As usual!'

'I think a little air would help first,' Torquil replied, as he hooked Fiona's arm and drew her away, out onto a balcony. Once there, he asked, 'Fiona, what the hell's got into you? You've insulted everybody you've talked to!'

But Fiona had instantly sobered up. She smiled and slid her arms about his waist. 'I was just having fun. All those prissy people. I needed to stir them up, to get each of them worried about my book.'

'But why?'

'Because it's a game, Torquil. Publishing is just a game. Bestsellers are more than literary effort — the book is just a part of the process — not necessarily even the most important part. Tonight is mainly about getting the publicity machine going.'

'Mainly?'

Fiona laughed and squeezed his waist. 'You're too clever for your own good, Torquil McKinnon. OK, I had a few — points to make with certain folk.'

'And what about me, Fiona? What part does the local inspector play in all this? Am I just part of the game?'

She raised her mouth to his and kissed him gently. 'I'm not playing with you at all, Torquil. I've got serious plans in mind for us.'

As they kissed, Torquil felt himself floating in a sea of bliss.

Then his mobile phone went off. Reluctantly, he gently detached himself and fished it out of his sporran to find the Padre's number flashing on the dial.

He raised the instrument to his ear.

'Torquil! You better get over here!' came the Padre's agonized voice. There was a rasping sound in the background, followed by a gentle thumping or slapping, then: 'I'm here at Ranald's place on the Machair Skerry with Ewan McPhee.' The strange rasping noise echoed in the background again. 'Ewan can't speak at the moment,' the Padre explained. 'Ranald Buchanan is dead. He's bashed his head and fallen in the water. His feet are all tangled up and his eyes, they, they — '

'They're what, Uncle?'

'They've gone, Torquil. The gulls have pecked them out!'

The rasping sound came again and Torquil vaguely heard his constable's voice cursing in the background. Then he realized that the rasping noise was caused by Ewan McPhee retching his guts out.

4

The post-mortem was held in the Kyleshiffin Cottage Hospital the following morning at seven o'clock, on the authority of the District Procurator Fiscal on Benbecula, whom Torquil had contacted after seeing the body.

It had been a sombre business from the moment of receiving the Padre's telephone call. Torquil had made his apologies to Angus MacLeod, briefly indicating that Ranald Buchanan had been involved in an accident and that he, as the senior officer of the West Uist Division of the Hebridean Constabulary, had been called to the scene. Despite MacLeod's attempts to extract more information Torquil had taken his leave with Fiona, much to the relief of several of the guests at the party.

Dropping Fiona outside the Bonnie Prince Charlie he drove to the police station where he swapped the car for his Royal Enfield Bullet and rode to Binacle Point where PC Ewan McPhee was waiting in the police *Seaspray* catamaran. A few moments later they were scudding over the moonlit waves on their way round the coast to the Machair

Skerry. Torquil could see that his constable was badly shaken by the events of the night — the Padre had contacted him as the duty officer, to take him over to the Machair Skerry after he had spotted Ranald Buchanan's boat through his binoculars.

'It's awful, Piper,' Ewan informed his superior officer. 'He looks like a dead seal that I saw once, its face all pecked by the gulls.' The thought of it produced another tide of nausea that made him reach for the side of the craft in order to vomit over the side. Torquil took over and steered the boat in towards the small skerry.

Ranald Buchanan's small motorboat was tied up to the iron spike on his primitive jetty. Standing smoking his pipe a few feet back was the Padre.

'He's here Torquil,' the Padre announced, tapping his pipe out on his heel and depositing the hot pipe in his breast pocket. 'I've given him the last rites, but I havena touched him. Ewan thought I'd better wait for you.'

Torquil hopped onto the stone jetty and flicking on his powerful flashlight knelt down to get a closer look at the body. Ranald Buchanan's feet were tangled on the mooring rope and the body was floating in the water a few inches below the surface. His straggly beard waving like seaweed around the already bloated white face gave him a macabre Neptunian appearance. The sight of the empty eye sockets was truly nauseating, the gulls having feasted on the eyes and the sea having washed away the blood. Torquil reached out and caught hold of the dead poet's waistcoat, then with both hands successfully turned the torso over in the water. The gaping wound at the back of the skull was just as nauseating, and despite himself Torquil winced. There was a great depression in the skull exposing a pulpy mass of brain and coagulated blood.

'That seems to have been the culprit,' said the Padre, pointing to a broad blood slick on the iron mooring spike. 'And look at these, a bottle and a copy of his new book of poems.'

Torquil looked at the empty bottle of peatreek and the thin volume of poems, '*Songs of the Selkie*,' lying open beside it, as if it had fallen as he was reading. He picked up the book and noted a few pencilled underlinings and scorings through words of the penultimate poem, entitled 'The Return of the Selkie'.

'He was too fond of his own peatreek,' mused the Padre. 'And when he was drinking, he was always his own worst critic. It looks as if he was walking back and forth on the jetty, fiddling with his latest work, maybe even working out which poems he was going to use in his reading tomorrow. Then he stumbled on the ropes, fell backwards and bashed his head and — '

'And drowned!' said Torquil. 'Aye, Lachlan, I agree, it looks like it.' He turned to Ewan, who was still looking decidedly ill. 'We'd better get him out of the water and take him back to Kyleshiffin, then I'll report the death to the Procurator Fiscal.'

Dr Ralph McLelland, the local GP and police surgeon, washed his hands after completing the autopsy. 'I'll have to do the histological examinations, of course, but from the morbid anatomical examination and surgical dissection it seems pretty obvious, he died from a blunt injury to the head and probable drowning.'

'Will a diatom test tell you anything?' Torquil asked, as he and the police surgeon stood looking down at the open body of Ranald Buchanan.

Ralph McLelland blew through tight lips. 'Not sure it will tell anything. Some algal diatoms will undoubtedly have crossed the alveolar junction into the bloodstream so I expect we'll find them in some of the histology samples. But whether he died from the head wound or from drowning is pretty academic, isn't it. It's a tragedy any way you look at it.'

'Aye, a tragedy right enough,' agreed Torquil. 'It'll take a few days for the inquest, so it'll be after the Gathering, I am thinking.'

'After the Gathering?' Ralph McLelland repeated. 'Do you think it will be respectful to carry on with it, Piper?'

⋆ ⋆ ⋆

An emergency meeting of the Gathering and Literary Festival Committee was held an hour later in the dining room of the St Ninian's manse, where Torquil announced the circumstances of Ranald Buchanan's accidental death. 'Of course, this is not official. There will have to be an inquest.'

'Had he any kin?' Angus MacLeod asked.

'None. He had been a widower for thirty years and he lost his only daughter about ten years ago,' the Padre replied. 'She had suffered from schizophrenia for a lot of years. And, of course, you will recall that she had a son that drowned twenty years ago.'

'I suppose the question that I, as the West Uist senior police officer, have to ask is — are you going to go ahead with the Gathering?'

Miss Melville was the first to reply. 'Of course we go ahead, Torquil. It's all very sad, but the life of the island has to keep going. We shall still hold Ranald Buchanan's poetry reading, but someone else will do the recitations. That is only respectful. We shall call it a celebration of his life.'

'I agree, Piper,' said the laird. 'The island is swollen with visitors. And not all of them have come to hear the Gaelic Poet. The majority, I would say, have come for the traditional Gathering. The sport.'

The Padre had struck a light to his briar and was puffing meditatively. 'Glad I am to hear you say this. I am thinking that it is what the old rascal would have wanted.' He looked uncertainly at his nephew. 'And maybe it would be an idea to allow the people who come to hear his poetry have a taste of what Ranald Buchanan was really about?'

'What are you saying, Uncle?' Torquil asked, suspiciously.

'Peatreek!' exclaimed the Padre with glee. 'It was what helped him with his poetic vision. Why not let folk enjoy a sample of his '*spirit*'.'

Torquil suppressed a smile, for he expected Miss Melville's reaction. 'You old fool!' she said. 'It sounds as if his peatreek killed him. Why should we be celebrating it?'

Angus MacLeod put a hand on the retired teacher's shoulder. 'I believe that Lachlan is playing with us, Miss Melville. He well knows that we cannot have anything to do with illicit liquor. But if toasting his memory is what you want, then I am prepared to donate six bottles of Glen Corlin Malt Whisky from my *legal* distillery for those who would wish to celebrate his life and work.'

The Padre clapped his hands. 'There you have it then, Torquil laddie. The show must go on! And if I might make a suggestion to the laird, about the use of his helicopter . . . '

* * *

Calum Steele had also been hard at work throughout the night, which had helped him to work off the hangover that he had anticipated after all the champagne at the ceilidh. Normally the *West Uist Chronicle* appeared twice a week, on Tuesdays and Fridays, but for the duration of the Gathering and the Literary Festival Calum had agreed to produce a special daily news sheet, every morning.

Reading it over a breakfast of boiled eggs, Ranald Buchanan's murderer was pleased to see a mere mention of the Gaelic Poet's demise, presumably from a tragic accident. Then followed a short biography about the fisherman-poet, with a promise of more information in the next issue.

'Poetic justice!' the murderer thought again on scanning the subheadings of the reviews of the Literary Festival lectures:

FIONA CULLEN TELLS ALL AND SACKS AGENT AND PUBLISHER

Our literary editor was well placed in the audience at the celebrated crime novelist's lecture to gather the mood of the meeting. Fiona, who used to work on the *West Uist Chronicle*, told the audience about the new book she is working on, which is entitled *Dead Writers Tell No Tales*. Then she surprised everyone by informing the audience that she was sacking her —

PROFESSOR'S BOOK PROVES THE REAL PURPOSE OF THE CRANNOGS OF WEST UIST

Everyone, our editor in chief included, has always accepted the traditional explanation about our beautiful crannogs being artificial Iron Age islets. Yet research over the years by Professor Neil Ferguson, head of the Department of

Marine Archaeology at the University of the Highlands, reveals that this is only a part —

GAME, FISH, STOVIES AND WHISKY
— WEST UIST
CULINARY SECRETS

Mrs Agnes Dunbar, former head cook at Dunshiffin Castle, has just published a small cookbook, which will give us an insight into what is really set before the laird for dinner. In fifty recipes stretching back to —

Anger seethed inside for a moment, threatening to show itself in some way. Then as it subsided there was a flash of inspiration, followed by an exhilarating sense of anticipation. Gulping down a mouthful of tea and folding the news sheet, lest anyone should notice anything unusual, the murderer smiled with satisfaction and pushed the empty plate aside.

Soon! Retribution was on its way!

* * *

Torquil and Morag heaved a sigh of relief after they had given the Drummond twins, the West Uist Division's two special constables, their instructions for crowd patrol. Never slaves to punctuality or to the hierarchy of the police force, the two fishermen had arrived late smelling slightly of herring, Heather Ale and tobacco.

'Och you should not be worrying. There will be no problems with the crowds,' said Douglas.

'None at all, for we shall be keeping a weather eye out,' added Wallace. The twins were even taller than Ewan, albeit more laid back and with far fewer collective brain cells. Nonetheless, everyone knew them and Torquil was sure that the twins would talk any rowdy revellers out of rowdiness; or bore them out of it.

Not that any problems were anticipated for at least a couple of hours, since it was not the islanders' way to begin drinking before midday. Any problems with rowdy behaviour was expected to come from incomers sampling the island's local Heather Ale at the Bonnie Prince Charlie or one of the other two hostelries in Kyleshiffin.

There had been a couple of well-attended lectures and writing workshops in the morning and now people were beginning to make their way to the village green on the hill above the town, in order to get a good seat or to see what was on offer at the several marquees set up around the roped-off arena.

Torquil called at Fiona's room at the Bonnie Prince Charlie to pick her up at half past eleven. She was still wearing a dressing gown and a cigarette was burning in the ashtray on her dressing table, beside a switched-on laptop and a mound of hand-written notes.

'Poor old Ranald,' she said, shaking her head, as Torquil filled her in on the events surrounding the Gaelic Bard's sad demise. 'Still, he probably went the way he'd have wanted, with a bottle of peatreek and a book of his poems.' Then picking a speck of invisible dust off his tweed jacket and smiling coquettishly up at him: 'You're the most fanciable man on the island, did you know that Torquil McKinnon?'

Torquil lay his bagpipes aside, encircled her waist and drew her close. 'And you are starting to get under my skin again.' He brushed her lips with his own. 'I think we need to have a bit of time on our own later, Fiona. We need to sort out what we're doing here.'

'We're having fun,' she said, kissing him on the nose. 'But first of all, you are going to win that Silver Quaich you've always wanted. Which reminds me, why the tweed jacket and not the full dress job like last night?'

'I'm an individual competitor,' he replied. 'The pipers from the pipe band will all likely be in the full kit, but I'm entitled to be more casual. Just the kilt, tweed jacket, tie and tam-o'-shanter beret.'

'But you're not as casual as me,' she said with a laugh, breaking away from him and pirouetting on her toes. And with a single pull she undid her dressing gown and allowed it to fall open to reveal her lithe naked body underneath.

Torquil closed his eyes and bit his lip. 'Dammit Fiona,' he said in mock agony. 'Like you said, I've got a competition to win. That's not fair.'

'Spoilsport!' she said with a laugh as she skipped into her en suite. 'I'll get dressed then. Like you said, we should talk later.'

* * *

A great banner emblazoned with the words '*Ceud Mile Failte* — One Hundred Thousand Welcomes' was strung above the entrance to the green. A light breeze billowed it slightly. At exactly twelve o'clock the South Uist Pipe Band, headed by Pipe Major Hamish Munro, led the procession into the arena. There were six pipers, a bass-drummer, then four side-drummers. As Torquil looked on he felt a tinge of nerves, since at least two of the pipers were above average ability and had their names down for the piping competitions, along with Hamish Munro himself.

Following them came the Chieftain of the Games party. In the centre marched a kilted Angus MacLeod, the current chieftain, his guests and the various specialist judges. Torquil felt Fiona stiffen at his side when she spied Roland Baxter and the surgeon, Dr Viroj Wattana, walking along with him and a coterie of long-legged blonde models in MacLeod tartan skirts with plaids slung over their right shoulders. The pipe band wheeled left and took up a position to the side of the main dais and continued to play, while the VIP party took their seats.

In the middle of the field a youth ceremonially pulled on the lanyard to raise the Games flag. It was timed exactly right, the flag reaching the top of the flagpole just as the band reached the last few bars.

When Hamish Munro whirled his staff to mark the end of their piece, Angus MacLeod stood and tapped the crackling microphone of the PA system. His speech was curt and to the point, welcoming all and sundry, especially Roland Baxter the Scottish Minister for Culture and his friend Dr Viroj

Wattana from Thailand to the Gathering and Literary Festival; thanking all of the organizers, including Miss Bella Melville and the Padre, Lachlan McKinnon. Then he gave a brief eulogy for Ranald Buchanan and asked for a minute's silence in his honour, before continuing.

'And now, may the competitors show their strength, speed, skill and dexterity, in whatever event they are competing in. May the spectators be entertained, the stallholders be prosperous and Jack Campbell the engraver be ever busy throughout the day, putting names on all the trophies.'

The noise of a powerful engine and rotating blades had gradually increased and from the direction of Dunshiffin Castle a helicopter with the AME tartan logo roared overhead and started on a circuit of the arena, before hovering over a sawdust circle at the far end of the field.

Angus MacLeod pointed at it. 'Our good Padre, the Reverend Lachlan McKinnon, has prevailed upon me,' he said, then paused for effect, 'I suppose you could even say, he has browbeaten me into making the AME helicopter available for the afternoon, to take sightseers on a trip around West Uist. Each spin will cost the munificent sum of two pounds a head, half to go to the Ranald

Buchanan Memorial Fund and half towards the West Uist Gathering Appeal for a permanent arena.' He waited for a round of spontaneous applause to subside, then looked heavenwards at the gradually darkening sky and added hopefully, 'And finally, in the hope that the heavens will not open, I declare the Gathering officially open.'

There was another round of applause accompanied by whistling, catcalls and general high spirits, then the crowd of people started flocking towards the clan tents, displays and various competitions. An almost undecipherable voice crackled on the tannoy to indicate where and when the various events would be taking place.

Torquil spotted the Drummond twins ambling around near the beer tent. For a moment he thought of going over to have a word with them, then he saw the familiar figure of the Padre hailing them, a glass of beer in his hand, and he thought better of it. Instead, he took Fiona's hand and nodded towards the far side of the green where a man with a loudspeaker was just announcing that the field sports were about to begin.

'Let's go and give Ewan a bit of support,' he said.

The big PC was standing outside the

hammer-throwing enclosure, wearing a tee-shirt and sporran-less kilt, with his arm around a red-headed, athletic-looking young woman of about his own age. 'Piper! I mean — er — Inspector McKinnon,' Ewan corrected himself. 'You're the very man I want,' he said, still looking a trifle pale after his adventures of the night before, yet with a smile across his boyish face. 'And Fiona. Come and meet Izzie Frazer.'

There was a thud in the arena parallel with them as a twenty-two-pound iron sphere attached to a four-foot wooden shaft plummeted to the earth from the first hammer-thrower.

Izzie smiled and Torquil could immediately see why Ewan had been so smitten by her. She was exactly his type. Redhaired like him, athletic with freckles and large orb-like breasts that amply filled her angora sweater. 'Ah, the famous Fiona Cullen!' enthused Izzie Frazer, her hazel eyes sparkling. 'I caught your lecture yesterday. Most interesting! And I've read every one of your books. I particularly liked *Flesh Trimmers*, your last one.'

The two women shook hands and naturally fell into conversation. While they did so, Ewan signalled his inspector aside and said in a muffled voice, 'Torquil, I'm sorry about this morning. Puking up on duty, I mean. I'm so bloody embarrassed.'

Torquil grinned back. 'Och, I can see that you are cross with yourself, Ewan. Well then, just use that anger usefully. Show Izzie what you can do with that hammer — assuming that you've got your trajectory right!'

Ewan grinned sheepishly at the dig about his mother's outhouse roof, just as his name was called out by the event referee. The big PC went and took his place behind the trig, the special throwing line. Torquil, Fiona and Izzie watched him swing the hammer round his head, gradually picking up momentum before hurling it over his shoulder to the accompaniment of a bestial roar. The hammer soared into the air and fell a full dozen feet further than the first competitor's marker. A cheer went up from the watching gallery, testifying to the big local police officer's popularity. Torquil noted with a grin that Morag Driscoll was on the other side of the field applauding and whistling, eschewing any professional decorum or neutrality that one might have expected from a uniformed police officer.

Izzie Frazer touched Torquil's arm. 'I thought they had to whirl round and round before they threw the hammer?'

'That's the Olympic hammer,' Torquil

explained. 'This is the Scottish hammer, and you have probably just seen the winning throw already.'

He noticed Izzie's cheeks flush slightly. 'He's a powerful lad,' she cooed enthusiastically.

'I understand that you are a writer as well?' Torquil asked, keen to change the subject.

'Not as famous as Fiona, but I'm trying. I've got three travel books under my belt so far.'

'Who is your publisher, Izzie?' Fiona asked.

'Wanderlust Press. They're a new publisher, a subsidiary of AME.'

'And where have you been in your travels?' Torquil asked.

'The East so far. I'm doing a series, you see. The titles are not very inspiring, but they seem to be selling.'

Fiona frowned. 'Oh they'll be selling all right, but if I were you I'd double-check the royalty statement. If Wanderlust have anything to do with Angus MacLeod Enterprises — you need to be careful!'

A female voice from behind them made Fiona spin round. 'And who are you maligning now, Fiona?' Allegra McCall asked. Torquil noted that the publisher had discarded her suit and was dressed in ski parka and green Wellingtons. Almost inevitably it seemed, a pace behind her was Genevieve Cooper, slightly out of breath as if she had been hard put to keep up with the publisher. 'Wanderlust Press is a perfectly good firm.'

'Allegra, eavesdropping is becoming a hobby of yours, I think!' said Fiona.

Genevieve put an arm about Izzie Frazer's shoulder. 'I heard what she was saying though, my dear. Perhaps Fiona is right, you should check your royalty statements. Authors don't always do that, being creative people. That's what a good agent will do for you, make sure you get the best possible deal. Do you have an agent, by the way?' And with the skill of a conjurer she pushed a card into Izzie's hand. 'That's me — Genevieve Cooper, the author's trooper,' she announced. 'Just ask any of my authors.'

There was another thud in the throwing area and they all turned to see a hammer fall ten feet short of Ewan's first throw.

Fiona squeezed Torquil's arm. 'I'm going to have to catch someone for a while, Torquil. You stay and watch Ewan and I'll meet you before your piping.' She stood on her tiptoes and pecked him on the cheek, then turned to see Izzie Frazer chatting with Allegra and Genevieve. As she went by them she touched

Izzie's shoulder and half-whispered. 'Remember what I said, Izzie! My best advice to you is to be careful of agents, publishers and cut-price booksellers.' She winked at her, and then smiled thinly at Allegra and Genevieve. 'We'll talk later, ladies.'

She left, oblivious to the looks of contempt bestowed upon her back by the agent and publisher.

⋆ ⋆ ⋆

Dr Viroj Wattana had been left to his own devices while Angus MacLeod went to give instructions to Captain Tam McKenzie, his helicopter pilot, about the trips round the island. He wandered in and out of the different marquees, feeling slightly bemused by this his first ever Gathering. It was a feeling that was not lessened when the Padre caught him by the arm and virtually frog-marched him into the beer tent.

Being virtually a teetotaller, Dr Wattana found that the Heather Ale Lachlan McKinnon had introduced him to went straight to his head. As a result, the sound of the music, the dancing and athletic events going on around all seemed to merge into a surrealistic fugue.

'And where did you train, Dr Wattana?' the

Padre asked, before quaffing a respectable mouthful of foaming ale.

'Chulalongkorn University in Thailand. Then after that I studied plastic and cosmetic surgery at Harvard in the States, then at Oxford in England, and then Edinburgh in — '

'In Scotland,' the Padre finished, with a wink and a quick drink. 'So you know a little of our strange Scottish ways then?'

Dr Wattana sipped his beer. 'Oh yes, I have some good friends in Scotland. I have known Angus MacLeod for some years and I am going diving with him and Neil Ferguson tomorrow.'

'Our celebrated professor of Marine Archaeology? How did you come to know him?'

'As you say, he is a famous archaeologist. He lectured at Chulalongkorn and he — er — he has been a patient of mine.'

'Enough said, doctor,' returned the Padre. 'I understand. Medical ethics and all that. You can't say any more. A bit like us, the clergy.' He eyed the surgeon's glass. 'But come on, doctor, you're hardly drinking. Let me get you a fresh glass then I want to pick your brain about something.'

As the Padre turned to the bar a hand fell sharply on his shoulder. 'Oh no you don't,

Lachlan McKinnon!'

The Padre turned, a crestfallen expression on his face. 'Ah! Miss Melville. I was just — '

'I don't care what you were doing, but I'll tell you what you are going to do now, Lachlan. You're coming with me, right now,' Miss Melville announced authoritatively. 'We need you in the Literary Festival marquee, where you are going to put your considerable persuasive talent for salesmanship to good use. You are going to sell at least one copy of every author's work.'

The Padre shrugged helplessly at Dr Wattana. 'Perhaps we can have another drink later, Dr Wattana.'

Dr Wattana nodded dumbly, for he had not been listening properly. He was looking out through the marquee opening beyond the Padre. He blinked hard. He was unsure whether it was the effect of the beer or whether he really had seen someone he had never expected to see again.

* * *

Ewan beamed at Izzie Frazer as she ran a French-manicured nail over his bulging biceps.

'You're a strong lad,' she purred. 'A powerful man. I like that.'

Despite himself, Ewan blushed. He raised the gleaming silver cup that he had just been presented with, breathed on it and rubbed it on his hip. 'Och, it was nothing special, Izzie. I didn't manage my record of last year. I just ken how to give the hammer a good hurl.'

'Hm, I like a man in a kilt,' she murmured. 'Your inspector, Torquil, he suits a kilt as well — but not as well as you!'

Ewan blushed. 'Will you come and listen to Torquil play his pipes? He's got a rare gift and he's — well, he's a friend as well as my inspector — I'd like to see him win.'

Izzie giggled. 'Actually Ewan, I'd rather not. I can't say that the bagpipes are my favourite instrument. I'll just have a look at that book fair in the Literary Festival marquee then I think I'll try and have a word with that literary agent, Genevieve Cooper. Maybe she can help my career.' And brushing his cheek with her lips she whispered something in his ear that made the big PC blush to the very roots of his carrot-red hair.

* * *

No one entering the Literary Festival marquee escaped the eagle eye of the Padre. Using his clerical collar shamelessly he homed in on anyone picking up a book and then successfully prised information from them about their literary tastes, their desires, ambitions and foibles. Within moments a sale was notched up, to the immense pleasure of Miss Bella Melville, who bagged each purchase, took the money then popped a complementary bookmark with Fiona Cullen's smiling face on it into each bag.

'These bookmarks are a popular gimmick,' said Miss Melville. 'That literary agent gave me a great stack of them. I've spread them about all over the place and as a result we've almost sold out of all of Fiona Cullen's books.' She shook her head sadly. 'She's a nice girl that agent. A pity that Fiona stabbed her in the back yesterday at her lecture.'

But Lachlan was not listening. He had spotted Professor Neil Ferguson chatting with a red-headed girl he thought he had seen cheering on Ewan McPhee at the hammer-throwing.

'Ah, it's Izzie Frazer, isn't it?' the Padre said, stepping up to interrupt their conversation. 'You're the travel writer. *My Sri Lanka* and *My Thai*. Those are your books, aren't they?' And before she could reply he had an arm about her shoulder and Neil Ferguson's and was bustling them towards the travel section. Before five minutes were up he had ensured that the professor had bought a copy of one of Izzie's books and that Izzie had purchased a copy of the professor's *Crannog* book.

'Padre, you have missed your calling,' Neil Ferguson joked. 'I believe that you could make a living selling tickets to hell and back.'

Lachlan tossed his head back and laughed as he stuffed thick-cut tobacco into the bowl of his briar pipe. 'Less of the blasphemy, if you don't mind, professor.' He struck a light to his pipe and beamed at Miss Melville as she handed over their purchases.

But before the professor could reply, the Padre had gone, a trail of tobacco smoke in his wake. He had spied a young hippy-looking couple perusing copies of Ranald Buchanan's latest work, *Songs of the Selkie*.

Good to see that the young were interested in Ranald's poetry, he thought. Let's see if I can persuade them to make a contribution to the old boy's memory.

5

Torquil handed the judge his list of selected strathspeys, hornpipes and *piobaireachds* and waited while the panel of three conferred. Then he bowed as the head judge, Major Mackintosh from Mull, handed the list back with ticks against the pieces the panel wanted to hear. He made his way over to the spectator area, just as Pipe Major Hamish Munro began to play his strathspey. Fiona was waiting for him.

'I've got you a programme,' Torquil said. 'There's a note inside that explains everything.'

'The mysteries of the pipes, eh?' Fiona replied with a smile. Then nodding at Hamish Munro, 'He sounds as if he knows what he's doing.'

Torquil frowned. 'Aye, he knows all right. He knows too bloody well, in my opinion.'

Fiona cuffed him playfully on the side of his head, knocking his tam-o'shanter-beret askew. 'Where's the famous McKinnon confidence, Torquil? You're going to win that Silver Quaich today, I just know you will. I spoke to the Padre over in the Literary

Festival tent,' she said, holding up a bag containing a couple of books. 'The old devil made me buy a travel book by Ewan's new lady friend and a cookbook by Agnes Dunbar. Anyway, he told me that the only person who can take the quaich away from you is yourself.'

They listened to Hamish Munro for a few moments, Torquil all the while getting more nervous and wishing that he had followed the Padre's oft-quoted advice to take a wee dram before playing in competition. Then all too soon it was his turn to take the dais. He kissed her then crossed the grass to the steps. He mounted them swiftly and awaited Major McKenzie's announcement that he was going to play the 'Haughs o'Cromdale', a stirring strathspey. Torquil tuned up and began to play.

It was a piece that he knew backwards and which always brought a tear to his eye, just as he was sure that it did to every piper. Originally, it had been a song written by the Hebridean shepherd poet James Hogg, telling of a lost Jacobite battle in 1690. But it was the fact that Piper George Findlater had played it with bullets flying around him to encourage his comrades to take a hill at the Battle of Dargai in 1897, despite having been shot in both ankles, that really moved him.

For this act of heroism he had been awarded the Victoria Cross. Torquil played as he thought of the words of the song:

As I came in by Auchindoun,
A little wee bit frae the toun,
When to the Highlands I was bound,
To view the haughs of Cromdale . . .

Playing virtually on auto-pilot, Torquil had fleeting impressions of what was happening in different parts of the field, beyond the judges' table. He saw Fiona standing watching him, looking so damned sexy in her black leathers, tapping a hand on the plastic bag containing her purchases. He saw Professor Neil Ferguson and Dr Wattana, deep in conversation, moving in her direction.

We were in bed, sir, every man,
When the English host upon us came,
A bloody battle then began,
Upon the haughs of Cromdale . . .

In another part of the field he saw Fiona's agent, Genevieve Cooper, in heated conversation with the publisher Allegra McCall.

But alas! We could no longer stay,
For o'er the hills we came away . . .

He saw the Padre jogging across the field towards the piping square, arms waving encouragingly at him.

Thus the great Montrose did say,
Can you direct the nearest way?
For I will o'er the hills this day,
And view the haughs of Cromdale.

Up above he saw the AME Enstrom Shark helicopter complete a circuit of the island and head in to land on the temporary helipad at the far side of the field.

The Drummond brothers were still standing near the beer tent, surreptitiously smoking.

Alas my lord, you're not so strong,
You scarcely have two thousand men,
And there's twenty thousand on the
plain . . .

Torquil played on, only dimly aware of the little tableau being played out on the field. Neil Ferguson and Dr Wattana were now close to Fiona, as was Ewan McPhee, coming from the other direction, with his mother — a small round woman with red hair streaked with silver — neither looking where they were going, so focused were they on the silver cup he was carrying. The inevitable happened. All five collided, Fiona stumbled, packages, parcels and purchases flying everywhere. Then they were all picking things up. Dr Wattana, Ewan and his mother looking awkward as Fiona seemed to make some cutting remark to the professor.

Stand rank and file on Cromdale.
Thus the great Montrose did say . . .

Torquil looked away, wary of becoming distracted from his playing. And his eyes fell on Genevieve Cooper and Allegra McCall. Genevieve seemed to stamp her foot, then the two separated, stomping off in separate directions. Nearby, as if not having wanted to interrupt them, Izzie Frazer walked after the retreating figure of Genevieve Cooper.

Turning back towards Fiona, he saw that the Padre had found her. Fiona was looking distracted for a moment, straightening out her purchases. Then at the Padre's nudge she looked up at Torquil, made a thumbs-up sign and winked.

Torquil closed his eyes, his heart soaring unexpectedly. He played on and on, eventually coming to the last few bars:

. . . Upon the haughs of Cromdale.
Of twenty thousand Cromwell's men,
Five hundred fled to Aberdeen
The rest of them lie on the plain
Upon the haughs of Cromdale.

He stopped, let his pipes down, bowed to the judges, then made his way down from the dais towards the grinning Padre, Ewan and his mother.

'Torquil you were magnificent,' said Jessie McPhee. 'A credit to the Constabulary.'

'Thanks Jessie,' replied Torquil with a grin. 'I just hope I've done enough there. We'll see what the judges think when they've heard the others.'

'It's in the bag, laddie,' said the Padre, stuffing tobacco into his pipe. 'Unless you've been handing out parking tickets to the judges.'

'Where's Fiona?'

The Padre shook his head. 'She said she had to go somewhere all of a sudden. Said you'd understand. Then she headed off for that thing she calls a motorbike.'

'She said she'll see you with the Silver Quaich, Torquil,' added Ewan.

The Padre had his pipe going to his satisfaction. 'And that's not a bad idea, my lad. You've got a hornpipe to play next, which isn't your strongest discipline. You have no need to be distracted by — a bonnie lassie!'

Despite himself, Torquil had to agree, and he forced away the image of Fiona standing in front of him with her dressing gown hanging open.

Later, he thought, suppressing a smile.

* * *

The rotary blades of the AME helicopter slowed down and Calum Steele pushed open the door and jumped out. 'Thanks Tam,' he shouted above the noise of the engine. 'I enjoyed every minute of that, so you'll get a good write-up in the *Chronicle*.'

He looked round and saw Fiona Cullen walking briskly in the direction of the car park.

'Now is as good a time as any, my girl,' he thought. And he rushed after her, turning into the car park in time to see her familiar form accelerating away on her Honda Fireblade.

'Oh no!' Calum muttered to himself. 'You won't shake the *West Uist Chronicle*'s editor off that easily, lassie.' He raced for his Lambretta — only to find that it was not there!

He cursed and ran back to the Gathering to find a member of the Hebridean Constabulary. His eye fell on the Drummond twins by the beer tent.

'I've been robbed!' he exclaimed, running across to Douglas Drummond and grabbing him by the elbow. 'My scooter has been stolen.'

Douglas Drummond eyed the newspaper-man with good humour, which Calum was pretty sure was fuelled by more than a mug or two of Heather Ale. Or possibly even a spliff or two of marijuana. 'And where did you leave this machine of yours, Calum Steele?'

'In the car park.'

'And did you leave the key in the ignition of your vehicle?' asked Wallace Drummond, equally good-humouredly, his eyes also looking slightly bloodshot.

'Of course I bloody well did. This is West Uist, no one ever steals anything here.'

The Drummond twins exchanged knowing glances. 'Ah, but there you are, Calum,' Wallace replied. 'You never can tell. You need constant vigilance.'

'Aye, constant vigilance,' Douglas repeated. 'Just about anyone could have taken it. If I were you, I'd report it to the station.'

'But there's no one at the station, you pair

of teuchters!' Calum exclaimed in exasperation.

'Of course not, Calum Steele,' returned Douglas. 'It's the Gathering today. Everyone is here.'

Calum cursed afresh and, ignoring their protestations about his language, he charged off, having spotted Morag Driscoll popping into the baker's tent with her three youngsters.

* * *

Torquil knew that he was up against it an hour later when, after having won the strathspey and the hornpipe and jig, he was sure that Hamish Munro would be out for revenge. He began his pibroch, having just heard a superb version of 'Squinting Peter's Flame of Wrath', by his arch-opponent.

But he was hopeful, as the Padre said he should be, since the judges had chosen to hear him play 'Cha till MacCruimean' — 'No more MacCrimmon', the pibroch that he had worked so hard on over the last few weeks.

He saw the Padre watching him, pipe fuming furiously as he beat out a tattoo on the back of his wrist, as if trying telepathically to send him the *canntaireachd*, the traditional teaching method. He closed his eyes and tried to picture the old boy singing the song, giving him the rhythm, the beat.

But it was emotion that was the key. And it was that emotion that Torquil had been striving so hard to put into his playing for all those practice sessions. It had been that which was missing whenever the Padre had accused him of playing like a constipated crow.

'*Hiodroho, hodroho, haninen, hieachin*.'

He played the final bars, and slowly opened his eyes to see the Padre ecstatically punching the air. He knew that the Silver Quaich was all but his. Fifteen minutes later, the competition over, he shook Hamish Munro's hand and mounted the dais again to receive the Silver Quaich, the traditional cup of welcome given to guests throughout the Highlands and Islands. But it meant much more to Torquil than that.

As he looked down he saw the Padre raise two fingers in salute, meaning that now there were two champion pipers in the family, and that there would be a Silver Quaich for each side of the mantelpiece in the manse.

Through tears in his eyes he saw the Padre wipe a drop or two from his own eyes. It was one of the proudest moments in his life.

* * *

The AME Enstrom Shark helicopter landed on the temporary helipad and the door was flung open. A moment later, before the great blades had even stopped, Captain Tam McKenzie, the pilot, was racing across the ground towards the piping square.

'Inspector McKinnon,' he cried, mounting the steps in two bounds. 'You've got to come,' he cried, grasping Torquil's sleeve and pointing to the helicopter.

Angus MacLeod saw his pilot's agitated manner and himself ran over to the foot of the steps, to meet them coming down. 'What's the matter, Tam?'

Torquil quietened the laird with a stern gesture. 'Tell me, Tam,' he said quietly. 'What's the emergency?'

'There's a body in the black tower ruins on the crannog in Loch Hynish!' he whispered urgently. 'I saw it as I passed over it. It's a woman's, I think.

'She's not moving, Torquil!' he added.

* * *

A few minutes later the AME Enstrom Shark helicopter zoomed over the waters of Loch Hynish, the blades causing waves to disturb the normally calm surface water.

'The wee free ferry is moored on the

crannog,' Torquil said, pointing ahead.

'It was there when I flew by,' Tam replied.

'There isn't room to land on the crannog,' said Morag Driscoll. 'Will you be able to land on the water, Tam?'

'Aye, the Shark has got fixed floats so we can land on sea or loch.'

Torquil was glad that he had been able to get hold of Morag rather than the squeamish Ewan McPhee. The sergeant had always proved to be one of the most level-headed of people.

'Can you just hover above the crannog first though,' said Torquil.

In answer Tam McKenzie manoeuvred the machine closer and hovered above the ruined tower on the crannog. Torquil looked down at the body sprawled inside, and felt a wave of nausea hit him like a battering ram.

The half naked body of Fiona Cullen was lying on her back in the overgrown interior of the ruined tower, her head turned at an unnatural angle. A ligature of some sort was visible around her throat.

'My God!' Torquil muttered in disbelief. Then he felt himself diving into a pool of dark unconsciousness.

PART TWO

Dead Writers Tell No Tales

6

Torquil came back to consciousness as soon as Tam McKenzie landed the helicopter on the loch surface, within stepping distance of the shore where the wee free ferry rowing boat was moored. His faint had been only momentary and he felt pretty sure that the pilot had not noticed it, although the touch of Morag's hand on his shoulder was enough to tell him that his sergeant had.

'Torquil, do you want me to . . . ?'

'No, I'm fine, Morag,' he replied as he pushed open the door, coughing to try to stave off the wave of nausea that remained. 'Let's take a look.'

His instinct was to rush out and pick Fiona up in his arms, but he had to be professional. He led Morag round the tower wall to the gaping doorway that was invisible from the wee ferry jetty, then pushed his way through the bracken and long grass to where she lay.

It was worse than he had thought. Her face had a blue cyanotic tinge and her mouth was hanging open with the tongue slightly protruding. Her eyes were open and staring into nothingness. Blood caked her blonde hair and blood had pooled from an ugly gaping wound at the back of her head.

'My God!' Torquil exclaimed, as he failed to feel a carotid pulse. He looked up helplessly at Morag. 'Should we try . . . ?'

Morag was on her knees beside him now, listening for a heartbeat and checking her other pulses. She put a hand on his shoulder and shook her head. 'She's dead, Torquil,' she said gently. 'I'm so sorry, but it is clear that she has been murdered. Our duty now is to get a doctor here for certification, then seal the crannog off as a Scene of Crime.'

Torquil nodded numbly. 'Someone murdered her,' he repeated. 'They murdered my Fiona!'

Morag slid her arm about her inspector's shoulder. 'Come on Torquil, the best thing we can do is to go outside for a while and wait.' She unclipped her police phone. 'I'll send Tam back in the helicopter and I'll phone ahead for the doctor.' She looked worriedly at her friend and senior officer who was clearly still in a state of shock.

Nightmares like this were not supposed to happen on West Uist.

* * *

Superintendent Kenneth Lumsden, Torquil's superior officer, was laid up with gout in his son-in-law's house in Benbecula when Torquil rang to report the murder of Fiona Cullen. Not renowned for his temper at the best of times, an attack of gout had rendered him touchy to say the least.

'So get on and investigate it, McKinnon! You are, I gather, an *inspector* now?'

'Yes sir, I gained my promotion six months ago. You were actually — '

'Yes, yes, I know, of course. So, what progress so far?'

Torquil had never liked the big man, a lowlander from Glasgow with an innate dislike for the islanders he now lived amongst. He filled him in on the finding of the body, the sealing-off of the crannog and the setting-up of an incident room in Kyleshiffin police station.

'Post-mortem?'

Torquil swallowed acid rising in the back of his throat. He coughed. 'It's going to be done almost as soon as I get off the phone to you, sir.'

'Let me have a report straight away. Fax it through. Any suspects?'

Torquil drew in a deep breath. 'Too early to say yet sir, but I think there may be a few.'

'Any motives? Always think of motivation, McKinnon.'

'Yes, sir.'

'Anything else then?'

'I think that in the light of this event we have to reconsider the death of Ranald Buchanan, the man who seemed to have died accidentally last night.'

'That sounds likely. The Procurator Fiscal will want to hold an inquest soon, so start investigating. Any possible link?'

'None that I can think of, superintendent.'

There was a noise from the other end of the phone, as if the superintendent had experienced a sharp pain. 'Right. You'll need to seal the island off. Cancel all ferries to and from the island until further notice. The companies won't like it, but they'll just have to lump it. Well get on McKinnon, you've got a sergeant and a constable, haven't you? Any specials?'

'Two sir, the Drummond brothers. But do you think that is enough? Shouldn't we get CID assistance?'

'Nonsense! The Hebridean Constabulary has never needed an independent detective service and we shan't start now. That's the Chief Constable's view, so we'll look after this ourselves. But I'll check it out with him, just for your peace of mind. Anything else?'

'There is just one thing, superintendent,' Torquil said hurriedly. 'What about a press release?'

'I'll leave that to you, McKinnon. Just let the local press know. That will be that Calum Steele fellow won't it? You mark my words; he'll soon see that it reaches the nationals and the television.'

'What about access, sir? Are we going to let outside reporters and TV crews in?'

Superintendent Lumsden's tone was pained, as if he was a teacher having to spend extra time explaining the simplest principle to a dim pupil. 'If the island is sealed off then no one can get in. That will be to your advantage, since you won't have busybodies getting in your way. If you just feed Steele a bit of news then you'll have some control. Nurture him. Keep me in touch.'

The phone went dead and Torquil was left looking at the receiver. 'Thank you for your support, Superintendent Lumsden,' he said, replacing it.

Morag handed him a mug of tea. 'You didn't expect anything else, did you, Torquil?' she asked. 'Drink this,' she ordered, moving into her natural maternal role. 'I've put in extra sugar for energy. You're going to need it.'

* * *

While Morag set about phoning round to cancel all ferry movements, Torquil left for the Kyleshiffin Cottage Hospital where Fiona's body had been taken. Dr Ralph McLelland was an experienced police surgeon who had trained with the Forensic Medicine Department at Glasgow University before heading home for the supposedly less stressed life of a Hebridean GP. He had been meticulous in his examination of the body at the crime scene, digitally photographing from every angle, taking pictures of the scene itself, measuring the positions of any loose objects in the area and bagging them for further analysis. He had loaded them onto his computer for Torquil to view.

'I never thought I'd be doing two post-mortems like this in one day, Torquil,' he said, as he continued to make notes of his general external examination of the body, which Torquil was relieved to see was now covered in a green plastic sheet. 'This is a really nasty one. After I do the actual post-mortem examination I should be able to tell you conclusively what caused her death, but at the moment it looks as if whoever did it was taking no chances on leaving her alive.'

'Meaning what, Ralph?'

‘She was hit with some sort of bludgeon and she’s been strangled. The question is, which came first? Was she knocked out, and then strangled? Or was she garrotted and then bashed on the head to make sure?’

Torquil felt a wave of nausea, mixed with anger. He took a deep breath and willed himself to be calm. ‘Was she — ?’

‘Raped? Not sure yet. Whoever did it had a good go at ripping her leathers off to have a go. I’ve taken swabs and scrapings from her nails and I’ll be looking at them under a microscope after I’ve done the actual PM. I need to see if she managed to take any chunks out of her killer’s skin. I can’t tell yet,’ he said, holding one of her hands and leaning forward to look at the nails. ‘They’re broken and there’s a lot of dirt under them. She might have struggled.’

Torquil felt his head spin and another wave of nausea threatened to make him topple forward. He reached out for the bench to support himself. The doctor saw his discomfiture and offered a spare stool. ‘Are you going to stay for the PM?’ he asked.

Torquil nodded. ‘Aye Ralph. I’m the investigating officer, so it’s my duty.’

‘As you wish,’ returned Ralph, laying aside his pen and turning to gown up. Once done he wheeled a waiting trolley over, upon which were rows of surgical instruments and saws. 'If you feel queasy at any time, just pop through to the side room.'

He picked up a scalpel and pulled back the sheet to reveal Fiona's naked body.

Torquil squeezed his eyes shut, wishing that he was not there, that he would not have to witness further violation of her body.

To his relief his mobile phone rang. He excused himself and went through to the side room.

'Torquil, I think you'd better come over to the Bonnie Prince Charlie,' came PC Ewan McPhee's excited voice. 'There's something odd going on. Mollie McFadden called me in when she heard about Fiona. The news has gone round the island faster than a summer squall.'

'What did she say, Ewan?' Torquil asked, trying hard to suppress the impatience in his voice.

'She said that she saw Fiona come in and go up to her room, but she never came down again. She's sure it was just before you went off in the helicopter.'

For a fleeting moment Torquil felt a glimmer of hope. As if there could have been some colossal mistake and that Fiona had just been sleeping in her room at the Bonnie Prince Charlie. Then the devastating image of her body lying on Ralph McLelland's mortuary slab made the hope vanish like smoke.

'Has she checked the room?'

'No, and I thought I'd better wait for you.'

'I'll be there in five minutes.'

Steeling himself he pushed open the door to the mortuary room and called through, without daring to put his head round. 'Ralph, I have to go. There may have been a development.'

'That's fine, Torquil. I'll have some news for you later maybe.'

The noise of an electric circular buzz-saw made Torquil beat a hasty retreat.

* * *

The Games had finished at about six o'clock and the crowds had all gradually dispersed, in search of food, relaxation, entertainment or drink. But just as Ewan had said, the news had spread about a body having been found on the crannog on Loch Hynish. That it was Fiona Cullen, the famous crime novelist, was also the news on the street and in the cafés, restaurants and bars. Already there was a sense of anxiety and murmurings about what action was being taken to find the killer.

Torquil, now in his police 'uniform', was

inevitably accosted several times as he walked the short distance downhill from the cottage hospital to the Bonnie Prince Charlie Tavern on Harbour Street. To all and sundry who asked him he replied that a body had indeed been found and that the police were making enquiries. He anticipated that the trickle of questions would turn into an avalanche as soon as people realized that the island was being sealed off and that those people who had planned to return to Lochboisdale in South Uist on the late-evening ferry would have to find overnight accommodation.

Or longer, Torquil thought to himself. He had visions of this taking longer than a day to sort out, even though it was just a small island.

He turned into the welcoming tavern and found Ewan standing at the bar, drinking tea with Mollie McFadden. The bar was busy, her staff dispensing Heather Ale and taking orders for food.

'Torquil, it is sorry I am to hear about Fiona. But I canna understand it. I saw her go upstairs to her room and she hasn't been down.'

'Let's get out of the bar, Mollie,' Torquil said. Then, once in the hall, 'When did you see her, Mollie?'

Mollie blinked and pushed her spectacles

farther back on her nose. 'About half past four, I think. There was no one here, of course, since the Games was still in full swing. I was just bottling up in the cellar and I heard that big bike of hers draw up into the back car park. I heard the door open and I went up to ask how the Games had gone. I saw her dashing up the stairs and I called out to ask, but she didn't seem to hear me. I heard her door close and thought no more about it.'

'You're sure it was Fiona?'

Mollie McFadden's eyes grew huge behind her thick spectacle lenses. 'She was wearing her black leathers and her helmet!' She grabbed his arm. 'Mother of God! Torquil, could that have been — ?'

'Ewan and I will see, Mollie. Have you a master key?'

Mollie scuttled into her small reception area and came back with a heavy key. 'Take care, the pair of you.'

Somewhat apprehensively Torquil led the way up to the Flora McDonald Room, where he had last seen Fiona alive that very morning. As he expected, the door was locked from within, and peering into the keyhole he saw that the key was still in the door.

'This key is useless,' he told his constable. 'We don't have enough time to wait, Ewan.

Will you do the needful?'

The big hammer-throwing champion nodded and with two shoulder charges the door burst open, to reveal a scene of devastation. The room was not just untidy; it had been destroyed, as if someone had trashed it in a frenzy of fury and passion. Fiona's helmet lay in a corner of the room as if it had been discarded and had rolled there. The bedclothes were scattered over the floor, her soft motorcycle panniers had been emptied and the contents thrown hither and thither. Torquil felt his anger rise as he spotted a pile of underclothes which had been slashed with some sort of sharp blade, just as had several loose blouses and the dressing gown that he had seen her wearing that morning. Several personal effects lay scattered about the floor.

'We've got a sicko bastard on our hands, Torquil!' Ewan growled, working his hands open and closed. 'If I could get my hands on him — '

But Torquil silenced him with a raised hand. 'We have to be professional, Ewan.' He pointed to the open window. 'The room looks out over the back car park. So that's how the killer, assuming it was the killer that Mollie saw, made off.' He crossed to the window and looked out. 'Her bike is there all right.'

'He must be a cool bastard, riding her bike back here,' Ewan gasped.

Torquil shook his head. 'We can't assume it was a man, Ewan.' He bit his lip, then mused. 'But why did whoever it was risk coming here? What did they want?'

Ewan pointed to the shredded frilly underwear. 'I told you, Torquil. A sicko!'

'Don't touch anything Ewan. We just need to get the room photographed and dusted for prints. Morag can sort that out. She's done her CID training and can bring her kit.'

He looked around the room; his eyes searching amid the mess for something that he knew should be there. He tapped his teeth with his fingernail as he contemplated. Then he snapped his fingers as realization dawned.

'Her notes and her laptop! They're not here. That's what the murderer came for, Ewan.'

'Sick bastard!' Ewan cursed, shaking his head in disgust.

* * *

Angus MacLeod was not himself. He was either angry, anxious or a combination of the two. The Padre could not quite work out which, as he sat with the laird, Miss Melville and the rest of the Gathering Committee in the Duncan Institute that evening. All of them were feeling shocked, of course, but needs must and they had to decide what to do now, since the news had percolated around that all ferries had been cancelled pending police investigations. The Padre had of course tried to contact Torquil to find out what was happening, and to try to console the lad, but as he expected Torquil was run off his feet and unable to talk.

Poor Fiona! Dead! Murdered! How could it happen to her? He had talked to her just a few hours ago, watched her head off on her motorbike, seemingly full of spirit and joi de vivre. And he was sure that a lot of that joi de vivre had been due to Torquil. It's a cruel world, he thought.

'I know that we're all more upset about Fiona Cullen than we could ever adequately express,' said Miss Melville, interrupting his reverie, 'but we do have to sort these problems out this evening. Sergeant Morag Driscoll has given me a list of all the pubs, bed and breakfasts, hotels and hostels that might be able to put people up for the night, but I think it might come to providing sleeping bags and blankets and finding whoever has got room for strangers to bed down in their living rooms.'

'You can put me down for twenty or so,

Miss Melville,' Angus MacLeod volunteered. 'Dunshiffin Castle is at your disposal.'

'And we can use the Duncan Institute,' piped up Rabbie Roberts, the caretaker. 'But I canna say that I can do anything about breakfasts,' he added, hastily.

'St Ninian's Hall is free, of course,' said Lachlan McKinnon. 'And of course, all of the marquees are still up. It might be a wee bit windy if there is a squall, but on the whole I think we should be able to manage.'

Angus MacLeod stood up, examining his wristwatch for the umpteenth time. 'Right then, if I can leave these things in your capable hands, I must be off. I have to look after Roland Baxter our esteemed Minister for Culture.' He shook his head. 'This couldn't have happened at a worse time,' he mused, making for the door. 'Just send however many people you want and I'll get the staff to make them comfortable.'

Lachlan also stood. 'And I'm afraid that I'm going to have to go as well, Ladies and Gentlemen.' He nodded and smiled at the other council members, in that reassuring way that the clergy manage during times of tragedy and suffering. 'I need to go and see Fiona Cullen's — body. It's time that I give her the Lord's blessing.'

'*A Thighearna bheannaichte*!' said Bella

Melville, her eyes immediately welling up with tears as she verbalized the thoughts of everyone in the room. 'Let the lassie rest in peace.'

* * *

The recreation room at the back of the Kyleshiffin police station had been converted into an incident room. The net of the table tennis table had been taken down and stowed away to provide room for all the documentation that was bound to accrue. Four large pinboards had been put up on the wall for all sorts of snips and snaps of information that may or may not be relevant. The whiteboard that was usually used to record table tennis scores and supply lists had been cleaned down in readiness and extra supplies of milk had been obtained for the innumerable brewings of tea that were anticipated.

Torquil, Morag and Douglas Drummond were sitting waiting for Ewan to come through from the front office so that the meeting could begin. But the heated voice of Calum Steele made Torquil shudder.

'Ewan will deal with the wee nyaff, Torquil,' Morag said, sensing her boss's irritation.

'No, I'd better have a word with him,' replied Torquil. 'Best to get the 'press conference' over and done with.'

'Ah, Torquil. At last! The organ grinder, not the monkey.'

Ewan smouldered. 'You just be having a care with your words, Calum Steele or I'll — '

'Ewan, why don't you go and brew up some tea while I talk to the editor of the Chronicle.'

'The editor has a complaint, Torquil,' Ewan returned, as he left the office. 'About his stolen Lambretta.'

Torquil leaned on the counter and rubbed his eyes. 'Calum, this is a bloody awful business. I'm going to nail the bastard that did this.'

'You will be having the full backing of the *Chronicle*. But I ought to warn you that the big boys, the nationals and the TV will be hard to handle. They have ways of inveigling information; they winkle it out of you.' He nodded meaningfully at the now closed office door. 'Some of your people may not be as adept as they need to be at keeping their mouths closed.'

'The only media involved will be the *Chronicle*,' Torquil replied. 'My superintendent has imposed a press embargo.'

The ghost of a smile flickered across Calum's lips. 'But you can't totally blank this from the news, man. Fiona Cullen is famous; it will need to be on the television news.'

'You can be the link, Calum. But the island is being sealed off, no ferries, boats or helicopters. Anyone landing will be arrested and held for questioning.'

Calum whistled. 'You're going to have to sort this out quickly, Torquil.' He winked as he drew out his ubiquitous notepad. He licked the end of a stubby pencil, then continued, 'Can you officially confirm that Fiona Cullen is dead.'

'She is. She has been formally identified by me and by her agent, Genevieve Cooper. We are treating this as suspicious.'

'Suspicious, I'll say,' agreed the little reporter. 'Half naked on a crannog in the middle of Loch Hynish. How did she get there?'

'We are making enquiries, Calum.'

'Any leads as to who did it?'

'We are following up several leads, but it is too early to report.'

'What about manpower? Have you enough folk on the job?'

'The West Uist Division of the Hebridean Constabulary is . . . *stretched*.'

Calum shook his head. 'Oh come on Torquil, give me something! I could have replied to each of those questions myself.'

They were interrupted by Torquil's mobile phone. Wallace Drummond's name flashed on the little view-panel. He excused himself and answered it, nodding as his special constable talked to him. 'OK, Wallace, get it covered and don't disturb it. We'll have to have it dusted for prints. Come back now, then you and Morag can check it after our meeting.'

Once he had finished, Calum asked eagerly, 'Have you got something there? A lead?'

'Perhaps, Calum,' Torquil replied. 'We don't know how Fiona Cullen got to the crannog, but we do have an idea as to how her murderer got out to Loch Hynish.'

'Well?'

'I had a suspicion that we would find something near the lochside. Wallace Drummond has just pulled a Lambretta out of the bracken.'

'Well I'll be buggered!' exclaimed Calum. Then, horrified, 'The cheeky bastard!'

* * *

Ralph McLelland arrived in time for the start of the meeting. He sat in the corner, his hands clasped over his slight beerbelly while Torquil stood by the whiteboard with a felt marker pen in his hand.

'OK, so we are here to hold the first formal meeting of the investigation into the death of Fiona Cullen.' Torquil talked slowly, enunciating every word, as if he still could not accept the fact that she was dead. 'This afternoon Dr Ralph McLelland conducted a post-mortem examination and he is now going to give us his findings.'

Ralph McLelland stood and took over from Torquil. He opened the file on the desk in front of him and began reading out his general findings at the murder site and then his observations of her body at the mortuary. As he did so, Torquil pinned the photographs of the murder scene to the first pinboard.

Morag and Ewan busily took down notes.

'It is not possible at this time to be certain about the cause of death. There was a major blow to the back of the head with a blunt instrument. That could have been fatal. But there was also a ligature around her neck with which she was strangled. Whether she was already dead or not, I cannot determine as yet.'

'Will further forensic testing tell you, Ralph?' Torquil asked.

'I'm not sure. The gross morbid anatomical examination can't tell me. Certainly there were punctate haemorrhages over the face, and in sections of the brain. That would occur with both a blow to the back of the head and strangulation, if either was a single event.' He bit his lip and frowned. 'There were no such haemorrhages in the lungs or upper airways, which is unusual in a case of strangulation.'

'Meaning what?' Torquil queried.

'That on balance, although I cannot be certain, my opinion is that she was already dead before the strangulation.'

Despite himself, Torquil heaved a sigh of relief. He had hated the thought of her being strangled. 'But what about the broken fingernails and the dirt under them?'

'It could have been reflex action after death,' the doctor replied without conviction. 'But again, my opinion is that her hands were raked along the ground after death. I didn't find anything except dirt on microscopy.'

'So it could have been done to make it look as if she'd struggled,' Torquil said with a shudder. 'What about the state of her clothes? She was half naked. Her leathers had been pulled off her top and halfway down her thighs. Had she — ?'

Ralph McLelland anticipated Torquil. 'No, I can say categorically that she wasn't raped. There were no signs of penetration, no bruising, no evidence of semen anywhere.

The murderer might have been interrupted or panicked and left.'

'Or it could have been done to make it look as though it was a sexual crime.'

'That's possible,' the police surgeon replied, picking up his mug of tea and draining it. He looked at his watch. 'Well, I think that's about all I have to tell you for now, Torquil. Do you mind if I get off? I have a couple of house calls to make.'

While Ewan showed him out, Torquil went to the whiteboard and wrote in the top-left corner three words: MURDER, INVESTIGATION, ARREST.

'OK, everyone,' he said, a few moments later as Wallace Drummond came in. 'We have a murder case on our hands.' In the centre of the board he wrote FIONA CULLEN, and underneath added arrows to subheadings of: writer, local girl, motorbike, the Gathering, Bonnie Prince Charlie. He tapped the board and spread out his hand to the other pinboards. 'This is the control centre and we're going to get this bastard, whoever it is. We're going to spend an hour putting all that we know up on this board and on these pinboards. We're going to build up a web of all the possible motives, all the possible suspects, anyone who had any dealings with Fiona while she was on the island, and any dealings before she came here for the Gathering.'

'Is it a sort of brainstorming that you are after having?' asked Douglas Drummond.

'Exactly,' Torquil replied. 'Absolutely anything goes up there, then we'll work backwards and establish links.'

'So we'll catch this bastard in the web!' exclaimed Wallace Drummond. 'Better put up Calum Steele and his Lambretta scooter then, boss.'

'Genevieve Cooper, her agent,' volunteered Morag. 'Allegra McCall, her publisher.'

Torquil put each name in a circle on its own, with little explanatory notes attached to each, and arrows linking them to Fiona's name at the centre of the board. He added the names of Professor Neil Ferguson, Roland Baxter, Angus MacLeod, Izzie Frazer, Miss Bella Melville, the Padre — Lachlan McKinnon.

'And I declare my own name,' he said, adding his name and circling it, annotating it with 'friend'.

'Torquil you were at the Gathering when this happened,' Morag protested. 'I saw you myself.'

'I was', he admitted. 'But we shall conduct this investigation with rigour and diligence. You shall interview me in due course, Morag.'

And so they worked for a good hour, dragging possible times, connections and hunches together and adding them to the board.

'Now let's just take a sidewards step.' The others looked curiously at him as he went to the other side of the whiteboard and wrote the name RANALD BUCHANAN in large letters, just as he had done Fiona's. 'Fiona's murder forces us to reconsider the death of Ranald Buchanan.'

Ewan spluttered. 'It was horrible, Torquil. Shall I go and make some tea, I feel kind of sick just thinking about it?'

Torquil nodded, and as the big constable retreated to the kitchen, he drew a dotted line between Ranald's name and Fiona's. 'Is there a link of any sort between them? I don't know.'

'They were both writers,' suggested Morag.

Torquil nodded and jotted notes. 'And Fiona's laptop and all her notebooks were missing.'

'Perhaps Calum Steele may have an idea,' Morag suggested. 'She used to work on the *Chronicle*, didn't she?'

'We will be speaking to Calum about his scooter and other things,' Torquil agreed.

Ewan came in a few moments later with a tray full of fresh mugs of tea. 'I heard what you were saying, Torquil, and it worries me. About Ranald and Fiona both being writers.'

'Go on, Ewan.'

'Well, all these people on the island are here for the Gathering *and* the Literary Festival. It might be a stupid suggestion, I know, but if there is a link and they were both killed, murdered I mean. Well, couldn't — ?'

'I see what he means!' Wallace Drummond exclaimed.

'A serial killer on the loose! On West Uist,' added Douglas Drummond.

Morag shook her head. 'Oh come on now, that's a quantum leap isn't it?'

Torquil shook his head. 'Maybe not, Morag,' he said, tapping the felt-tip pen against the whiteboard. 'Do you remember the title of Fiona's next book?'

The sergeant's eyes rolled up in alarm.

'That's right,' said Torquil, as he began to write the title in capital letters: DEAD WRITERS TELL NO TALES.

'We need to find that manuscript,' he said. 'Or at least we need to know what it was going to be about.'

7

The alarm went off at 7 a.m. and woke Torquil from a wretched nightmare. He shot up in bed bathed in cold perspiration.

In his dream he had seen Fiona row out to the crannog on Loch Hynish, a peal of laughter following her as she left him on the shore. Unable to get across to the island he kept calling out her name, only to be greeted by more laughter. And then he heard a noise, a scream he thought, followed by someone else's laughter. But still he could not get out to her and he called more frantically. Then he heard the whirring blades of a helicopter, getting louder and louder until their noise reached a crescendo, and he found himself sitting up in bed, his hand stretching out to switch off the alarm.

The stark realization that Fiona was dead was like a knife through his heart.

Yet the content of the dream would not leave him as he rose, shaved and showered. There was something in the dream — something important that he could not quite put his finger on.

He descended the stairs to the smell of

porridge, but found the big kitchen was empty. A simple note on the large deal kitchen table read:

Torquil,
There is porridge in the bottom of the Aga. I'm on the golf course if you need me.
Lachlan.

Torquil read the note in disbelief, then screwed it up in his hand and contemptuously threw it in the pedal-bin.

'Oh man man!' he exclaimed as he served himself porridge and sprinkled salt over it. 'How the hell can anyone play golf at a time like this!' He poured milk and forced himself to eat, despite having no desire whatever for food. When he had managed half of the portion he shoved the bowl aside and rose to make tea. But that too, had no taste and picking up his mobile phone and wrapping his tartan scarf about his neck he left the house, strode down the path and out the iron gate, over the road and onto St Ninian's Golf Course.

The Padre was nowhere to be seen.

But then Torquil heard him. Or rather, he heard the repeated click of an iron club hitting balls and he realized where his uncle was. Jogging across the dunes he crested a rise and saw him standing on the ninth tea, hitting ball after ball over the small hill towards the out-of-sight green.

'Ah Torquil, laddie,' Lachlan called, seeing his nephew strutting towards him. 'I needed to come out and hit a few balls at *Creideamh*.'

'I wondered what you were doing out this early — playing golf, today of all days!' Torquil replied stiffly. 'Fiona is dead you know!'

The Padre nodded his head. 'I know that Torquil. And I cannot believe it any more than you. Do you know why I called this hole '*Creideamh*', when I designed it?'

'Of course. It means Faith. It's beside the kirk and the cemetery and it takes an act of faith to knock it between them.'

The Padre hung his head and swished the club along the grass. 'It was partly that, Torquil. But it was to remind me that life goes on.'

'Not for Fiona,' Torquil snapped. 'She was murdered yesterday. And I'm going to find her murderer.'

'And do what, Torquil? Have your revenge?'

'I'm going to bring whoever did it to justice. I'm going to get justice for Fiona.'

'I hope you do, laddie, I hope you do. Just

make sure it is justice and not revenge.' He pulled his pipe out from his top pocket and began filling it from his dilapidated pouch. 'But you know as well as I do that your parents are both buried in that graveyard. You never want to talk about it, but the fact is that they are there. I designed this golf course so that I could test my faith to keep going whenever I came this way.'

'Like you are testing it now? By hitting golf balls?'

The Padre tamped the tobacco down in the bowl of his pipe. 'That's right. Your parents died tragically, Torquil. Drowned in the Minch on their way to the mainland, and I became your guardian.'

'And I'm grateful, Uncle.'

The Padre shook his head. 'I don't want your gratitude, Torquil. You are my brother's son and I was happy to look after you. Just as I have been proud of all the things you have achieved, like the Silver Quaich that you won yesterday.'

Torquil waved his hand dismissively.

'No Torquil, I am proud. But this hole, Faith, has meant a lot to me. It hasn't always been easy bringing a lad up all on my own. And I don't think that I made a half bad job of it. But I've always been able to test my faith here on this little golf course.'

'I don't like to think about my parents being here,' Torquil admitted, hanging his head.

'I know that Torquil. And I know that you think I'm showing disrespect by hitting golf balls the day after Fiona — passed over. But I'm testing my faith again. I'm hurting inside. I'm sad and I'm as angry as hell. And these golf balls are feeling every little bit of my anger.' He gave his nephew a wan smile. 'And when I'm angry I mis-hit the ball, just as Fiona did the other day. Like when she hit Professor Ferguson.'

'What are you getting at Padre?'

'Let your emotion out, laddie! Your task is to find whoever did this dreadful thing, but you can't do it when you're full of anger and hate. Hit some balls, or go to St Ninian's Cave and play a few tunes, just do something to let it out. Then you'll be able to get things in perspective, be able to ask the right questions.'

'You mean about things like Fiona's reaction when she hit Professor Ferguson?'

The Padre struck a light and applied it to his pipe. 'Aye, Torquil. Questions just like that.'

* * *

Torquil rode the Bullet fast along the snaking Loch Hynish road towards Kyleshiffin. And as he did so, putting the machine through its paces, he realized that the old boy was right, as he so often had been. Riding aggressively, losing some of his frustration was therapeutic.

There were so many issues going through his mind; so many things that had given him cause for anger, yet he had pretty well suppressed them. He was good at that. His parents had died in a freak accident in the Minch when he was a youngster of five. He barely remembered them, having bonded with the Padre and been brought up by him. And in that he realized that so many of the Padre's interests were now his, like motor-bikes and the bagpipes.

But not the faith! Early on, Torquil had expressed disquiet about religion and the Church. He had assumed it was because he didn't like to think that his parents were lying dead in the cemetery. Yet now he knew that it was more than that. It was to do with a feeling of anger that he had about God.

He opened up the throttle and accelerated out of a corner. And it was anger at his parents for getting themselves killed.

A shiver ran up his spine and the involuntary movement made the bike wobble dangerously.

Fiona! Was he angry with her for getting killed?

He applied the brakes and skidded to a halt. 'You bloody idiot, Torquil McKinnon!' he screamed at the top of his voice. And as if suddenly startled by his cry, a flock of gulls rose from the sandy machair and squawked noisily across the loch. 'I loved her! I always loved her and I should have been there to protect her!'

Anger coursed through him like hot lead. And again the Padre's words struck a chord. '*Just make sure it is justice and not revenge*.'

He wasn't sure which he really wanted. First of all he just needed to find the bastard. And in that respect the Padre was right. He needed to be dispassionate and clinical. A thinking machine.

He started up the Bullet again and headed for Kyleshiffin.

First, find the bastard! he thought. Then I'll see what I want.

* * *

Morag was hard at work by the time Torquil arrived at the station. Despite having had less than four hours' sleep, for she had gone with Wallace Drummond to photograph and fingerprint Calum Steele's Lambretta immediately after the meeting the night before, she looked as fresh as a daisy. No mean task since prior to setting off she had to organize her three children. Torquil admired his sergeant's ability to multitask, which she was forever telling him and Ewan, was a quality of the female sex.

'Tea, boss?' she asked, handing him a copy of the morning's special festival edition of the Chronicle. 'Calum wasted no time there. Look at the headline.'

The words stood out boldly:

THE GATHERING MURDER!
FAMOUS WRITER'S BODY FOUND

Torquil winced as he read the report of the finding of a body on the crannog on Loch Hynish as the Gathering drew to a close. In his most sensational journalese Calum Steele recounted how the famous crime writer Fiona Cullen had mingled with the crowd at the Gathering, then disappeared for a while, only to be found after her body had been sighted by the AME helicopter, which had been giving visitors aerial trips around the island all afternoon.

Somewhat indignantly he had added the theft of his Lambretta, hinting strongly that 'the police suspect the killer may have used the editor-in-chief's vehicle to get to Loch Hynish'.

Torquil looked up from the paper and asked, 'Did you find anything on the scooter?'

Morag put a mug of strong tea by Torquil's elbow. 'Nothing at all. The handlebars had been wiped clean. It's probably never been so clean, actually. You know how scruffy Calum Steele is.' She wrinkled her nose at the thought of the local journalist. 'And I think he must have been on the phone to the mainland newspapers and TV channels straight away. Did you see the news on Scottish TV this morning?'

'No. I had other things on my mind than television,' he replied, feeling a tad guilty over his contretemps with the Padre.

'The TV is always on at my breakfast table,' Morag said. 'It keeps the kids occupied while I do their eggs or kippers. Anyway, they basically gave a résumé of Calum's article.'

'Well let's hope we can get a swift result before the media circus is forced upon us. Where's Ewan?'

Morag had picked up a pile of reports and had begun arranging them into alphabetical order. 'I sent him out in the *Seaspray* to do a reconnoitre to make sure we don't get any investigative reporters from the big papers trying to break the embargo.'

'It won't be easy to stop them, Morag. You had better get Fergus McAllister the harbour master to keep a watch as well and let us know if any boats try to land.'

'I've done that, boss.'

Torquil grinned. 'You're a wonder, Morag. What would I do without you?'

She saw his face suddenly pale and she patted his shoulder. 'You're going to be all right, Torquil,' she said soothingly, in her big-sister manner. 'We'll nail this bastard.'

'Bloody right,' he replied, picking up his mug and swallowing tea. Then, slapping the desk with the flat of his hand, he added, 'OK then, time to get started on the interviews. We'll have to split them between us.'

'Who do you want to see first, boss?'

Torquil's lips tightened. 'Professor Neil Ferguson. I want to know why he was ferreting around the St Ninian's cemetery the other day.'

* * *

Professor Neil Ferguson had breakfasted on orange juice and half a slice of toast, his usual morning fare, at about six o'clock before heading out to sea in his 28-foot cabin cruiser. He anchored about a quarter of a mile from the west coast, donned his wetsuit and dived into the sea.

Ewan spotted the boat as he came round the Machair Skerry on the north of the island and headed towards it. He sounded the claxon, then cut the engine and coasted alongside just as the professor was hauling himself back on board.

'Good morning!' he called out. 'It is glad I am to be finding you, professor. There are two good reasons,' he explained. 'First, it is not permitted for anyone to leave the island at the moment.'

'Ah, I'm sorry,' Neil Ferguson replied, sitting down and removing his face mask and snorkel. 'I wasn't thinking. And what is the second reason, constable?'

'My inspector wants to interview you. He just called from your hotel.'

The professor nodded, showing no surprise. 'Of course. I rather thought he would want a chat.'

Ewan eyed him suspiciously. Why isn't he surprised? I had better tell Torquil about that, he thought.

⋆ ⋆ ⋆

Dr Viroj Wattana had been unable to sleep. There were so many questions buzzing through his mind, so many anxieties.

The bitch was dead!

Yet the implications were awesome. The whole afternoon at the Gathering had been a blur, partly due to that idiot priest and the alcohol he forced down him. But he had been sure that he had seen — ! Yet it couldn't have been, surely not?

Unable to toss and turn any longer he rose, dressed and silently made his way through the corridors of Dunshiffin Castle, passing several rooms from whence a cacophony of snoring was being emitted by the multitude of largely unwanted guests that had been billeted at the castle the night before.

Fresh air. He needed to get outside so that he could think what to do next.

* * *

A muscle flinched in Torquil's jaw as Ewan reported to him about how he had found the professor of Marine Archaeology snorkelling off the side of his cabin cruiser.

'Is he in the interview room?'

'Aye Torquil, he is that. With a cup of coffee.'

'And you followed him back to the Kyleshiffin harbour?'

'I did. I waited for him to set off. I thought

that would be best.'

'And you left a marker buoy over the spot where he was swimming?'

The big constable's face went puce and he fidgeted from foot to foot. 'I — er — no, Torquil. I didn't think about that.'

Morag was watching from her desk, all too aware that Torquil's temper was beginning to rise. She half expected an eruption any moment; as did Ewan. But it didn't come. Torquil merely nodded. 'That's a pity, Constable McPhee,' he said coldly. 'It may be of no importance whatever — or it could be vital information that we have now lost.'

'I'm sorry — er — inspector,' Ewan blustered. 'But why would it be important?'

Torquil turned to Morag. 'Explain, will you, sergeant,' he said, heading for the interview room. 'I'm going to have a chat with the professor.'

When he had gone, Ewan turned desperately to his superior. 'Morag, what have I done? I've never known Torquil pull rank like that before.'

'Oh sweet Lord!' Morag exclaimed with a gentle shake of the head. 'Just think Ewan. A murder has been committed with some sort of bludgeon. Where do you think would be a good place to lose it if you were a murderer?'

Ewan gasped as realization dawned. Then

he quickly shook his head. 'But you can't be serious. No one could think that Professor Ferguson could have done it.'

Morag clicked her tongue. 'Ewan, my love, right now everyone on West Uist is a suspect!'

* * *

Professor Neil Ferguson was used to public speaking. He had taught in lecture halls full of two hundred students, given papers at world scientific conferences of several hundred, and presented a popular television series, *The Treasures of the Deep*. Despite this, he was more nervous about his interview with a Hebridean police inspector than he had ever been before.

'Had you known Fiona Cullen for long?' Piper asked, after briefly informing the professor of the purpose of his interview, namely that it was part of his investigation into the murder of the famous crime writer.

'A few years. I first met her when she was a reporter with your local newspaper here.'

'That would be five years then,' Piper volunteered. 'Before she left to become a full-time writer. Have you read any of her books?'

The professor shook his head. 'No, crime fiction isn't my thing.'

'Were you on friendly terms with her, Professor?'

The academic raised his eyebrows slightly at the use of his title. A frequent visitor to West Uist for the better part of twenty or so years, he had always been on first-name terms with Torquil McKinnon.

'We used to be.'

'What changed that?'

Neil Ferguson looked down at the table in front of him and wiped an imaginary speck of dust away. 'I'm afraid that she blamed me for the death of a friend of hers.'

Torquil was making notes as they spoke, rather than using the more formal tape recorder. He gestured for the professor to explain.

'As you know I have a certain reputation as an expert on crannogs, the artificial islands to be found on the lochs and lakes of the northern parts of the British Isles. The majority date from the Iron Age. Originally they seem to have been constructed as defensive islets, but later on they became a sign of power, of wealth. Sort of archaic follies.'

Torquil could see that the professor was warming to his subject and beginning to relax.

'I have studied the crannogs of the

Hebrides extensively over the last twenty years or so. I did my doctoral dissertation on the crannogs of the Uists.' He sucked air in between his teeth. 'What I'm trying to say, inspector, is that I have a detailed knowledge of the way the crannogs were constructed. I can outline the different styles, just as an expert drystone waller can look at a dyke and tell you all sorts of things about the way it was built, and why a particular technique was used.'

'Your point being?'

Neil Ferguson sighed. 'Egyptology is the sexy side of archaeology, inspector. Everyone and his dog knows about the pyramids of Egypt. They were built with massive man-power over decades with ropes and pulleys. We all know that.'

Piper was beginning to feel his irritation rise, just as the professor's nerves seemed to be calming. 'Has this a bearing on my investigation, Professor Ferguson?'

'Absolutely! Despite the fact that we know scientifically how the pyramids were built, there are still people — New Age folk — who are convinced that the pyramids were built by some extraterrestrial beings or by survivors from the lost civilization of Atlantis. They are called 'Pyramidiots' by bona fide Egyptologists. Well,' he took a breath, his face a picture of exasperation, ' — we have the same problem in Marine Archaeology. There is a thriving market in Atlantean and extraterrestrial theories about crannogs. We have oddballs insisting that the crannogs were built as landing platforms for UFOs, or as islands on which to build mini-Atlantean-style temples to encircle the globe.'

'And you think that is nonsense?'

Neil Ferguson shoved his fingers through his thick brown hair. Although now in his forties he still had the look of a man ten years younger. 'Of course it's rubbish. And that is what I said — perhaps a trifle forcefully — on a TV chat show one afternoon. You may have seen the sort of show. A husband-and-wife team sitting on a sofa, sipping tea and giving all kinds of eccentrics an easy ride. Anyway, this woman, Esme Portland, was expounding about her book, *Mini Temples of Atlantis* I think it was called. I was there as a supposed tame archaeologist. Only I didn't feel tame about the rubbish she was spouting. It demeans my profession.'

'And the result of the interview was what?'

'I showed her up as a simpleton on TV.'

'And?'

The professor bit his lip. 'I'm not sure there was an 'and'! he replied. 'I mean, I don't know whether one can make a connection between the television programme and the — er — '

'The what?' Torquil asked blandly, making it seem as if he was unaware of any of this.

'Esme Portland cut her wrists the evening of the show. Fiona Cullen was a friend of hers. She phoned me up and told me that I was responsible for her friend's death.'

'Did you have any other contact with her?'

'She harassed me for a few months. Phone calls, letters, that sort of thing. I ignored them actually.'

'And when was all this?'

'About eighteen months ago.'

'And there was no further contact between you.'

Neil Ferguson shook his head. 'Not until I came to West Uist, when I saw her with you and the Padre.'

'Ah yes,' Torquil admitted. 'On the golf course — or rather, in the St Ninian's cemetery.'

Almost unconsciously the professor touched his forehead where a slight bruise was visible. 'What was she doing there?' he asked.

This was potentially tricky ground, Torquil knew. It would be so easy to lose the initiative if he allowed himself to have the interview turned on him by a clever interviewee. And there was no doubt that the professor was a clever man.

'She wanted to have a chat with the Padre as one of the Literary Festival judges,' Piper replied, then added, 'But more to the point, what exactly were you doing in the cemetery, professor?'

The archaeologist seemed to ponder this for a moment before replying. 'Research. I was following up on a story I came across recently about the 1745 uprising and the hunt for Bonnie Prince Charlie after Culloden.'

'Indeed? Tell me more.'

The professor shrugged. 'I'm not sure about the veracity of the tale. I was told that in 1746, when Bonnie Prince Charlie was on the run throughout the Hebrides, there were eight days that have never been properly accounted for. As you probably know, it is believed that he spent five of those eight days on West Uist and three days sailing between here and the other Western Isles trying to liaise with the French vessel sent to pick him up.'

'You mean the *Hirondelle*?'

'No, that was the vessel that finally did pick him up from Skye. No one knows much about this other French vessel, except that it is thought to have sunk somewhere off West

Uist in deep water after holing its hull on rocks.'

'Aye, we all know the tale,' Torquil said. 'But it's always been linked up with the Selkie legend. The seal-folk took the souls of the sailors.'

Neil Ferguson nodded. 'Yes, I was told that the whole crew drowned, except for the ship's pet marmoset monkey. It floated onto the beach on driftwood and was promptly hanged as a French spy by English Dragoons stationed on the island.' He took a deep breath. 'I was looking for the grave of the monkey in the cemetery.'

Torquil forced a laugh. 'That's a new one on me, professor. But I'll check it with the Padre. He'll know.' He made a few more notes then laid his pen down on the table.

'I seem to recall that you said you'd be going diving with friends over the next few days.'

'With Angus MacLeod and Dr Viroj Wattana around the crannog, and maybe a bit of deep-water diving.'

'You realise that will not be possible now?'

'Of course, inspector. You don't want us muddying the waters around the murder site.'

Torquil nodded. 'I'm glad you understand, Professor Ferguson. Now, let me ask you candidly, did you like Fiona Cullen?'

The marine archaeologist looked as if he wished he was somewhere else. Perhaps underwater wearing a mask to protect himself from involuntary facial expressions. 'Are you suggesting that I need a lawyer with me now, inspector? Are you suggesting that I know something about this unfortunate death?'

Torquil was unflustered by the professor's sudden irritability. He shrugged. 'I will be asking all interviewees similar questions, Neil. It is just routine.'

The professor seemed to relax at the use of his Christian name. 'In that case I can say that I honestly had no strong feelings about her at all. I think she felt an antipathy towards me because she thought I was in some way responsible for her friend suddenly snapping and committing suicide.'

Torquil jotted down a few more notes. 'And what exactly were you doing this morning when PC McPhee found you swimming from your boat?'

'I often go for an early morning swim when I'm here. The water is so clear at this time of the year. Apart from that I wanted to check out a new wetsuit and some equipment before I met up with my friends.'

'You weren't disposing of anything?' Torquil asked bluntly.

Neil Ferguson shot to his feet. 'Absolutely

not! What the hell do you mean?'

'Just routine questioning,' Torquil replied with a soft smile. 'So where were you yesterday afternoon at the end of the Gathering?'

'I was watching you, actually. I had a chat with Viroj Wattana and then, when he went off, he had a headache from drinking Heather Ale with the Padre, I had a look at some of the clan tents.'

Torquil nodded. 'Oh, just one more question — why did you decide to come to the Gathering this year?'

The ghost of a triumphant smile hovered over the professor's lips. 'Your uncle, Lachlan McKinnon, asked me to come.'

Torquil nodded and closed his notebook. 'Thank you, Professor. That will be all for now.'

* * *

Dr Viroj Wattana was in an ill humour. And the cause of that ill humour was the man standing opposite him, lecturing him about being discrete.

The little Thai surgeon was smarting, but he merely bowed. Soon, there would be a levelling of scores, he thought.

8

Miss Bella Melville was giving Morag Driscoll a hard time. Having taught every member of the West Uist Division of the Hebridean Constabulary, she maintained, in her own mind at least, the right to talk to them as if they were still her pupils.

'And I don't care what your superior officers are telling you, Morag Driscoll, I am telling you that you will not be able to keep the island sealed off. It is unfair to the local people and it is grossly unfair to the tourists who want to leave.'

Morag smiled as sweetly as she could. 'We *are* investigating a murder, Miss Melville.'

'And don't try that tactic with me, young lady,' returned Miss Melville. 'I am as deeply upset about Fiona Cullen as anyone else. I taught her as a wee girl, you know.' Her cheeks reddened slightly beneath her carefully applied Elizabeth Arden make-up. 'The media will have a field day with you all unless you play ball with them. You do yourself and Torquil McKinnon a favour and get him to telephone his superior officer now and get this silly rule overturned.'

Morag nodded conspiratorially. 'I'll have a word with him, Miss Melville.'

'Be sure that you do. I know he's under pressure at the moment, but just give him one other message from me.'

'Yes, Miss Melville? What?'

'Tell him that Miss Melville said TDG!'

'TDG?' Morag repeated.

Miss Melville came close to smiling. 'That's right Morag Driscoll. He'll understand.'

And indeed, ten minutes later when Piper emerged for a cup of tea, having let Professor Ferguson out of the station by the back door, he knew only too well what his old teacher meant.

'She used to tell me to 'Take a Dose of Gumption',' he explained as he and his sergeant sipped hot strong tea in the office. 'She used to think that I was sometimes too timid. That I needed to be more like the Padre and show more gumption, more oomph!'

'Och, you've done just fine, Torquil,' Morag said defensively, shifting effortlessly into big-sister mode. 'Look at you. You must be about the youngest inspector in the whole of the west of Scotland.'

'But she's right, Morag. We can't just seal off the island like this. I need to talk to the superintendent again. That's what she meant — I should do it straight away and not procrastinate.'

Morag looked doubtful as Torquil reached for the phone.

As usual it seemed to be a pretty one-sided exchange.

'I think he'd had second thoughts himself,' Piper told her as he put the receiver down after his call. 'He's apparently talked it over with the Chief Constable and they agree, we have twenty-four hours to investigate, then the ferry service must resume as normal.'

'And what about media coverage?'

'We've still to use Calum Steele as a go-between.'

'So we have twenty-four hours to catch this maniac?'

'There's worse, Morag.'

'Out with it, boss.'

'Twenty-four hours and then he may come across himself.'

Morag groaned.

* * *

After he had hit enough balls to raise blisters on the insides of both thumbs, the Padre went into his study and tried to write a sermon. But it was a thankless task. His mind would not settle. He kept thinking of Fiona and Ranald Buchanan. Finally, he went out, got on the Red Hunter and chugged around the island to Ranald Buchanan's cottage, *Tigh nam Bàrd* — the House of the Bard. He had no particular purpose in mind; he just felt that he needed to think. And he suspected that if he just stayed and pottered about the manse, he would be bound to receive a call from Bella Melville.

Also, there was something worrying about Ranald's death. They had all been too quick to assume that he'd slipped on that jetty while he was drunk and bashed his head on that spike. The fact was that Ranald Buchanan had always managed to function even when he'd drunk enough peatreek to sink a battleship.

The House of the Bard was a fairly basic croft, literally built within a stone's throw of the sea. There was a jetty where he moored his boat, and just a hundred yards distant the Machair Skerry jutted out of the sea. The Padre stood looking at it for a few moments, seeing the water lapping at the jetty on the skerry, where they had found Ranald's body floating just under the surface. And behind it was the shack where he kept his fishing tackle and a good quantity of his best peatreek.

The Padre turned to look at the cottage, a

three-roomed affair, surrounded by a low wall containing a garden overgrown with nettles and thistles. Behind it there were several large corrugated-iron outhouses where, everyone knew, the Gaelic Bard made his fishing flies, repaired fishing tackle and distilled his peatreek — a cottage industry in every sense of the word.

The Padre walked round the outside of the cottage, looking in through the windows and marvelling at the primitive furnishings and the lack of proper amenities. He pulled out his pipe and stuffed the bowl with the dark thick-cut tobacco that he favoured. Aye, basic was the way you liked it, wasn't it Ranald, he mused as he strolled on, leaving a trail of smoke in his wake.

But it wouldn't have been much of a life here for her or the boy, he thought. And he felt sad to think of how tragic Ranald Buchanan's life had been. His daughter going mad after the birth of her son, and then her son drowning beyond the Machair Skerry. I guess that's where the creativity came from, Ranald, the Padre thought out loud.

He walked over to the outhouses where he had found Ranald distilling his peatreek on so many occasions. He smiled as he thought of the old chap's defence — 'Mind that dog collar o' yours, Lachlan. You cannot tell anyone! It would be unethical for a man of the cloth to grass on his supplier of peatreek.' Then he would lock the padlock and take him round to sample one of his best flasks of peatreek in his front parlour.

The Padre was still grinning when he realized that the padlock he had been thinking of was not securing the door, but was lying open in the dust.

He was about to try one of the doors when he thought better of it. He was on his own at a deserted croft, and there was an unknown murderer somewhere on the island. What on earth was he thinking of? He made his way back on tiptoe to the Red Hunter, slipped on his goggles and kick-started the bike into action.

When he had ridden a quarter of a mile along the road he stopped, pulled out his mobile phone and called Torquil.

⋆ ⋆ ⋆

'Where's Ewan?' Torquil snapped after speaking to his uncle on the phone.

'He'll be back in a moment,' replied Morag. 'I sent him out to get some milk. He's upset that you're cross with him, Torquil. About not leaving a buoy. He's kicking himself.'

Torquil frowned. 'We're all going to have to be on our toes, Morag. So far we've no idea who did this thing. Ewan occasionally needs a prod.' He stood and made for the door. 'That was the Padre. He's just been to Ranald Buchanan's croft — Lord knows why — and it looks as if someone's tampered with his sheds. I'd better go and have a look.' He scowled. 'I was going to interview Genevieve Cooper, but I think you'd better do that while I'm out at Ranald's place.'

'Any particular line you want me to take, boss?'

'The quickest one to the truth. We know that Fiona was going to fire her, but we don't know why.'

'I'll go as soon as Ewan comes back.'

Ten minutes later Torquil coasted to a halt beside the Padre, then together they set off back to the House of the Bard. Over the years they had enjoyed many a ride together on their classic bikes, had many a breakdown and repair session, and occasionally one or other would have a spill. More often than not their trips had been full of good spirits, yet now there was no sense of enjoyment, just urgency and desperation to get to the bottom of this tragedy as swiftly as possible. And it was just possible that a break-in at Ranald Buchanan's could be relevant.

'What were you doing out here, Lachlan?' Torquil asked as they dismounted by the moss-covered garden wall in front of the cottage.

'Seeking inspiration. My sermon wasn't going very well,' the Padre explained. 'Come on,' he said, leading the way round the back to the corrugated outhouses. 'You know what he kept in these sheds, don't you?'

Torquil gave a thin smile. 'Peatreek, of course. But I didn't think it was doing any harm, so I never made an issue of it.' He bent down and, without touching it, he examined the padlock that lay on the ground. From his pocket he pulled out a handkerchief and laid it over the padlock, using a few pebbles to stop the handkerchief from blowing away. 'Morag will come and do the forensics on it later.' And so saying he inserted a pen into the door crack and pulled the door open.

The smell of alcohol that was released was almost overpowering. Dozens of bottles lay smashed on the ground, their contents having seeped into the earth floor.

'Looks like someone went berserk in here,' Torquil said, pointing to the evidence of bottles having been indiscriminately smashed on the corrugated walls. 'And it was done a while ago.'

'Not long after he died, I expect,' the Padre agreed.

'We'd better have a look in the house, Lachlan.'

'The door won't be locked, of course,' the Padre said. 'Ranald had nothing he considered of any value in his house.' He cast a sad look at the detritus in the shed. 'This was what he thought he was really good at. Making peatreek.'

'How much did he make? How many folk did he supply?'

'Around the islands? To his fishing cronies and customers?' the Padre pouted reflectively. 'Enough for his meagre needs and much more, I guess.'

As the Padre had predicted, the door was unlocked. Inside, the house looked as if Ranald Buchanan had just left it and intended to return shortly. There was the odour of stale cigarettes and marijuana smoke. Thick dust covered the furniture, a few used coffee mugs and fishing paraphernalia littered the table, while in the grate and over the hearth there was a heap of black ash. To the side of the fire was a broken bottle with some amber-coloured liquid still in the bottom.

'Looks like either Ranald or someone else has been burning papers,' Torquil said, bending and inspecting an unburned fragment of paper. 'It's part of a poem, I think,' he said. He nodded at the broken bottle. 'It looks as if someone, probably the breaker of all his bottles, kept one bottle to burn a stack of paper.'

'His poems! His work!' exclaimed the Padre, in exasperation. He shook his head. 'That wouldn't have been Ranald. He was too conceited ever to do anything like that.'

Torquil stood up to face his uncle. 'I agree with you there, Lachlan. It looks like someone wanted to destroy all that Ranald Buchanan held dear. His peatreek and his poetry.'

'He was murdered, wasn't he, Torquil!'

'I believe so. I'm sorry. I know that you were close to him.'

The Padre shrugged. 'He was an eccentric, laddie. We need folk like that.' He puffed up his cheeks. 'Oh he could be a cantankerous old fool. And in his younger days he'd been a bit of a — er — well, a bit of a lecher, but he wasn't a total bad lot.'

Torquil nodded. 'And a poet. One of the last great Gaelic poets. West Uist has lost a lot with his death.'

The Padre inexplicably tossed his head back and guffawed. After a moment, he took a deep breath, then said, 'Well I agree that he was a Gaelic speaker, Torquil — but a great poet? Never! He wrote doggerel. As a poet he was a non-starter.'

'Are you serious, Lachlan?' Torquil asked incredulously.

'Afraid so, laddie. Ranald Buchanan was a rogue in many ways. A likeable rogue, I thought, but a rogue nonetheless. He was a versifier, a doggerel-peddler. If he wrote in the straight dialect, like William McGonagal, he would have been denounced straight away, but because he wrote in the Gaelic, and since most people no longer speak the native tongue, he is forgiven for his mistranslations into English. Patronage! That is what made Ranald Buchanan's reputation. It does no harm having a large chain of bookshops pushing your work.'

'You mean AME Books?'

'Exactly.' The Padre looked over Torquil's shoulder. 'What does the fragment say?'

'It's just a few handwritten words. Presumably lines from a poem: 'by the providence' and 'Selkie returns'!' Then he added, 'And they're in English, not the Gaelic,' he added.

'Hmm. I expect that was a translation of a poem. As far as I know, he composed in Gaelic, then translated.'

Torquil took out his pocketbook and inserted the fragment inside the cover. He then turned to his uncle, 'Do you have a list of all the writers who attended the Festival?'

'Of course. Back in my study. Why?'

'Because it's possible that some of them could also be at risk.'

The Padre eyed his nephew quizzically and Torquil explained about Fiona's missing laptop and notebooks. 'Her latest novel was to have been called 'Dead Writers Tell No Tales',' he said. 'It looks as if we've had the murder of two writers. We don't want a third.'

* * *

It did not take Morag long to track Genevieve Cooper down. She had left her room at her bed and breakfast after a frugal repast, consisting of a glass of orange juice, an Aberdeen buttery and two back to back Gauloise cigarettes, then gone for an amble along the bookstalls and stands that were still up and running. Her distinctive appearance in the small harbour town made her easy to stalk. Morag followed the sightings to Henry Henderson's Bookmakers, where she had placed a few bets, then into the Bonnie Prince Charlie, where she found her in a corner seat nursing a large vodka and tonic and smoking one of her trade mark French cigarettes.

'Genevieve Cooper?' Morag asked, holding out her warrant card. 'I'm Sergeant Driscoll of the Hebridean Constabulary. May I have a few minutes of your time?'

'Ugh! The dreaded interview,' Genevieve returned, downing her drink in one go. 'I think I'd better have another of these before we start.'

Morag waited for the literary agent to return from the bar with a fresh drink, and then produced a silver pen and notebook. 'I'm afraid that I need to ask you a few questions about Fiona Cullen.'

In answer, Genevieve dissolved into tears, which immediately merged into an attack of hiccups. Another few moments passed while they gradually subsided. Then, with a freshly lit cigarette, Genevieve sat back and smiled. 'Ask away then sergeant dear, Genevieve Cooper, the author's trooper, is at your service.'

'How long had you been Fiona Cullen's agent?' Morag asked, poised with her pen.

'Five glorious years. I guided her from rags to riches. And never a cross word spoken between us.'

'Yet I understand that she recently announced that she was firing you?'

Genevieve blinked several times as if her brain was having difficulty registering the question and computing an answer. Then she replied, 'Not firing me, just parting company, dear.'

'Is there a difference?'

'You get fired when you've done something wrong. I hadn't.' She puffed her cigarette then waved her hand extravagantly. 'These things happen between authors and agents.'

'Has it happened to you before, Genevieve? Have other authors parted company with you?'

Genevieve blushed and reached for her vodka and tonic. 'I may have had a lean patch recently.'

'Any reason for that?'

'It's a mystery.'

'It couldn't be anything to do with gambling, could it?'

The literary agent suddenly stiffened. 'Why do you ask that?'

Morag made a play as if she was doodling. 'Oh, just because you've been seen in Henry Henderson's Bookmakers several times so far. And you placed a couple of bets already today — the day after Fiona Cullen was murdered. Some people might think that was unusual. They might even suggest that you had a problem, an addiction.'

Genevieve stubbed out her cigarette in the ashtray and immediately lit another. She looked at the cigarette and shrugged. 'OK, so I admit that I have an addictive personality. But my drinking and gambling have nothing to do with our parting company.' She coughed. 'Not directly, anyway.'

'So it had an indirect effect?'

Genevieve bit her lip. 'Look sergeant, I may not be the best literary agent in the world, but I'm not bad. I have a knack for certain things and not others. I'm good at getting authors published, getting them linked up with the right publisher and ironing out any flaws in that vital first contract. And I'm good at getting people to keep an interest in an author. Sometimes I may go too populist, that's all.'

Morag looked puzzled. 'But surely every author wants to be popular?'

Genevieve smiled. 'They want to be popular, not populist! I may be too brash for some people.' She inhaled deeply on her cigarette then tapped the lengthening ash off. 'Fiona said I didn't consult her often enough, and that my taste in advertising could be a bit tacky. She thought I sometimes went too far down-market — like getting her to do a sexy pose in Japan. She said that I dumbed down her writing and created the image of her as a kind of literary slapper.' She shook her head emphatically.

'As if I'd do that to one of my authors!'

Morag felt herself warming to Genevieve. 'Can you give me an example of what she meant?'

'She criticized me about some of the publicity pieces I managed to get into magazines. She wanted to be in the literary reviews not the girlie mags. In a way she was a snob, I think. She saw herself as a real writer, a potential Booker prize-winner, rather than a crime writer.'

'Was her writing good enough for that?'

Genevieve took a meditative puff on her cigarette. 'No,' she said decisively. 'She was a born story-teller, but her writing was a little crude. The truth is, my lovely, that although we all want to live in a class above our own, only the extraordinarily talented make it work. I don't think I could have gotten a literary publisher to look at her stuff.'

Morag grimaced. 'That sounds harsh.'

'But realistic, sergeant dear. Fiona on the other hand was not realistic. I think she had a thing about tackiness. What she didn't realize was that tackiness was her bread and butter. It wasn't a literary audience that was buying her books; it was tacky old Joe Bloggs and his sister Sharon who liked her work.'

She took a final drag on her cigarette then stubbed it out. 'I think that's why she took such an aversion to the bookmarks I had made up.'

'The bookmarks that were given away with each new purchase at the Literary Festival?'

Genevieve nodded. 'I think they were a tour de force. Everyone would see her in Osaka — and it is a sexy pose, but it's also sophisticated, whatever she said — and want to buy a copy of one of her books.'

'But she didn't like it?'

The agent vigorously shook her head. 'She hated it! I still don't know why. And that's when she said we should part company.'

'When exactly did she say this?'

'On the ferry over here.'

'Oh!' Morag exclaimed in surprise. 'So you had plenty of time to mull it over!'

* * *

Calum Steele had a strong Walter Mitty streak, which he was blissfully unaware of himself. He saw himself as a man of letters, an editor of literary excellence and an investigative journalist at heart. He loved the celebrity status that being editor of the *West Uist Chronicle* gave him, even though the population of the island was small enough for most people to know the majority of their neighbours anyway. The flipside of the coin, to his chagrin, was that because so many people knew about other people's business, there was little scope for actual investigative journalism. Until now! The sudden swell in the island's population, and the murder of the celebrated Fiona Cullen, meant that not only was he the main link to the outside world, but he was also in a position to do some real investigating and maybe even find the murderer before Torquil McKinnon did.

And to best Torquil at anything would give him great pleasure. All his life he had played at least second fiddle to Piper, and although he was probably one of his best friends, it pissed him off! To outstage him — to have a national scoop — would, he felt, salve the wound he had received on that day in Miss Melville's class when Torquil had won the Robert Burns Poetry Recitation Prize for his rendition of 'To A Mouse', after Calum had stuttered and stumbled over his potted version of 'Tam o'Shanter'. It hadn't so much been the fact that Torquil had won that bothered him; it was more the fact that Fiona Cullen, an eight-year-old blonde angel, had been inspired to give the winner a kiss. And then, twenty years later, after she had worked for Calum then gone on to far bigger and better things, she had come back to West Uist and had Torquil in her sights.

When she was working for him as his reporter, she had slept with Torquil! It still hurt, even though he was sad that she was dead.

He rankled inside. Perhaps he could scupper Piper in the media. He had the power. Or perhaps he could do it more effectively some other way. It was nice, he reflected, to have some choice in the matter.

Arming himself with this knowledge, he stepped up to the unusually quiet public bar of the Bonnie Prince Charlie and winked at Mollie McFadden, who peered myopically at him, her expression that of mild suspicion.

'And what can I do for you, Calum Steele?'

'I'll take a pint of your best Heather Ale to begin with, Mollie.'

He watched her pull the pint, her right forearm noticeably more developed than her left after having pumped a seaful of beer over the years. Calum took a hefty swig then wiped foam off his upper lip as he replaced the glass on the counter.

'A sad business,' he remarked casually. 'A bad ending to the Gathering.'

Mollie leaned on the bar. 'Terrible. And it makes me feel awful, her having stayed here in my tavern.'

'Fiona used to work for me, you know,' Calum said. 'We were at school together.

Same class as Torquil.'

'Aye, I recall. That was before she became famous.'

Calum's cheeks burned and he took another swig of beer. He hadn't realized it before, but he was jealous of his former employee. They had both gone off to university, as had Torquil, and they had all come back to West Uist. Both he and she wrote words for a living, but she had achieved something really big, while he was still reporting on Gatherings, the price of fish and who was selling what at the church jumble sales. He forced the emotion from his mind, for now he was chasing the biggest story of his life, ironically thanks to Fiona!

'Was she working while she was here?'

Mollie smiled at the *Chronicle* editor's efforts to winkle information from her. 'Aye, she was working on her new book, just as she said at her talk the other day.'

'Have the police taken her things away? Her writing, her notes and everything?'

Mollie shook her head. 'You will have to be asking Inspector McKinnon that question, Calum Steele. And while you're at it, you'd better ask him about the ghost!'

Calum raised his eyebrows quizzically, his journalistic antennae quivering. 'Did you say *ghost*?'

'Aye, a ghost. I saw Fiona Cullen go up those stairs to her room yesterday at about five o'clock, when they say that her body had already been found.'

Calum leaned closer and dropped his voice. 'Mollie, do you realize what this could mean to you?'

'Aye Calum, I do. I'm sorry about poor Fiona, but I'm a working lassie with a living to make.'

'You know that I'm handling all the media coverage at the moment?'

Mollie McFadden's eyes gleamed behind her spectacles. 'That's what I heard. Would you care for a dram of malt to follow that pint?'

Calum nodded with a sly smile as she poured a good measure of Glen Corlin from one of the special bottles that she kept under the bar. 'The public has a morbid streak of curiosity, Mollie. If the publicity about Fiona Cullen's ghost is handled right it could prove very profitable in the long term for the landlady of the Bonnie Prince Charlie Tavern in Kyleshiffin.'

As he sipped his malt and imagined the headlines in *Scottish Life* magazine, Mollie greeted another customer. 'I'll just serve this gentleman,' she whispered, 'then we can have a wee chat over in the corner.'

'*Slàinte mhath*,' said Calum, as he downed the rest of the glass. He smiled as the fiery water of life hit the spot.

⋆ ⋆ ⋆

At the same moment, Genevieve Cooper put her glass down on the table and snapped her Zippo lighter to puff a further cigarette into life. Morag, a passionate non-smoker, suppressed a wince and sat stoically enduring the smoke. 'Did you arrange many trips for her?'

'Loads. France, Germany, Japan and Thailand. I got her published in eight languages and arranged tours in each country.'

'Are there any of her foreign publishers here?'

'No, this is just an experiment. It's hardly the Edinburgh Festival, is it? As far as I've seen, the only person from foreign parts is that funny little Dr Wattana.'

'Did Fiona have a literary connection with him?'

Genevieve laughed. 'Good Lord, no! Fiona often combined business with pleasure when she was away.'

'She had a relationship with him?'

This time the agent sniggered. She

dropped her voice. 'She had a boob job in Thailand.'

'He operated on her?'

'Yes, but not to her satisfaction. She ranted about him botching the job. Didn't use big enough implants. There's a court case between them.'

'Do you know what he's doing on West Uist?'

'No idea, my lovely. But I think they had words at the Gathering yesterday.'

Morag made another entry in her notebook, then continued, 'She was an attractive woman. Any men in her life?'

A twinkle formed in Genevieve's eyes. 'I rather had the impression that there was a current man in her life, a certain inspector of the local police.'

Morag glossed over the remark. 'I meant before she came to West Uist for the Gathering.'

'Fiona was socially gregarious. She had quite a few men friends. She liked to party. She was close to Angus MacLeod for a while, and I think — only think, mind you — that she may have had a fling with Roland Baxter.'

'The Scottish Minister for Culture?' Morag asked in surprise.

Genevieve stubbed her cigarette out. 'I don't know details, but Fiona hinted that the minister was — er . . . ' She hesitated a moment, ' . . . less potent than people might imagine.'

Morag jotted a few lines. 'One more question. Would losing Fiona Cullen's custom cause you cash flow problems?'

Genevieve Cooper stiffened. 'Why ask that?'

'This is a murder investigation. It's my job to ask questions, no matter how unpalatable or unpleasant. Henry Henderson tells me that in the short time you've been in Kyleshiffin you've laid several bets and lost over seven hundred pounds.'

A muscle twitched near the corner of the literary agent's mouth. 'I like a flutter. I've told you that already.' She hesitated, then nodded, as if having made up her mind about something. 'OK, so maybe I like it a bit too much, but I've always been strictly honest and fair with my authors. That's maybe more than some pub — ' She bit her lip and leaned forward. 'Look sergeant, I don't want to say anything out of turn or get anyone in trouble.'

Morag eyed her sternly. 'I repeat, Genevieve, this is a murder investigation. Withholding information could get *you* in trouble. So come on, what do you mean?'

'Christ! Look, Fiona Cullen was a very sexual woman. What you may not know is that she swung both ways.'

'Go on.'

'She had an on-off affair with Allegra McCall for a couple of years. I think that Fiona ended it because she thought . . . ' Once again she hesitated and looked doubtful, but a look from Morag urged her on. 'She thought that Allegra may have been holding money back. Rooking her! Not paying her for various print-runs, that sort of thing.'

'Any truth in that, do you think?'

Genevieve shook her head. 'I think Allegra McCall is one of the most honest publishers I deal with. I think it was another of the bees that Fiona got in her bonnet.'

Morag shook her head sadly. 'But now she is no more. Tell me though; what were you doing at the close of the Gathering?'

Genevieve Cooper gave a small guilty-looking smile. 'I was avoiding people. I had a bit of a tiff with Allegra actually. Nothing serious, I think we were both just pissed off with Fiona. I went to see if the bookies was open — but of course it was closed for the Gathering.'

Morag glanced at her watch and put her pen away. 'Thank you, Genevieve. You've been most helpful.' She rose to go.

'Could you do me one favour, sergeant?'

Genevieve asked. 'Please don't tell Allegra I said anything.'

Morag maintained her professional poker face. 'All I can say is that we never divulge our sources.'

* * *

PC Ewan McPhee was feeling miserable. Manning the station desk had been really tough since he had had to deal with a constant stream of queries, complaints and all manner of sightings and suggested theories from locals and tourists. Dutifully he had recorded them all, dealing with them as best as he could. The problem was that he was feeling bad about letting Torquil down, especially when he must be going through his own personal hell and grief. It had been clear to everyone that he and Fiona had been picking up on their old relationship.

He was only half listening to Annie McConville as she gave him the benefit of her advice, while Zimba her large Alsatian sat patiently beside her.

'So if you want to scour the entire crime scene for clues, just get back to me. Zimba has a better sense of smell than any bloodhound; you just take it from me.'

Ewan nodded and forced a smile as the old

lady turned to go. 'I'll tell my Inspector, Annie.'

His forced smile turned into a real one a moment later when Izzie Frazer came in. She was wearing jeans and a green poncho, her shoulder bag slung diagonally across her breasts like a bandolier.

'Am I glad to see you, Izzie,' Ewan said with relief. 'I need something to cheer me up. It's been a bloody awful time. I — '

She reached across the desk, grabbed both of his ears and pulled him forwards to plant a kiss on his lips.

'Is that better, Ewan?'

He grinned like a Cheshire cat. 'Aye, it's just got a lot better.'

Izzie shivered. 'I can't believe it. I talked to her at the Gathering yesterday and now she's gone. How could something like this happen?'

Ewan bit his lip. 'I don't know, Izzie. I feel so sorry for Torquil, and he's got the job of finding the bastard. At a time like this when he must be going through hell himself.'

'I missed you after the Gathering, Ewan.'

'Aye, I know, it was just pandemonium. But did you manage to get hold of that agent woman?'

Izzie shook her head. 'No. It was odd. I saw her leave the grounds and I ran after her, but she just seemed to disappear. She's faster than she looks.'

'What are you doing now?'

'Visiting you, silly. I thought we could have lunch or something.'

The big constable shook his head. 'I'm afraid I've got to man the fort. But maybe we could meet this evening — whenever I get away. But it could be late, awful late.'

Izzie reached out and tousled his hair. 'It doesn't matter how late, Ewan. I think with everything that's going on I could do with a cuddle from a big strong constable.'

Ewan flushed to his roots again.

9

Ewan grimaced when Morag came in. He nodded in the direction of Torquil's closed office door. 'The boss has been buttonholed by Calum Steele. The sly dog was in here thirty seconds after Torquil and almost demanded to have a word with him. I think he sees all this as a chance to get famous.'

'How long have they been in there, Ewan?'

'About twenty minutes — and without any request for tea or coffee.'

'The boss is obviously not wanting to encourage him then,' Morag murmured. Then she smiled. 'But I could do with a cup, my wee sweetheart.'

Ewan grinned. 'Coming right up, sergeant.'

And while he was in the kitchenette rattling cups and making tea, Morag went through to the incident room, sat down and wrote up her report from her notes. Ewan joined her a few minutes later with a tea-tray and the biscuit barrel.

'Any progress?' he asked, dunking a ginger biscuit in his mug of tea.

'A lot of interesting facts that may or may not be relevant,' Morag replied, sipping her tea and reluctantly ignoring the biscuits since she was in one of her diet phases. Although only a few pounds overweight she felt a duty to stay as fit and slim as she could in order to prevent a heart attack, like the cruel early one that had taken her husband away in his thirty-third year and left her a widow with three children to look after.

Torquil's outer office door opened and they heard the inspector walking Calum Steele to the door.

'I'll have to let this one out, you know that, don't you, Piper.'

'Just the facts, Calum. No embellishments and no theorizing.'

Calum Steele's voice was indignant. 'I'm a responsible journalist, Piper McKinnon! You know I always shy away from sensationalism.'

The rest of the conversation was inaudible to them. They heard the outer door close and a few moments later Piper came in. He spotted the tea then shook his head as he poured himself a cup. 'Calum Steele may prove a liability to this investigation!' he volunteered. 'Somehow or other he found out that someone went into Fiona's room after she was murdered. He was trying to find out about what she was writing. The sly dog.'

Morag pushed the biscuit barrel across the desk, then enquired, 'What about the Padre's call, boss? Was everything OK?'

Torquil munched a ginger biscuit. 'Are these your mum's biscuits, Ewan?' The big constable flushed and began to nod. 'They're delicious! Thank her for me, will you.' He flashed a smile at the constable. 'Sorry I snapped this morning, I was — '

'Upset,' Ewan interjected, eagerly. 'Of course you were, boss. Losing Fiona like that.' His face went crimson and his voice trembled. 'And what with me acting the gowk! I'll think next time, you just wait and see!' And picking up his mug he stood. 'Maybe I'd better man the desk — unless I can do anything the now?'

Torquil winked. 'You're a good lad, Ewan. I'll brief you later.'

When they were alone Torquil picked up a felt-tip marker pen, stood up and tapped its end on the whiteboard, beside Ranald Buchanan's name. 'There's no doubt, it was murder, Morag!' And he told her about his investigation with the Padre. 'We'll need to forensic the place, of course. I'm thinking that you may need some help from South Uist, so if you do — '

'I'll manage, boss. We want to sort this ourselves, don't we?'

Torquil gave her a half-smile and then drew a box around Ranald's name. 'And what about your interview with Genevieve Cooper?'

'Here's my report, boss. Hot off the press and illuminating.' But as he reached out for it she held the papers firmly for a moment. 'But I think you should just steel yourself, Torquil,' she said concernedly. 'You may find out a few things about Fiona that you didn't know.'

* * *

Kyleshiffin was thrumming with activity. The market stalls on Harbour Street were doing a roaring trade and so were all the shops as people resigned themselves to their enforced stay on West Uist.

Torquil was pleased to leave the hustle and bustle for a while and headed off on his Royal Enfield Bullet for Dunshiffin Castle. After reading Morag's report he decided to put off his interview with Allegra McCall, at least until he got his head cleared. News that Fiona had had an affair with another woman had thrown him and he felt the need to disconnect for a while.

But as he rode into the Dunshiffin Castle forecourt he found himself transported back to the ceilidh of the other night. There were people all over the place, just as there had been then.

Of course, he told himself. They've been staying here. Billeted by the Padre and Miss Melville!

People were getting into cars and mini-buses, presumably to be transported back to Kyleshiffin in search of food and refreshments.

He stripped off his gauntlets, goggles and Cromwell helmet.

'Ah, Piper McKinnon! Up here!'

He looked up at the sound of his name and saw the elegant torso of Angus MacLeod, the laird of the Dunshiffin estate, beckoning him from an open first-floor window.

Jesmond, the laird's butler-cum-general-factotum, met him at the door and directed him up the great stairway to Angus MacLeod's sumptuous oak-panelled study, where the man himself was sitting on the corner of his desk, puffing on a large Havana cigar.

'Ah, Piper, come in. Have a seat. A cigar?' He held out his hand.

Torquil shook hands, but refused the cigar humidor and sat down. 'Angus I need some information.'

Angus MacLeod nodded as he blew a stream of smoke ceilingwards. 'About Fiona Cullen's murder, of course.' He shook his head. 'I'm afraid that I probably know nothing of any use to you. I was at the Gathering all afternoon.'

Torquil raised a finger. 'We'll talk about Fiona in a minute. In fact I'm here to investigate two murders. It's the first that I want information about.'

Angus MacLeod stared at him in amazement. 'Two murders?'

'Aye. I'm investigating the murders of Fiona Cullen and Ranald Buchanan.'

The Laird of Dunshiffin visibly paled. 'Are you serious? You think that Ranald Buchanan was murdered too?'

Torquil nodded. 'That I do. And I believe that you have important information for me.'

Angus MacLeod stared at the glowing tip of his cigar. 'And why would you think that, Piper?'

'Because, for one thing, you were his sponsor. You've been pushing his books in your chain of bookstores all over the west of Scotland. You brought him to prominence, made him famous.'

'He deserved his success. I just gave him a hand on the way.'

'Am I right in thinking that it was you who first called him 'the Gaelic Bard'?'

The laird puffed his cigar and blew a ribbon of smoke from the corner of his mouth. 'Who told you that?'

'The Padre.'

Angus MacLeod smiled. 'The Padre doesn't miss much does he? But that still doesn't detract from the fact that Ranald deserved his success. He was a great poet and his book sales back that up. He is one of the few Scottish poets to ever make the bestseller lists.'

Torquil gave a slow whistle. 'Now that's no small feat for any poet is it? I thought it was a miniscule market. They can get great kudos, but it's basically pocket money stuff. The Padre tells me that not even the poet laureate makes a living from his poetry.'

'Perhaps the Padre knows less about the book industry than he thinks.'

Torquil smiled and leaned forward. 'Do you know, I think I will take you up on that offer of a cigar. Ordinarily I only ever smoke when I'm amongst the midges, but that aroma is tempting. Havana isn't it?'

'The finest. Montecristos. Help yourself.'

Torquil opened the humidor and selected a cigar. He snipped its end with the gold cigar clipper that lay inside and picked up the box of Swan Vestas. The laird watched him through narrowed eyes as he methodically lit it.

'Hmm. That's good,' said Torquil. 'Did Ranald like cigars?'

'Why do you think I should know that?'

'Because he was often here, wasn't he?'

'He was. And now that you mention it, I don't think he ever did smoke cigars. He was addicted to those foul little roll-ups of his.'

Torquil savoured his cigar. 'Did he smoke tobacco here, or weed? Marijuana, that is.'

'Tobacco, of course!' snapped the Laird. 'Look Piper, what are you getting at?'

'Ranald Buchanan smoked cannabis regularly. You know it and I know it. I admit that I never pulled him in for it, since he was not exactly causing a problem on the island.'

'Magnanimous of you.'

Torquil shrugged. 'That's the way things work in life, though, isn't it, Angus? People do each other favours.'

'I don't follow.'

'Well, I've always wondered why you, as the owner of Glen Corlin distillery, the only West Uist distillery, didn't try to stop Ranald Buchanan from supplying half the islands with his peatreek.'

Angus MacLeod shot to his feet. 'Illicit alcohol! Are you suggesting that Ranald Buchanan ran an illicit still?'

Torquil looked at the accumulating ash on his cigar. 'That's exactly what I'm saying. And I believe that you knew that very well — as just about the whole island did.'

The laird smiled triumphantly. 'So you admit that you, an officer of the law, knew about this?'

'I suspected, but never investigated. It was hardly in the public's interest. Besides, the distilling of peatreek is a traditional craft of the outer isles.'

'But it's illegal. Immoral even.'

Torquil smiled benignly. 'I don't think it is all that immoral.'

'It's dishonest then. It deprives the government of revenue.'

'Ah, dishonest. You mean less than honest?' Torquil stood up and took an extra puff on his Havana. He walked across to the bay window, leaving a trail of smoke in his wake. 'Tell me, Angus, do you think that touting a meagre talent and pretending that it was a major one was strictly honest?'

'What do you mean, McKinnon?'

Torquil turned and grinned at the laird's obvious discomfiture. 'Come on Angus. We both know that Ranald Buchanan smoked cannabis, that he was an illicit distiller — and that he didn't rate as a poet! Yet somehow you ignored his peatreek making, which was directly against your personal financial interests, and for some reason you pushed his books in your bookstores.'

The laird seemed to have gone slightly

pale. Torquil noticed him unconsciously looking towards the tray of assorted decanters on the side table, as if he suddenly felt in need of a drink. But the laird quickly regained his composure. He picked up the box of matches and slowly relit his cigar. 'OK! I admit that I helped him by pushing his books in my shops. What's the problem there? He was a fellow islander and I wanted to see him become a success.'

'But how do you account for the number of books you sold, Angus? That many people just don't like poetry.'

'What are you suggesting?'

'That perhaps for some reason someone bought his books in large quantities.' He smiled sarcastically. 'Perhaps the books were literally cooked.'

Angus MacLeod sat down in the plush leather chair behind his desk. 'I think you should be careful what you say, Inspector McKinnon.'

'Oh I will, Angus. Which of course brings me to the second murder.'

'You still haven't told me why you think Ranald Buchanan was murdered,' the laird interrupted.

'That's police business at the moment, and I can't discuss it.' Torquil laid his cigar in the ashtray and brushed the palms of his hands against each other. 'Fiona Cullen had a grudge against you, didn't she?'

Angus MacLeod shrugged his shoulders. 'She didn't approve of my bookstore policy. Many authors don't. They want sales, big sales, but they don't like cut-price books, or anything that could affect their royalties.'

'And you sell cut-price books?'

'I'm a businessman. I make money for the publishers, the authors and myself.'

'Do you deal directly with the publishers?'

'Quite often, yes.'

'And could some of the deals affect an author's income?'

The laird considered for a moment, then nodded. 'In a way, yes, that's possible.'

'Did you do a deal with Fiona Cullen's publisher?'

Angus MacLeod folded his arms. 'I'm not prepared to say.'

Torquil nodded and decided not to pursue the matter. Instead, he asked, 'Did you ever have a relationship with Fiona Cullen?'

The laird's face reddened and he too laid his cigar in the ashtray. 'I may have done — for a while.'

Torquil felt the hairs at the back of his neck begin to rise. But he dared not allow any personal emotions to show through. 'A sexual affair?'

'Of course!' the laird replied curtly. 'But not for long. Only a month or so. It started at one of my parties.'

'And it ended when?'

'When I caught her cheating on me.' He frowned, got up and crossed to the tray of decanters. He poured himself a couple of fingers of Glen Corlin, which he downed in one go. Then, through gritted teeth, he added, 'With Allegra McCall, her publisher at Castlefront's, as it happened. I was furious, I stopped stocking her bloody books altogether. And any others by Castlefront.' He pulled a handkerchief from his breast pocket and dabbed his forehead. 'There! Are you satisfied now, McKinnon?'

Torquil felt anything but satisfied and was about to reply when the noise of an engine starting up was followed by the gradual build-up of whirring rotor-blades.

'What the hell is that?' Torquil blurted out.

'It's my helicopter,' Angus MacLeod replied nonchalantly. 'Roland Baxter has to get back to the mainland. I said he could get Tam McKenzie to fly him back today.'

'Like hell he can!' Torquil snapped. 'I'm investigating what could be a serial murder case and no one leaves West Uist until I say so.'

The laird raised his eyebrows. 'I think you

may be too late, inspector.'

Torquil stepped very close to the laird. 'And I'm asking you to get straight on your radio to Tam McKenzie and tell him that he must under no circumstance leave West Uist. I want to talk to Roland Baxter — right now!'

* * *

The Padre had gone on from Ranald Buchanan's to do a couple of pastoral visits before riding into Kyleshiffin for a meeting with the Literary Festival Committee about the situation. He had parked the Red Hunter beside the harbour wall and was just stripping off his goggles and helmet when he spotted Dr Wattana a little further along the harbour trying to peep through the cabin window of a cabin cruiser, which was gently bobbing up and down next to the police *Seaspray* catamaran.

'Dr Wattana,' the Padre called out in greeting. 'Do you fancy a boat like that?'

The little doctor turned and blinked at him. 'Ah yes, you're the drinking priest!' He exclaimed. 'I was just looking for a friend of mine.'

The Padre had mechanically struck a light to his briar pipe and tossed the match carelessly into the gutter. He looked right and left to make sure that no one was in earshot. 'Actually, I'd rather you didn't use that particular description, doctor,' he said with a twinkle in his eye. 'It doesn't do for a man in my profession to have that sort of reputation.'

Dr Wattana blushed and executed a nervous little half-bow. 'I didn't mean offence — that is, I only meant that you introduced me to your beer.' He shook his head as if recalling an unpleasant memory. 'It made my head spin.'

The Padre gave a short laugh. 'Good old Heather Ale!' He pointed to the sign above the door of the Bonnie Prince Charlie Tavern. 'Would you care for a half pint?'

Dr Wattana held his hand up and looked horrified. 'No! I mean, I need to find my friend and talk to him. I hoped that he would be here.'

The Padre glanced at the cabin cruiser, with the name 'Unicorn' emblazoned across its prow. 'So you're looking for Neil Ferguson? This is his cruiser.' He snapped his fingers. 'Yes, of course, I remember you telling me you were supposed to be going diving with him and Angus MacLeod today.'

Dr Wattana bobbed his head. 'But everything has changed now. This regrettable murder — !'

'Aye, awful, isn't it. Nothing like it has

happened on West Uist before.'

'She was so — *talented*,' mused the little surgeon, as if carefully selecting his words.

'How about a cup of tea if you don't want beer?' the Padre suggested, tapping his pipe on the harbour wall and immediately shoving it into his breast pocket.

'Thank you, but no. I have just seen someone I'd rather not speak to right now. I must go. And I need to speak with that police inspector most urgently.'

The Padre looked at him in surprise. 'You mean Torquil? Well if you like I could — ' But Dr Wattana had already gone and had scurried towards the crowds still milling around the market stalls.

A hand dropped on his shoulder and he turned to see the grinning face of Calum Steele. 'Wasn't that the wee Thai surgeon?' Calum asked.

The Padre nodded. I wonder how he knew to avoid Calum, he thought with a grin.

* * *

Roland Baxter, the Scottish Minister for Culture, was in a furious mood when he stormed into Angus MacLeod's study.

'Just who the hell do you think you are, McKinnon?' he barked at Torquil. 'I'm a minister in the Scottish parliament and I have important business to attend to.'

'Since when?' Torquil asked with an innocent smile.

'Don't push your luck, inspector.'

Angus MacLeod had stood up to try to placate the irate minister. 'Easy now, Roland. Inspector McKinnon is investigating a murder after all.' He glanced at Torquil, then added: 'Two murders actually.'

Roland Baxter looked amazed, but before he could get a word out, Torquil interrupted. 'Angus, I'd be grateful if we could have the use of your study for a while.'

In answer, the laird nodded. 'Of course.' And, addressing the minister, 'Take it easy Roland.'

Torquil gestured the minister to the plush armchair. 'So minister, could you answer my question? Since when did you have important business to attend to? As I understood it, you were planning to stay a few days on West Uist with your friends.'

The minister seemed to have regained his composure, the only sign of any antipathy or stress being a slight flaring of his nostrils. 'That was the plan, yes. I was going to enjoy a break and go fishing with Angus.'

'Not diving?'

'No, I don't dive myself. But Neil Ferguson

was going to take Angus and Dr Wattana out for a dive around the crannog, and probably also do a bit of deep-water diving too.'

He crossed his legs and flicked an imaginary speck of dust off his immaculately pressed trousers. 'What did Angus mean, you're investigating two murders?'

'We have reason to believe that Ranald Buchanan was also murdered.'

'By the same person?' Roland Baxter asked in disbelief.

Torquil shrugged. 'I am not yet in a position to answer that, but it is suspicious. Let's talk about Ranald Buchanan first. What was your relationship with him?'

Baxter looked bemused. 'I had no relationship with him. None that is except for my position as Scottish Minister for Culture and his status as a major Gaelic poet. As such he had to be regarded as a national asset.'

'Yet you are not a fan of the Gaelic?'

Roland Baxter gave a dry smile, the practised smile of a politician. 'I am not personally in favour of extending the use of the Gaelic, because I see it as potentially divisive. But I am in favour of promoting anything to do with Scottish culture. I see Ranald Buchanan's significance as a poet, Gaelic-speaking or not.'

'And Fiona Cullen? How significant did

you see her?' Torquil asked in an attempt to catch the minister on the hop.

'She was an able crime writer.'

'What was your relationship with her? Were you involved with her?'

Roland Baxter eyed Torquil with a hint of hostility. Then again the politician took over. 'We had been involved, but not for long.'

'Tell me about it.' And once again he felt an inner heat, as if his temper was rising, but he suppressed it as best he could.

For a moment it looked as if the minister was not prepared to cooperate. Then he shrugged. 'We had a fling for less than a week. It was after a party at Milngavie in Glasgow. A friend of hers had just written a book and she was expecting great things. I was — '

'Who was the publisher?'

'Castlefront. They publish a wide range of books. A strong fiction list, but also strong on equestrian, crafts and New Age stuff.'

'And Fiona Cullen was a Castlefront author?'

The minister nodded. 'My presence at the party lent it a certain — respectability and solidity. Fiona was pleased for her friend, because she thought it would help the book. It — '

'Did the book do well?'

The minister looked put out by Torquil's repeated interruptions to his narrative. 'No! I'm afraid it had a bad TV review.'

'Was that TV review after your affair with Fiona Cullen?'

Roland Baxter stared open-eyed at Torquil as if his question had suddenly answered a question of his own that had been posed over and over in his mind. Then slowly, he replied. 'Yes, as a matter of fact it was. It seemed that for some reason Fiona decided we weren't going anywhere.' A muscle in his jaw twitched, then he stiffened and sat upright. 'Fiona Cullen was one very complex woman.'

Torquil found himself nodding his head. A complex woman indeed.

'Finally, where exactly were you between four and five o'clock yesterday?'

'I was at the Gathering all afternoon. I'm the Scottish Minister for Culture, damn it! Everyone knows me and would have seen me there.'

Or they would think they had, you pompous git! Torquil thought.

* * *

Superintendent Kenneth Lumsden had been feeling reasonably well until he switched on the news. Kirstie Macroon, the bonnie red-headed newsreader for Scottish Television, was a particular favourite of his. Yet when she reported on the murder inquiry on West Uist he jumped to his feet and experienced a sudden lancing pain that shot from his big toe straight up his spine. His leg buckled and he fell down with a yell.

Thirty seconds later he was dialling the Kyleshiffin police station. It took a further thirty-five minutes before he was connected to Inspector Torquil McKinnon at Dunshiffin Castle. The superintendent was not a happy man.

'What the hell is happening?' he thundered down the phone. 'Why haven't you got an arrest? Why haven't you reported back to me with a progress report? And why on earth is Scottish Television giving a report about ghosts?'

Torquil had not seen any of the reports, so asked the superintendent to explain what he had heard. After he listened to his superior's histrionic rendition of the news he replied: 'I wasn't aware that the newspapers had given the television that information, sir.'

Superintendent Lumsden was not impressed. 'Well you bloody well should know, McKinnon. You give that Calum Steele his information, don't you?'

'That must be information he's given out

himself, sir. It didn't come from us. It's just a bit of sensationalism. But what harm can that do?'

'What harm! The harm lies in the fact that we have no arrest. What are you playing at, McKinnon? It's a tiny bloody island.'

Torquil took a deep breath. 'We are investigating two murders, sir.'

'Exactly! So why no arrest yet?'

There was silence for a moment then Torquil asked, 'What do you suggest I do, Superintendent Lumsden?'

'Get out and arrest a suspect! You have until tomorrow, then I'm coming over.'

There was a click then Torquil found himself staring at his phone.

'And thank you for your support, Superintendent Lumsden,' he said softly.

* * *

Piper left Dunshiffin Castle and took the long snaking coastal route back towards Kyleshiffin. As he sped along the chicane of turns and bends leading to the lay-by overlooking St Ninian's Cave, he momentarily wished he had his pipes in the pannier. His mind was swimming and his heart ached as if the blood flowing through it carried a mix of negative emotions. Anger, guilt, jealousy and an almost unbearable sorrow each seemed to rise in peaks, then plummet downwards to be replaced by a different emotion.

He gunned the Bullet as he changed gear to take the final bend, and as he did so he saw the large four-wheel drive parked in the lay-by. He braked and stopped beyond it. The vehicle was empty.

Then suddenly the air was broken by a woman's scream.

10

Torquil jumped down to the beach and sprinted across the shingle towards St Ninian's Cave, from whence the screaming continued to ring out.

Allegra McCall was on her knees inside the cave, her head in her hands as she stared upwards screaming like a banshee.

Torquil spotted the half empty bottle of clear spirits beside her.

Thank Christ! he thought with relief. For a moment he had thought someone was being — !

He pushed the thought from his mind and went over to the woman, his emotions turning from relief to a mixture of anger and jealousy. Anger that the woman was intruding in his cave, tainting its echo with her screeching. And jealous that she might have slept with Fiona!

He shook her gently and called her name. 'Miss McCall! Allegra!'

But she didn't even seem to register his presence. Her eyes seemed to be looking upwards, staring straight through the rock of St Ninian's Cave.

You're drunk and hysterical, he thought. His hand itched to strike her, to slap her across the face and jolt her back to reality, just as they did in the old movies. But his logical side told him that was the worst thing you could do to someone in such a state. Apart from that, the islanders' innate respect for womankind was like a solid barrier to such an act.

Damn you! Stop it! He yelled internally.

He picked up the bottle and sloshed it across her face. The effect was instantaneous. Shocked out of her screaming frenzy by the cold liquid she stared up at him for a moment before falling forward and dissolving into tears. Torquil let her lie there for a few moments then gently eased her up onto her knees.

'I . . . I'm sorry,' she eventually gasped, her eyes focusing hazily on him. 'You're him, aren't you? Fiona's latest conquest.'

Torquil scowled. 'Actually, I was an old conquest,' he replied bitterly. 'Or maybe a rediscovered one.'

'The bitch!' Allegra McCall cursed, before once more dissolving into uncontrollable sobbing and screaming.

Once again Torquil came close to slapping her. And once again his scruples kept him in check.

* * *

The Padre and Miss Melville had spent a couple of hours trying to placate disgruntled visitors who wanted nothing more than to leave the island. Explaining that the enforced quarantine was none of their doing didn't seem to help overmuch. Accordingly, they opted for the strategy of trying to provide further entertainment and diversion with lectures and workshops. Fortunately, several of their authors were more than willing to help, yet they knew that there would only be so many talks and lectures that people would be willing to listen to.

It had clouded over and started to drizzle as Lachlan headed for his Red Hunter. On his way he saw Professor Neil Ferguson striding along the harbour towards his cabin cruiser.

'Ahoy there, professor!' he yelled, trotting along the quay with the intention of persuading the marine archaeologist to give another talk.

'Ah, Padre,' said the professor, turning quickly with a pile of magazines and assorted paperwork cradled in his arms. The inevitable happened and several magazines slipped from his grasp into a puddle. 'Damn! I was just going to put some of this stuff into the hold.'

Lachlan helped him gather up an assortment of soggy archaeological journals, magazines and programmes from the Gathering. The professor took them from him and swiftly climbed on board. 'Back in a moment,' he said, sliding open the cabin door and disappearing inside with the pile.

'I want to be ready to go as soon as I can,' he said a few moments later when he emerged again. 'I've had enough of West Uist for a while — and of police interviews!'

'Interviews?'

'Piper had a lengthy chat with me this morning,' he explained. 'I'm afraid I'd been a bad boy and broken his embargo in my boat. I went out for an early morning swim. I didn't think it would matter.'

'He gave you a rough time, did he?'

'A bit.'

The Padre had mechanically filled his pipe from the yellow oilskin pouch that he seemed to keep several ounces of tobacco in at any time, and struck a light to the cracked briar bowl. 'Torquil is a bit upset himself, Neil. Don't worry if he seemed a bit abrupt.'

Neil Ferguson sighed. 'Of course, I feel guilty about her.'

Lachlan blew out a thin stream of blue smoke. 'Guilty? Why ever should you feel guilty?'

'Because I don't think . . . ' He sighed again and bit his lip. 'I've explained it all to Piper this morning,' he replied, after seeming to consider his words. 'I expect he'll tell you himself.'

The Padre shook his head. 'I doubt it, Neil. Torquil is the senior officer in a murder investigation. I'm not sure that he'll feel able to confide in his old Uncle Lachlan.' He shook his head then repeated, 'He's a bit fraught himself.'

Neil Ferguson nodded his head. 'It will be a relief when they catch the bastard. Then we can all go home.' He touched Lachlan's arm. 'Tell Torquil I'll . . . ' He hesitated, then added, 'Tell him I'll catch up with him later.'

The Padre nodded and clenched his pipe between his teeth as he watched Neil Ferguson walk off in the direction of the Bonnie Prince Charlie. The professor was out of sight before he realized that he had not asked him about giving another lecture.

* * *

Sitting in Allegra McCall's Mitsubishi Shogun four × four after having phoned to Morag to send the Drummond twins over to bring her and her vehicle back to Kyleshiffin, Torquil hefted the empty bottle of vodka in his hand. Outside, the rain was lashing the windows.

'Why Allegra? Why the vodka?'

The publisher looked back at him with red-rimmed, bloodshot eyes. 'I haven't drunk all that. It was only half full.'

'But you've drunk too much to drive back to town. We may only be a wee island but we have the same laws as the mainland.'

'So breathalyse me!' she said indifferently.

'I should do, Allegra. But I want information from you and I want you to give it to me.'

She bent her head and trembled. Her hair was astray and she did not look remotely like the straight efficient bastion of respectability he had seen at Angus MacLeod's ceilidh and at the Gathering. She pulled back a sleeve to glance at an ornate expensive-looking Rolex watch that Torquil reckoned would be worth half a year's salary to him, then she took a deep breath and eyed him unsteadily. 'How do you know that I was planning to come back to Kyleshiffin at all?'

Torquil raised his eyebrows. That surprised him. 'What do you mean, Allegra?'

'That I was toying with the idea of killing myself.'

'Now why would you want to be doing that?'

For a moment her cheeks suffused with colour and he feared that she might be about to drift back into hysteria. But then the colour disappeared just as suddenly and her shoulders dropped. 'Because I don't know if I want to live any more. The person I loved is dead. Killed by some . . . ' she hesitated as she sought for a word, 'some monster's hand.'

'And how did you plan to do it?'

Allegra McCall shrugged matter-of-factly. 'I was going to drink enough not to care, then I was going to load my pockets with stones just like Virginia Woolf.'

Torquil eyed her dispassionately. 'Why kill yourself though? Did you feel guilty about Fiona's death?'

'Of course I bloody did.'

'Did you kill her, Allegra?'

Fires blazed in her eyes, then just as suddenly extinguished themselves. 'That's a stupid question! I loved her.'

Torquil maintained his dispassionate poker face. 'You were her publisher, so you mean that you loved her as an author?'

Answer that, he thought, but then he realized that he was pushing her, not because he wanted her to give him information, but because he wanted her to give him a reason to validate the emotion of hate that was rising within him just then. He had a demon on one shoulder and an angel on the other, each prompting him one way or the other. The demon wanted to bully her, to make her say things that stoked up his internal fires. The angel tried to calm him down, telling him to be calm, clinical and dispassionate. So far the demon had been winning, but now the angel was gaining the upperhand. Yet in that he felt his heart aching, for he had to negate his own feelings.

You have to be detached, the angel's voice said in his head. For just now you have to think that Fiona meant nothing to you — that she was someone unfortunate enough to get herself killed — and you have to find out who killed her.

Allegra McCall sniffed. 'I was her publisher, inspector. I was the person who first lifted the stone and let her crawl out. I nurtured her, groomed her, I turned her writing into something the world wanted.' She took a deep breath. 'Yes, I loved her as a writer, but I . . . I . . . just loved her.'

Torquil refused to let her off the hook so easily. But now he was pursuing his questioning with a more professional motive. The effect was just as brutal. 'You mean in a sisterly manner?'

Allegra McCall looked sober for the first time. She shook her head. 'I loved her, inspector. And she told me that she loved me too.' She smiled and her eyes went misty, as if she was looking into the past and seeing a happy memory rekindle itself. 'We were lovers for two years.'

Despite himself, Torquil was aware that the angel had suddenly dropped off his shoulder.

⋆ ⋆ ⋆

Roland Baxter and Angus MacLeod were drinking malt whisky in the laird's oak-panelled library-cum-billiard room. They had both felt unsettled ever since Piper McKinnon had left, and their tempers were fraught. None of this helped their ball-potting and neither of them had much interest in the game of snooker they were playing.

'You were a fool to ever get involved with him!' said Roland Baxter. 'He could drop you right in it.'

Angus MacLeod picked up his smouldering cigar and puffed thoughtfully on it for a moment. 'Yes, it has all suddenly gotten out of hand. I thought having him here would have sorted everything out.'

'Well it hasn't, has it!' the minister snapped.

Angus MacLeod's voice was as silky as ever. 'But you know what they say, Roland

— mud sticks.' He blew out a ribbon of Havana smoke. 'And of course, mud also splashes and gets on other people.'

'Are you threatening me, Angus?'

'Just warning you, old chap.'

Roland Baxter leaned over the table and lined up the black ball, then deftly potted it in the corner pocket. 'In that case we'd all better be careful hadn't we?'

* * *

Although Morag's report on her interview with Genevieve Cooper had already prepared Torquil, Allegra McCall's answer struck home like a dart dipped in the poisonous cup of jealousy.

But she has valuable information that might lead to the murderer, he chided himself. I have to get her to tell me. 'Was she faithful to you during that time?' he forced himself to ask.

'She was never faithful. She liked sex. Lots of it.'

Torquil swallowed a hard lump that suddenly appeared in his throat. 'And were you faithful to her?'

'She was all I ever wanted.'

'And so what happened?'

The publisher shook her head. 'I don't

really know. She just suddenly became suspicious of me. She started to think that I was holding money back on her.'

'Were you?'

'Don't be ridiculous. I loved her and would have done anything for her. In fact I was doing everything possible to help. Genevieve Cooper and I transformed her from a small island journalist into what she is — ' She stopped, her face mirroring the pain that she felt. 'We turned her into the Queen of Scottish Crime. She was rich, well on her way to millionaire status.'

'Tell me about Angus MacLeod.'

Allegra stared blankly back at him. 'Tell you what?'

'Where did he fit in? Why did she dislike him so much?'

She darted her eyes heavenwards and whistled. 'Again she had a crazy idea that he was making money out of her and not letting her reap her just rewards. You know that he runs a string of cut-price bookshops along the west of Scotland?'

'AME Books.'

'That's right. The thing is that he sells vast numbers of books. She was still getting her royalties, but she hated the idea of her books being sold for less than the recommended retail price.'

'That was all?'

'As far as I know.'

'Could she have been having an affair with him?'

'No way!'

'What about our esteemed minister for culture, Roland Baxter?'

Allegra hung her head. 'Yes,' she replied, almost in a whisper. 'She used him, I think. Used his power, used him for sex, and then bad-mouthed him.'

'How so, Allegra?'

'She put it round that he was impotent. And she hinted that she was going to do an exposé of him in her next book. Just like she did in her last one, *Flesh Trimmers*.'

'Explain that to me, Allegra.'

The publisher waved her hand in front of her eyes as a mini swarm of midges opportunistically flew through the slightly open window and began biting. She flicked the automatic window button and the glass slid up. 'Mind if I smoke?' she asked, reaching into the glove compartment and taking out a pack of low-tar cigarettes. Torquil declined one and waited as she lit up; feeling grateful for the smoke that so rapidly discouraged the midges.

'You do realize that Fiona more or less wrote to a formula. She used a *roman-à-clef* in each of her books.'

'My schoolboy French tells me that means a novel with a key? I don't understand,' he lied. He recalled Fiona's very own words at her lecture. 'What does that mean?'

'It means that some of the characters were thinly disguised allusions to real people. Effectively, she wrote a crime novel round real-life celebrities, generally doing a real hatchet job on them, showing all of their inadequacies or peccadilloes so that the reader would cheer when they were bumped off, as they invariably were. Take her last book, *Flesh Trimmers*, for example. The person she based it on, Dr Viroj Wattana, is suing her for defamation of character.'

Piper stroked his chin and nodded. 'Does he have a case?'

'He has a gripe. I guess he could legitimately claim to be upset, but for him to win his case he would have to prove that he was her subject for the cosmetic surgeon in the book. And he may have a job doing that.'

'What's so bad about being in the book?'

'She implies that he doesn't do straight cosmetic surgery, and that he is a butcher and a botcher.'

'Was he definitely the subject of the book?'

'Yes. And she used him because she wasn't happy with the boob job he did on her. She felt that he left one breast higher than the other.' She took a long puff on her cigarette and let out a plume of smoke. 'And she was right, there was a slight difference, but nothing to speak of. I thought her breasts were beautiful.'

'Could he have had a motive to kill her, do you think?'

She eyed him quizzically. 'Is that an ethical question, inspector?'

'Murder is an unethical business, Allegra. I'll do whatever it takes to find Fiona Cullen's murderer.'

She nodded. 'He had no warm feelings for her and a court case would have been costly. It could have crippled his reputation if he lost.'

'And what about her new book?' he asked.

'I don't know much about it, except that it was to be called *Dead Writers Tell No Tales*.' She shivered involuntarily. 'God! That's eerily prophetic.'

'Was it going to have a *roman-à-clef*, too?'

'I expect so.'

'And if that is the case then whoever was going to be the main character could have been in for a hatchet job?'

Allegra nodded. 'The full Fiona Cullen treatment! Poor sod!'

And Torquil realized that there were indeed several people who could have found themselves inside the covers of her new book — a number of people with a possible motive for wanting her dead.

That made it ever more important to find that missing laptop.

⋆ ⋆ ⋆

Morag had been busy. After Torquil had left Kyleshiffin for Dunshiffin Castle she had been working at the duty desk dealing with the constant stream of tourists, idlers and busybodies. Then a young couple had come in. A young man with long lank hair and a girl with long corn-blonde hair with ringlet extensions. They were both dressed in baggy jeans and tee-shirts; each had a rucksack on their back. Morag noticed the gleaming new wedding ring on her hand.

'*Latha math*,' Morag greeted. 'Good morning to you.'

The young woman smiled. 'I just love that Hebridean accent. Is the Gaelic easy to learn?'

Morag smiled. 'I cannot be saying very easily, I have been speaking it all my life. Now what can I be doing for you?'

The young man slid his rucksack off his

back. 'We found something and wonder if it could be important.'

'Important in what way?' Morag queried.

'In your murder investigation,' the young woman replied. 'Show her, Simon.'

Morag watched as Simon opened his rucksack and pulled out a plastic bag. He laid it on the counter and unrolled the plastic. 'I didn't touch it,' he said with a half smile. 'I know that you'll probably want to send it for forensic analysis.'

Morag leaned closer and saw a battered black plastic case. It was unmistakably a laptop computer that someone had tried very hard to smash to bits.

'Look,' said Simon triumphantly. 'You can see her nametag on it. Fiona Cullen.'

Morag nodded non-committally. 'It could be useful,' she said, wrapping the bag round the laptop again. She raised the flap on the counter. 'Perhaps we'd better have a word through here.'

* * *

Genevieve Cooper was smoking even more heavily than usual. Ever since she had received the call on her mobile from *him*.

Damn him! Why was *he* pushing her now of all times?

Everything was going wrong. Desperate measures might be called for.

* * *

Ever methodical, Morag made notes as she interviewed the couple:

> *Mr and Mrs Simon Sturgess, newly married, enjoying honeymoon on West Uist. Came for the Gathering and Literary Festival. Both recently MA graduates in Scottish Studies from Dundee University (Carol with a first, Simon with a lower class second).*
>
> *Both passionate about poetry and crime fiction.*
>
> *Met Ranald Buchanan in his shop two days ago, and purchased a copy of his book,* Songs of the Selkie.

'And how have you spent your time on West Uist?'

'At the Gathering and just ambling around the island. We've bought loads of books, talked to lots of authors,' Simon volunteered. 'Carol wants to be a writer.'

Carol flushed. Morag noticed that she seemed to blush easily. 'One day, maybe,' Carol said. 'I'd like to be a crime writer, like

Fiona Cullen. Or a poet, like Ranald Buchanan.'

Who are both dead, thought Morag. She jotted notes, smiled at Carol, then said to Simon: 'And where did you find this laptop?'

'In a bin in a car park.'

'Which car park?'

'The one behind the Bonnie Prince Charlie.'

Morag involuntarily took a deep breath.

'I'm surprised that the police hadn't found it. What with her having stayed there.'

Despite herself, Morag felt she was beginning to take a dislike to Simon Sturgess as he sat back looking smugly at her. 'And why were you looking in a bin in that car park?' she asked.

He grinned. 'Carol wants to be a crime writer. Me, I want to be a detective. I thought it would be fun to investigate a real-life murder.'

'Interesting,' Morag mused as she continued to make notes.

* * *

Wallace Drummond drove Allegra's Shogun back to her hotel in Kyleshiffin while Douglas went on, under Piper's instructions, to check that nothing had been touched at the crannog on Loch Hynish, and in particular that there were no ghoulish tourists. Torquil rode back to the station on his Bullet, stopping at Miss Melville's main Festival book stall to buy a copy of Fiona Cullen's last book, *Flesh Trimmers*.

Morag had gone out some ten minutes previously, Ewan informed him when he arrived back at the station.

'She tried phoning you, Piper, but she said your phone wasn't picking up. She's pretty excited about something and said she'd explain when she came back.'

'Did she say where she was going?'

'To find the Padre, actually. Would you like a cup of tea, Piper?'

Torquil nodded and retreated to his office, while Ewan went to get him some stewed tea. Slumping into a chair he thumbed through the book, trying to get the gist of Fiona's *roman-à-clef*. He quickly found the first description of the main character and realized that it did not take too much imagination to identify the maverick surgeon in the novel as Dr Viroj Wattana. It was as if she had based the novel upon the Thai doctor, describing him exactly. Then, scanning the first chapter, he gained some idea of the fictional surgeon's activities.

'*Mac an diabhoil* — son of the devil!' said

Ewan coming in with a tray of tea and biscuits. 'An evil bugger that doctor is.'

Torquil glanced at the gory book cover, illustrating a masked, bespectacled surgeon with a blood-stained scalpel in his gloved hand. 'Have you read this book, Ewan?' he asked in surprise.

'Och, I have read all of Fiona's books,' Ewan returned, his eyes narrowing. 'Haven't you?'

Torquil shook his head. 'None of them. I'm not a fiction fan really.' And as he said it he felt a deep regret, almost mounting to guilt.

Ewan pouted, then shrugged his big shoulders. 'She's really good, Torquil. She can — ' then he knocked the side of his head with his knuckles. 'There I go again. Talking without thinking. I meant that she told a good story, kept you guessing.'

'Well go on Ewan, tell me about this book. Why don't you like this surgeon?'

Ewan looked doubtful. 'But I don't want to spoil the story for you, Piper!'

Torquil picked up his mug. 'I need to know, Ewan. This could be important for the investigation. You will save me time by giving me the low-down.'

Ewan sat down and picked up his own mug of tea, dunking a ginger biscuit in it. 'It's all set in Thailand, you see. This surgeon is supposed to be a posh cosmetic surgeon, but he makes most of his money by doing cheap organ transplants and sex change operations for rich foreigners. Oh yes, and he also has a sideline in doing operations for the gangs. Instead of the gangsters shooting people's knee-caps off like they do in London and places, the gangsters arrange castrations. He does it for them at a special clinic.'

'I can see why you don't like the guy,' Torquil remarked.

Ewan grinned. 'But don't worry. Fiona made sure that he got his just deserts.'

Torquil nodded and sipped his tea. And maybe that is why the real Dr Wattana had a grudge against Fiona!

Putting down his mug he rose and went through to the incident room where he began adding notes to the whiteboard.

* * *

The Padre was enjoying a ploughman's lunch at the bar of the Bonnie Prince Charlie when Morag caught up with him. He beamed at her over the rim of a glass of Heather Ale. '*A Mhorag, slàinte mhór*,' he called across the crowded bar.

'And good health to you, too, Lachlan,' she

returned, refusing his offer of a drink. 'I need a bit of information.' And she described the young couple she had just interviewed.

'Aye, I remember them clearly. Bookish types. They were at all of the lectures. She was quiet, but he seemed keen to ask questions of all of the lecturers. As my auld faither would say, he'd speir a snail out of its shell.' He sipped some beer then wiped foam off his upper lip. 'Why the interest in them, Morag? They seemed an innocent enough couple.'

'You're probably right, Lachlan. But they found Fiona Cullen's laptop.'

The Padre raised his eyebrows. 'Does Torquil know?'

'Not yet. He hasn't picked up his phone for a while.'

'And why are you suspicious of them?'

Morag shook her head. 'I don't know if I am or not. It's just that she says she'd like to be a crime writer like Fiona or a poet like Ranald.'

'It is a commendable ambition to be a scribe.'

'And he says he wants to be a detective. To tell you the truth, there's something morbid about him that I don't like.'

The Padre popped a piece of oatcake with Orkney cheese into his mouth. 'And why did you come to me, Morag Driscoll, and not Bella Melville?'

Morag grinned at him. 'I'm still frightened of her.'

Lachlan began to chuckle, then elbowed her and dropped his voice. 'I don't blame you, lassie. She still scares me!'

Morag's mobile beeped and she accessed a text message, with a puzzling smile. 'Piper's back,' she announced. 'And he said I have to find you and bring you with me!'

* * *

In the incident room they looked down at the smashed laptop. 'Will we be able to find out anything that was on it?' Torquil asked.

Morag shrugged. 'Who knows. The Forensic Department at Dundee University may be able to, but it just depends whether the hard drive has been destroyed or no. My cousin is a dab hand with computers. I can get him to look at it if you like.'

'Please do. It'll be quicker than getting it over to Dundee. Were there any CDs or floppies?'

'This was all they found. He seemed smug that he had found it and that we hadn't.'

Torquil leaned back in his chair with his hands linked behind his head. 'Uncle, I have a couple of things I need to ask you.'

Despite the no smoking signs the Padre had already filled and struck a light to his pipe. No one except Bella Melville ever had the nerve to ask him to desist from his pipesmoking. 'Ask away, laddie.'

'What do you know about a monkey's grave in the St Ninian's cemetery?'

The Padre puffed furiously for a few moments, as he often did when deep in thought. Then he tapped his teeth with the stem of his pipe and shook his head. 'There is no monkey buried in St Ninian's. Maybe you are thinking of the legend about the Boddam monkey. It's a fishing village near Peterhead, where it is said the villagers found a wrecked ship after a storm. There was no one on board except a monkey. Knowing that according to the law of salvage they had no right to it, because there was a living creature aboard, they hanged the monkey.' He tamped the tobacco down in his pipe with his thumb. 'That is the source of the monkey story, I think.'

'That's interesting,' Torquil said after a moment, 'because Professor Ferguson tried to tell me that he was researching a tale he'd been told about a wreck associated with Bonnie Prince Charlie. He said someone had told him about the ship's marmoset having made it to shore and then been hanged by English dragoons.'

'I think someone was pulling his leg.'

'Or he was pulling mine,' Torquil replied. 'I was asking him what he was doing in the cemetery the day Fiona and I met you on the golf course.'

'The day she hooked her ball and hit him? I tell you what, laddie — I'll go and have a look at all those graves and report back to you.'

'Before you go, Uncle,' Torquil said, picking up the copy of Fiona's book *Flesh Trimmers*, 'You had a chat with Dr Wattana at the Gathering, didn't you? Did you realize that Fiona may have used him as a *roman-à-clef* in this book?'

The Padre nodded his head. 'Aye, I had a drink with him at the Gathering. But I didn't know about the book. Is that significant?'

'He may have had reason to be happy about Fiona's death.'

The Padre whistled softly. 'He's a nervous little fellow. I saw him earlier today, hovering about Neil Ferguson's boat. He seemed a bit preoccupied, a bit distressed in fact. Said he wanted to talk to you.' The clergyman looked pensive for a moment. 'As did Neil Ferguson. I saw him afterwards.'

Torquil looked over at Morag, who had

remained silent as she took notes. 'I think it's time we brought Dr Wattana in for questioning. Send Ewan on this one, will you Morag.'

* * *

Ewan had telephoned Dunshiffin Castle to see whether Dr Wattana had returned, but had been greeted with a stiff negative from Jesmond, the Dunshiffin butler. Other enquiries at hotels, pubs and restaurants also drew blanks. So Ewan met up with the Drummond twins and together they set off to see whether the doctor could be found anywhere in Kyleshiffin.

The rain meanwhile had turned into that extra fine variety called Scotch mist, which typified the Western Isles. Halfway between drizzle and mist, it was wet enough to drench you slowly and thick enough to get lost in.

Parked up a side alley behind the lifeboat house, they found the AME car the Thai doctor had been seen driving about in that day.

Suddenly, the noise of a powerful boat revving up broke the silence that had hung over the harbour ever since the embargo had been passed on using boats. All three rushed down the alley in time to see a boat accelerating out of the harbour and disappearing in the mist in the direction of far-off South Uist.

'That's Professor Ferguson's boat, the *Unicorn*!' cried Ewan. 'Come on you two, let's get the *Seaspray*. I don't know what he thinks he's up to.'

'He's going to have a good start, Ewan. We'll be pushed to catch him,' said Wallace as the trio broke into a run.

'I'll catch the bugger!' returned Ewan. And this time I won't be letting Piper down, he thought to himself.

PART THREE

The Selkie Returns

11

The catamaran scudded across the waves, in and out of patches of sea spray and mist, gradually gaining on Professor Ferguson's *Unicorn*. They could hear the drone of its powerful engine as it raced on towards the slow-rising silhouette of South Uist. As they came within hailing distance Ewan picked up the microphone and flicked on the loudhailer.

'This is the Police. You are ordered to stop. Cut your engine immediately!'

But the boat raced on regardless.

'What are you thinking we should be doing, Ewan?' asked Wallace Drummond.

'Aye, how will we be stopping him if he doesn't want to be stopped?' Douglas queried.

Ewan rubbed his lantern jaw. A thorny problem it was proving, right enough. They could hardly ram the boat. Far less could they draw alongside at this speed on a choppy sea and try to board.

'We'll keep on his tail and take him when he stops,' Ewan said, decisively. 'At this rate, it will be in Lochboisdale. Then we'll arrest the bugger.'

Wallace wiped sea spray from his eyes. 'Why would the professor be making a run for it? He's nothing to hide, has he?'

Ewan bit his lip at the recollection of his encounter with the marine archaeology professor earlier in the day. 'Maybe he has, maybe he hasn't,' he mused, deciding that the twins did not need to know about his slip-up with the buoy. 'But running away from the island when all boats are banned from leaving is suspicious in my book. As is ignoring police orders to stop!'

The professor's boat started to veer towards starboard, describing a slow turn.

'He's making for Barra, I think,' Wallace suggested.

Then the boat started to chug, its engine spluttering.

'He's running out of fuel!' Ewan cried triumphantly. 'Now we'll have him, lads.'

And sure enough a few moments later the boat's engine gave a final splutter then went dead; with its speed cut, the boat began to flounder.

Ewan again flicked on the loudhailer. 'This is the police, Professor Ferguson. You are under arrest for leaving West Uist without permission. Please anchor and submit yourself.'

Wallace took the helm and manoeuvred the

Seaspray close to the *Unicorn*. There was no sign of movement aboard.

'I am not liking this!' said Douglas Drummond. 'It's like the bloody *Marie Celeste*!'

And as the mist started to curl in around them, all three police officers felt shivers run up their spines.

'I don't like it either,' agreed Wallace.

* * *

Calum Steele was drinking a whisky and water at the bar of the Bonnie Prince Charlie and going over details with Mollie McFadden for his next news bulletin to Scottish TV.

'It's going to be the making of this pub, Mollie,' he said with a wink.

Mollie tapped him on the back of his hand. 'Like my auld mother said, Calum. You scratch my back and I'll scratch yours.' With this she ambled off to the other end of the bar to serve another customer.

Calum swallowed the last of his whisky and stood contemplating the bottom of his glass when someone coughed next to him. It was the cough of someone wanting to attract his attention. He turned to find a young couple standing smiling at him. He recognized them from somewhere, possibly from one of the lectures at the Festival, he thought.

'Can we buy you a drink, Mr Steele?' Carol Sturgess asked.

'We love your paper and the articles you've been writing about the Gathering,' enthused Simon. 'This murder is going to make you famous.'

Calum felt slightly nonplussed, an unusual feeling for him. 'Sure, it's a sad way to gain recognition,' he said at the same time nodding at the offer of a drink and tapping the bar to attract, Mollie's bar-helper's attention. 'What can I be doing for you both?' He had spotted their wedding rings: 'Mr and Mrs . . . ?'

'Sturgess — Simon and Carol. We've been here for the Festival,' Carol volunteered, while her husband ordered a round. 'I want to get into the media like you, too.'

Calum accepted his whisky and topped it with an equal measure of water from the small Bonnie Prince Charlie jug on the bar. 'Well, journalism is a hard life. Rewarding though.' He raised his glass. '*Slàinte mhór*!'

'Could we have a word with you, Mr Steele?' Simon asked, pointing to a corner table under the portrait of the Young Pretender, Charles Edward Stuart. 'In private.'

'We have some information that you might

want to use. We found something, but the police didn't seem too interested . . . '

Calum eyed them with renewed interest. 'Come away with me, my friends. You'll not find Calum Steele uninterested.' He put a hand on Simon's arm and dropped his voice. 'But I'm afraid that the *West Uist Chronicle* doesn't have a very big cheque book.'

Carol squeezed his arm. 'Don't worry, Mr Steele. You won't need a cheque book.'

* * *

Having secured the becalmed *Unicorn* with grappling hooks, Ewan jumped on board. There was no one at the wheel, which had been locked off. He slid back the cabin door. The twins watched him disappear below, prepared to leap to his assistance should the occasion merit it. But after a few moments the big constable reappeared, his face pale and confused-looking.

'What the hell!' he exclaimed. 'There's no one here. There's a dreadful mess though. Bottles and pills and papers everywhere. I think the professor has flipped and done away with himself!'

'He must have jumped into the sea before now and we missed him in the mist,' Wallace deduced. 'We'd better get on the blower and get the coastguard helicopter out.'

'And we'd better get on back and see if he's still alive,' said Douglas. He thumped his head with his fist. 'Gah! We're a right trio of fools!'

'Oh Boy!' Ewan exclaimed. 'I'd better phone Piper first and see what he wants us to do.'

* * *

Torquil was not in a good humour when Ewan called him. 'Right, you'd better bring the boat in. Have you got enough fuel?'

'Aye, there's spare in the boat and we've got reserves in the catamaran in any case.'

'Good, you'd better get going then in case he's managing to stay afloat. But don't touch the cabin, Ewan, whatever you do. Use gloves and make minimum contact with the controls.'

'That's what I was planning, inspector.'

'Do a good sweep and get the Drummonds to do the same. It'll not be easy but try and chart a course on the way back, as close as you can to the route you took there. And leave — '

'Leave a buoy! I know, sir. I've dropped one already.'

'On you go, Ewan.'

Damn it! Torquil thought a moment later as he put the phone down. If Neil Ferguson was a killer the last thing he wanted was for him to commit suicide. He had wanted to look Fiona's killer in the eye. Or even better, catch him alone somewhere!

The commotion from the outer office was an irritation he felt he could have done without. He tried to ignore it, sure that Morag would deal with it quickly. But in this he was not quite correct. A few moments later she tapped on his office door then popped her head round. 'Torquil,' she mouthed. 'I think you'd better come through. Professor Ferguson is here and he's hopping mad because someone's stolen his boat.'

Torquil stared at her incredulously for a moment. Neil Ferguson was alive! So who the hell was on the boat? Things are getting crazy, he decided with a silent shake of the head.

And in fact, hopping mad was an understatement to describe the professor's state of agitation. He was furious. Almost irrational, Torquil thought. When questioned as to why he was so angry the marine archaeologist replied: 'My research papers, my work over the last year is on that boat.' He crossed his arms as if expecting this answer to explain everything. 'There's at least a quarter of a million words in that cabin.'

'Well, we'll see if it's all still there, Neil.' Torquil replied. 'Ewan is bringing your boat back now.'

* * *

Calum Steele woke up in the camp bed that he kept in his office for emergencies when he was either working late or when he felt too drunk to ride his Lambretta home. His tongue stuck to the roof of his mouth and a pounding headache made him groan as he fought to recall just how he had gotten there. The fact that it was still daylight confused him. Then he remembered getting into a drinking session with that young hippy couple, Simon and Carol Sturgess. Not that they seemed to have drunk as much as him. Three pints of Heather Ale and about four whiskies; a mere bagatelle for him under ordinary circumstances. He hadn't really wanted to drink all that much, but he felt flattered by their attention. Especially by hers, sticking her tits at him that way. And then they had left the Bonnie Prince Charlie — he remembered waving to Mollie who had eyed him in that withering, disapproving way of hers — then they had come back to the *Chronicle* office. And then what?

The whirring of distant helicopter blades impinged upon his thoughts for a moment, which seemed strange, what with the ban that Piper had placed on all travelling from the island. But then a sudden gut-wrenching spasm of utter nausea and dizziness overcame him and he leaned out of the camp bed and vomited on the floor. Then he felt himself slipping into a pool of unconsciousness.

* * *

The coastguard helicopter was joined by an RAF helicopter from RAF Macrahanish which had been quickly scrambled after Morag had sent off the details of a person lost overboard. While they continued to sweep the area, the Drummond twins came in with *Seaspray*, followed by Ewan in Professor Ferguson's *Unicorn*.

Torquil was waiting for them at the harbour.

'No sign of anyone?' he called out as he caught the rope to secure the *Seaspray*.

'Not a — ' began Wallace Drummond, suddenly seeing Professor Neil Ferguson approach along the harbour. 'The professor is alive!' he gasped, as if he had just seen a ghost.

'Of course I'm alive,' Neil Ferguson

snapped. 'Who stole my boat? Who have you got there?'

Ewan had cut the engine of the *Unicorn* and hopped ashore to tie up. 'We've no idea, Professor Ferguson,' he said with a half-smile. 'But we are glad to see you.' He shook his head and looked at Torquil. 'It's a mess in the cabin, though, inspector.'

Torquil boarded. 'You haven't touched anything have you, Ewan?'

The big constable shook his head.

'I'll tell you if anything is missing,' said Neil Ferguson, climbing aboard after Torquil.

But Torquil stopped him with a hand on his arm. 'I'll go first, Neil. You can come, but I must insist that you don't touch anything. This is still an official investigation you know.' He looked back at Ewan, then continued, 'Give Morag a bell. I want her down here pronto with her camera and fingerprint kit.'

Slipping on a pair of rubber gloves from his pocket he slid the cabin door open and went down the steps with Neil Ferguson close behind.

'Bloody hell!' exclaimed the professor. 'All my papers have been scattered. And some bastard has drunk a bottle of my best whisky.'

'Was it a full bottle, Neil?'

The professor nodded.

'And what about this empty bottle of paracetamol?'

'That wasn't mine.'

Torquil knelt down to look at another empty bottle that was lying on its side on the floor. 'And this wasn't yours either,' he said. 'This bottle was made out to Dr Viroj Wattana. Nitrazepam — sleeping tablets.'

'Viroj!' the marine archaeologist exclaimed. 'You think Dr Wattana was here?'

Torquil straightened up and shrugged. 'I'm not saying anything, Neil. But an empty bottle of tablets made out to Dr Wattana is lying on the floor of your boat. I'd say it looks suspicious, wouldn't you?'

'Do you — Do you mean he's killed himself?'

'That is a possibility,' Torquil replied, looking round. Then, having sighted a loose paper on the floor underneath the cabin table, he exclaimed, 'Hello, what have we here?' He bent and picked up the single sheaf of paper by its corner and laid it flat in the middle of the table. In a shaky hand was written the name 'Fiona' followed by a pattern:

FIONA ขอโทษ

Neil Ferguson looked over his shoulder and whistled softly.

'Do you know what that means?' Torquil asked.

'It's Thai, Piper. It says 'Fiona', then 'I am sorry'.' He looked at Piper. 'Does that mean . . . '

A muscle twitched in Torquil's jaw. 'Does it mean that we've found Fiona Cullen's murderer?' He bit his lip, then nodded. 'It could be a confession before he killed himself. I'm afraid it looks like it.'

'I can't believe that, Piper. Not Viroj — '

But he did not finish. He flinched as Piper McKinnon suddenly leaned forward and pounded the table with his fist.

'*Mac an diobhoil*!' Torquil cursed. 'I wanted to take him alive!'

* * *

By 7 p.m. Morag had photographed the cabin of the *Unicorn* and dusted it for fingerprints. In a corner of the cabin, underneath a pile of scattered journals and papers, she found a pair of wire-rimmed spectacles.

'Those are almost certainly Dr Wattana's,' said Torquil as he, Morag, Ewan and the Drummond twins sat round the table in the incident room after tea that evening. Outside, mist swirled against the window panes.

The helicopter teams had been in contact, informing Morag that they were going to do one further sweep before returning to their respective bases. They had found nothing whatsoever and the sea squall and mist were making the search hazardous.

While Morag had talked to the helicopter crews Torquil had been on the telephone to report on the finding of the boat to Superintendent Kenneth Lumsden, who was still staying at his son-in-law's house in Benbecula.

'Well, I think it sounds clear that the chap has done himself in,' the superintendent had barked down the phone. 'Do you feel confident about it?'

'I'd like to go over things with my team, sir.'

'Do so, then ring me, then we can let folk off the island and back to civilization.'

As usual Torquil had been left staring at the receiver as the superintendent disconnected without courtesy or warning.

Well let's deliberate, he thought as he looked at the wire-framed spectacles, one lens of which was cracked, presumably after the doctor had thrown them down in a semi-drunken, drug-fuelled haze, or when they had been skittering around the floor during the boat chase.

'Did you go over the ship's inventory with the professor?' he asked.

Morag nodded. 'There was a spare anchor. That's gone.'

'I am betting that he used that to weight himself down,' Douglas Drummond volunteered.

His brother nodded sombrely. 'Aye, to take him down to Davy Jones's Locker.' He made a sign of the cross over his heart. 'Poor man!'

'If he was a murderer then he was not a poor man,' Torquil rebuked sharply, standing up and going over to the whiteboard. He picked up the marker and wrote the name 'Viroj Wattana'. Under it he made several notes:

Doctor/Thailand/cosmetic surgeon
Book character/Legal action
Spectacles
'Fiona, I am sorry' (written in Thai)
Boat/missing spare anchor
Whisky/paracetamol/Nitrazepam
(sleeping tablets)

Then he drew lines between Wattana's name and that of Professor Neil Ferguson and Fiona Cullen. He tapped the board with the end of the marker. 'What do we make of it then? Anybody?'

'He did it!' blurted out Douglas Drummond. 'It is as plain as day.'

'I am in agreement with my brother,' said Wallace. 'He was cross about Fiona writing her book about him.'

Ewan nodded. 'That's right, Piper. I told you about it, remember?'

'Well,' Wallace went on. 'While we were all at the Gathering he persuaded her to meet him at the crannog on Loch Hynish, then he — did her in!' He saw his inspector's sudden pained expression and frowned. 'Sorry Piper, I mean that he murdered her.'

His brother took over, as if they were thinking along the same train of thought. 'But with all this police investigation he panicked. Decided to do away with himself and so he stole Neil Ferguson's boat and headed out to sea.'

Ewan nodded again. 'I think that makes sense. And while he was out there he drank a bottle of whisky for courage and swigged a couple of bottles of pills, then threw himself overboard.'

'And what about the note?' Torquil prompted.

'That confirms it,' Douglas said eagerly. 'It stands to reason he'd say it in his own language.'

Torquil looked at his sergeant, Morag Driscoll, who had remained silent with her lips pursed pensively. 'What do you think, Morag?'

Morag clicked her tongue. 'It seems logical. But there are still a lot of loose ends. That and — '

'Go on, Morag.'

'Well, he had a motive, perhaps. Means — who knows? Anyone could have stolen Calum Steele's Lambretta. As for opportunity — yes he had that, too — but so did a lot of people. His note says sorry, but it doesn't say what for.'

'And we don't have his body either, do we?' Torquil added. 'There weren't any oxygen cylinders missing were there?'

Morag shook her head. 'No, I specifically went over the diving equipment. Everything is just where it should be.'

Again Torquil tapped the whiteboard. 'Like you I'm not entirely happy. And it's not just the loose ends, either. It's the connections as well. We've got a board here that's beginning to look like a spider's web. Two webs even. Too many connections.'

'I still think he did it, Piper,' said Douglas.

Torquil sighed. 'Certainly, at the moment Dr Wattana is our chief suspect. And the very fact that we can't find him makes the theory that he may have taken his own life seem very likely. And if that is so, it strengthens the case against him.' He laid the marker down again. 'I think I'd better contact Superintendent Lumsden again.'

* * *

Despite her great sorrow, Bella Melville had enjoyed her day, what with organizing talks, and dashing here and there between showers in her best schoolmarm manner trying to keep tempers calm. It had been tough, challenging and draining all at once. Quite like the old days, she reflected, when she had striven to keep the Kyleshiffin School running with the minimum of support from the Highland and Island Education Department.

The news on the street about the professor's boat and the fact that the helicopters had been dashing back and forth in the lashing rain and the mist had led to a mass of rumours.

He's struck again!

The murderer has been caught!

The bastard committed suicide.

Like the sensible Hebridean woman that she was, Bella Melville had squashed each rumour that she came across with the irrefutable logic that you could not come to a proper conclusion without knowing the facts. When Sergeant Morag Driscoll telephoned her with the news that the embargo on travel had been lifted and that a special Macbeth ferry was on its way from Lochboisdale, she was delighted. And curious!

'And tell me why it has been lifted, Morag Driscoll? Who has been found?'

Morag was silent for a moment. 'No one has been found, Miss Melville.'

'Now remember what I used to tell you about being obtuse, Morag. Now just tell me — '

'I suggest that you listen to the news, Miss Melville,' Morag blurted out. 'I'm not at liberty to divulge anything else.' And with a hasty goodbye, she had rung off.

Torquil nodded at Morag as she replaced the phone. 'I think we can leave it to Bella Melville to alert the whole of West Uist,' he said with a half-grin. 'I bet she's loving being in charge again.'

'Does the superintendent feel comfortable about letting everyone go now?' Morag asked.

Torquil nodded. 'He just wanted a quick answer so that we can get the island back to normal. He thinks it is an open and shut case.'

'But you don't, do you, Torquil?'

'I'm uneasy, Morag,' he admitted. Then

with a sigh he added, 'Still, I guess it's time that we got Calum over here to give him the news.'

* * *

Torquil himself called at the *Chronicle* office after being unable to get hold of the newspaperman by telephone, either land line or mobile. Letting himself in by the back door (knowing from experience the loose brick behind which Calum kept his spare key) he ascended the stairs to find Calum in his underpants, huddled over his toilet.

'A bit early for you, isn't it, Calum' he said, upon smelling the alcohol-vomit odour that emanated from the bowl.

'That bloody hippy couple spiked my drinks!' Calum moaned between retches. 'And they've robbed me!'

Torquil patted Calum on the back and poured him a glass of water from the tap. 'Here, drink this, brush your teeth, then tell me what happened. If you've been robbed, we'll get the culprits. And maybe you'll want to know the news!'

Upon hearing the last words Calum Steele took a deep breath then steeled himself manfully. 'What news?' he asked, pushing himself to his feet and reaching for the water.

'Teeth first!' Torquil insisted. 'I'll make tea while you get ready.'

And with a greasy-looking patched dressing gown about his shoulders and a mug of sweet tea clutched in his hands, his teeth chattering and his face alabaster pale, Calum Steele reported his theft as Torquil insisted.

'They've taken all my notebooks, Piper. And my camera and photographs. Everything to do with the case.'

'That's bizarre, Calum.'

Calum curled his lip contemptuously. 'They're a bizarre couple right enough.' He cringed. 'They could have done anything while I was out cold. They could have killed me!'

'We'll bring them in for questioning, Calum,' Torquil soothed. 'And if they have any of your things we'll charge them.' He took a sip of tea, then gave the local newsman an update on the boat chase and the disappearance of Dr Wattana.

'He was a weird wee man,' said Calum, jotting it all down on a scrap of paper, his hands visibly shaking. 'He was talking to the Padre earlier today, by Neil Ferguson's boat as it happened, but he skedaddled as soon as he saw me coming to chat with him.'

'Did he indeed?' mused Torquil.

* * *

The late Scottish TV newscast that evening was given by a glamorous red-headed reporter standing on the quay at Oban in front of a newly arrived Macbeth ferry. It was a synopsis of the report that Calum had rang through.

'The murder enquiry on the Island of West Uist, into the death of the celebrated crime writer Fiona Cullen, has taken a huge leap forward. The West Uist Constabulary, headed by Inspector Torquil McKinnon, had been anxious to interview a Doctor Viroj Wattana, a cosmetic surgeon from Thailand, who is believed to have stolen a motor launch and headed off in the direction of Bara. When the boat was finally boarded by police officers, it appears that Doctor Wattana had vanished overboard.

'A coastguard helicopter was joined by a rescue helicopter from RAF Macrahanish, but no body was found. The search was discontinued due to adverse weather conditions, but will continue tomorrow morning.

'Happily, movement to and from the Island of West Uist is now returning to normal service.'

The camera shot then zoomed in on the ferry, just as a great hoot resounded from the boat.

Allegra McCall sat on the edge of her bed in her hotel bedroom and flicked the remote control to change channel. On the table in front of her was a half empty bottle of vodka, which she had purchased from the hotel bar upon her return to Kyleshiffin. She raised the glass.

'Fiona! Why? Why?'

Her head slumped forward and she dissolved into tears, unaware of the soft footsteps behind her.

There was a dull thud and a moment later she slithered to the floor, a patch of blood flowing from a wound at the back of her head.

12

The Padre had bathed and was comfortably settled in his study dressed in an ancient maroon dressing gown, his pipe billowing plumes of smoke as he worked on the eulogies for Ranald Buchanan and Fiona Cullen, when Torquil arrived home.

'Are you OK, laddie?'

Torquil nodded, although he was unsure how he actually felt. 'Did you hear about Dr Wattana on the news?'

'Aye. Do you think he did murder Fiona?'

Torquil sighed. 'It certainly looks like it. Then his nerves or his conscience got the better of him and he ended it all.'

The Padre blew smoke ceilingwards and laid his pipe down in a large brass ashtray. 'He seemed a nervous, vulnerable little chap to me.'

'Calum Steele said something similar earlier. He also mentioned that he saw him talking to you on the harbour, but that he scuttled away when Calum approached.'

The Padre had crossed to a side table and picked up a decanter of malt. 'That's right. It was near Neil Ferguson's boat, I told you, remember?'

He poured two good drams, topped them up with water and handed one to his nephew, then perched on the corner of his desk. 'He was trying to look into the boat. He said he was looking for Neil Ferguson.' He gave a rueful smile. 'He made a wee jibe about me being the 'drinking priest'. I asked if he was supposed to be going diving with Neil and Angus MacLeod, and he went all sad and said everything was different after Fiona's 'regrettable' murder. It seemed a strange word to use about a murder, but I don't suppose there can be an appropriate one. And he did dash off. I just assumed it was because he didn't want to get pinned down by our local newshound.'

Torquil sank into the big armchair and sipped his whisky. 'Maybe so. But talking of Neil Ferguson, did you check out those graves?'

Lachlan put down his drink and picked up his pipe. 'As a matter of fact I did,' he said, tapping the pipe out and reaching for his oilskin tobacco pouch. 'There was no monkey grave, of course. But there was a grave there that I had just about forgotten all about. It was Flora Buchanan's. Strange that I didn't remember it being there.'

'Wasn't she Ranald Buchanan's daughter?'

'Aye. She was a chronic schizophrenic, ever since her son was born. You may recall that he was drowned out beyond the Machair Skerry. Dr Crompton McLelland, Ralph's father, thought that some trauma had unhinged her mind. She had to be committed to a mental hospital on the mainland, and there she lived and died. She was buried here ten years ago.' He struck a light to his pipe. 'I remember that Ranald himself had engraved her headstone, but I had never noticed until now the inscription he had written underneath her name.'

'What did it say, Lachlan?'

'He wrote '*Finally safe from the Selkie*'.'

'And why is that significant?'

The Padre puffed on his pipe. 'Don't you see, Ranald had a thing about the Selkie. It was a common theme in a lot of his poetry. A cynic might say that he capitalized on it.'

Torquil nodded slowly. It was becoming clear. Part of Ranald Buchanan's success seemed to depend upon the fact that his grandson had drowned, and that the island folk had been willing to accept the rumour that a Selkie, a seal man, had impregnated Ranald's daughter and then had come back years later to claim the boy as his own and carry him off to his home beneath the sea. The superstition about drowning was somehow embedded in the islander psyche.

'Who was the father?'

The Padre shrugged. 'I honestly have no idea, Torquil. Ranald would never talk about it, except to affirm his belief that it had been a Selkie.'

'What was the child's name? And how old was he when he drowned?'

Lachlan screwed his eyes up as he delved into his memory. 'Archie. Young Archie and he was four. Ranald had brought him up himself after Flora was committed.'

'Four years old?' Torquil gasped. 'How the hell could a four-year-old go out in a boat all on his own? That's impossible, Lachlan.'

The Padre nodded. 'Nowadays it would be considered so. But it was just assumed that the youngster had somehow gotten into the rowing boat at Ranald's jetty and managed to untie the mooring.' He shrugged. 'When Ranald discovered the boat had gone a search was started. The lifeboat went out and found the boat about a mile out from the Machair Skerry. It would have drifted that far. Young Archie's scarf was hanging over the side, but the lad had gone.'

'But that's negligence. Why was there no action against Ranald?'

'Things were different then. Ranald seemed

to be broken. I suspect it was felt that he'd been through enough. It was just considered an unfortunate accident. West Uist folk have always lived with the sea, as you know yourself.'

Torquil sipped his whisky. Selkie legend or not, he thought, it was strange that Neil Ferguson should be looking in St Ninian's cemetery for a grave. Clearly it wasn't for the grave of a monkey as he had told him. But why would he have been looking for Flora Buchanan's grave? And did this somehow indicate a link between the deaths of Ranald Buchanan and Fiona?

* * *

Roland Baxter and Angus MacLeod had dined and were sitting in the library of Dunshiffin Castle drinking brandy and smoking cigars.

'I never thought Viroj would do anything stupid like that,' said the Scottish Minister for Culture.

'Suicide, you mean?'

'Actually, I meant murder. He was a cold-blooded fish as we both know, and I think he would have been perfectly capable of taking a life, but only in cold blood. Careful planning and clinical execution would have been Wattana's way. A crime of passion doesn't seem his style.'

Angus MacLeod idly swirled his brandy. 'But he hated her all right,' he said reflectively. Then continued, 'Do you think he's done us a favour?'

Roland Baxter's eyes shot up. 'Only if he hasn't left any records.'

The laird shivered involuntarily. 'If he has, we're buggered!'

'You mean you are, Angus.'

A cold, humourless smile flickered across Angus MacLeod's face. 'No Roland, I meant what I said. *We* would be buggered.'

Ever the practised politician, Roland Baxter smiled genially as he savoured his brandy. 'In that case we'd better see that there are no silly pieces of paper left lying around. I assume that you can check on that?'

'I suppose I'll have to,' the laird snapped. 'But what about Ferguson?'

'What about him?'

'Could he . . . ?'

The Scottish Minister for Culture pursed his lips and blew out a perfect smoke ring. 'I think that I can put the right type of pressure on him.'

* * *

Its head rose majestically out of the water and stared at him with large brown eyes. He stood transfixed, hypnotized even, as it swam towards the shore. Then once it reached the shallows it shuffled its great body onto the shingle beach, never once taking its eyes off him.

And then it transformed itself, its lower half tapering, its back flippers elongating, changing into legs. It rose, and began walking towards him.

The Selkie! He wanted to scream, to run away, yet he could not move. In desperation he held out the Silver Quaich.

But it ignored him. It walked past him, towards the waiting motorbike. It mounted it, kicked the engine into action and accelerated away.

He must stop it! His legs seemed unwilling to move, as if they were anchored in mud. But gradually they obeyed his will until he was running, chasing after it with all his might. He hated it. He would kill it. He ran faster and faster until he lost his balance and began to fall, down the edge of the cliff.

Torquil landed with a thud in a tangle of bedclothes, his mind swirling, his skin damp with perspiration and his heart pounding. It was pitch-dark, the luminous hands on his bedside clock showing that it was almost five o'clock.

So the Selkie returned after all, he mused. He lay pondering the events of the last few days for another half hour then flung himself out of bed and showered.

By the time the Padre shuffled downstairs at six o'clock, his usual time to rise, there was a delicious aroma of fried herrings emanating from the kitchen.

'Come in Uncle,' Torquil greeted him with a grin as he dished a pair of oatmeal-coated herrings from a skillet onto a couple of warming plates. 'I have to be off in a few minutes.'

'You seem in brighter spirits than I've seen you for ages, laddie.'

Torquil had already started to work on his herring. 'I had a dream last night.'

'I heard a bump. I thought you'd had a nightmare.'

'A revelation, actually. I dreamed that a Selkie came out of the water for me.'

The Padre stopped with a forkful of fish halfway to his mouth. 'It must have been our chat last night about Ranald Buchanan.'

Torquil took a sip of tea. 'Maybe. But in any case it showed me something that's been puzzling me since the murder. How did the murderer get from Loch Hynish to the

Bonnie Prince Charlie Tavern on Fiona's motorbike without anyone spotting him?'

'I thought Mollie McFadden saw him — or her? She thought it was Fiona, didn't she?'

'Exactly. And so whoever it was must have been in leathers — right?'

'Aye. You have Mollie's testimony there.'

Torquil shook his head. 'But I don't think they were wearing leathers. They certainly weren't Fiona's. She was wearing hers.' He shuddered, then shook his head as if to clear it of the image of Fiona Cullen's body with her leathers half pulled off. 'Lachlan, I think the murderer was wearing a wetsuit.'

The Padre thumped his fist on the table. 'And so — '

Torquil nodded. ' — and so it would explain how he was on the crannog waiting for her. He'd swum out. And it explains why the wee ferry was still tied up at the crannog. Fiona had used it to row out to the crannog, but he swam back. Then he simply pulled on her crash helmet and rode back to the Bonnie Prince Charlie on her Fireblade.'

Lachlan poured himself a cup of tea. 'It could have been Wattana, right enough. He was a slight chappie, and in a wetsuit from behind he could easily have fooled Mollie.'

Torquil polished off the rest of his herring and took a mouthful of tea. 'Now I need to head off to the station. I've got to sort a few things out. Will you be staying here?'

The Padre nodded. 'I'll be chained to my desk all morning. I have the funeral service and a suitable sermon to prepare, then I have a pile of unanswered correspondence to attend to, thanks to the Gathering and Festival. Why, do you need me to do anything?'

'Just let me know if a fax comes through from Thailand. I've broadened the net a little and I'm waiting for some information to come back.'

Once Torquil had gone the Padre finished his herring, drank another cup of tea and then went across the road to his Kirk. And there he knelt before the altar and muttered prayers for the departed spirits of Ranald and Fiona, and for his dearest nephew and ward, Torquil.

* * *

The whiteboard in the incident room now looked like a complex spider's web, for Piper had added several other connecting lines linking the two webs together. The pinboards were covered with a mass of papers and photographs, and the desk was laden with piles of notes and the contents of Neil

Ferguson's cruiser cabin. It was this heap that Torquil was now meticulously working through. There was something there, he knew. The problem was that he was not entirely sure how to find it.

By his side was a blown-up photograph of the note that Wattana had left.

He leafed through a couple of scientific papers that the professor of marine archaeology had obviously been working on. Then he looked at a sheaf of letters from various institutions. They all seemed to be from his opposite numbers at the universities of Oxford, Massachusetts and Chulalongkorn.

'What's this?' he said, sitting upright to read a handwritten letter on letter-headed notepaper from Chulalongkorn University in Bangkok. Only he could not read a word, for it was written in Thai.

So you really are fluent in Thai, aren't you Professor Ferguson? he mentally asked, glancing again at the photograph by his side.

While he did so he reached across the desk for his cup of coffee and inadvertently knocked over another pile of papers which went crashing to the floor. With a shrug he bent to pick them up, his eye being drawn to a programme for the Gathering. A bookmark with Fiona's smiling face had fallen out and startled him. Then he saw that the programme was open at the listing of the main events, and there were a few notes written in the margin in ballpoint pen.

Dhuine, Dhuine! he breathed in amazement. This is my writing! And this is the programme that I gave Fiona myself! What the hell is it doing in Neil Ferguson's papers?

* * *

Sergeant Morag Driscoll had been up half the night nursing a semi-delirious eight-year-old daughter with tonsillitis. She had been on the verge of calling Dr McLelland out when the temperature finally broke at six o'clock and she had stumbled back to bed, to doze fitfully until her official waking-up time at seven. The bedside telephone rudely intruded upon her slumbers five minutes before then and she struggled up onto one elbow to answer it.

'Morag, I've found something!' Torquil's voice rapped out. 'Neil Ferguson had Fiona's programme among his things.'

Morag swung her legs out of bed. 'I'm sorry Torquil, but what programme?' She tried to force her mind to focus.

'He had her programme of the Gathering events,' Torquil explained. 'And that means that it looks as if he swapped programmes with her at the Gathering. I had made some notes in a programme explaining about the tunes I was going to play in the piping competition. I am thinking that he must have swapped programmes and inside his was a message to meet him at the crannog on Loch Hynish.'

'I see!' gasped Morag. 'So what do we do now, boss?'

There was a pause for a moment, then Torquil spoke. 'It's still all a bit flimsy, but there are a few things that Neil Ferguson needs to explain. I'm going to go and see him now.'

'Are you arresting him?'

'Maybe. There's nothing concrete yet, so I'll have to play it by ear. I'll have gone by the time you get in.'

'Be careful, Torquil. Are you sure you don't want Ewan to come with you?'

'You look after Ewan, Morag,' Piper replied sardonically, then hung up, leaving Morag looking at the buzzing receiver in her hand.

* * *

Calum Steele had managed to control his thundering headache and successive waves of nausea for long enough to produce another 'special edition' of the *Chronicle*. Having then sent off the handful of teenagers who delivered it to the outlets across the island he settled down to watch the early morning Scottish TV news with a mug of sweet tea and a couple of rounds of jam and bread.

He smiled at the sight of Kirstie Macroon, the pretty redheaded newsreader with pert breasts that he lusted after and fantasized about. She was sitting in front of a backdrop of Kyleshiffin harbour as she read the latest bulletin:

> *The search for the body of Dr Viroj Wattana continued at first light this morning, but without success. The surgeon from Thailand was wanted for questioning by the island police who have been investigating the murder of Fiona Cullen, the famous crime writer, whose body was discovered on a crannog on Loch Hynish.*

The picture behind her changed to one of the crannog, with an inset photograph of a smiling Fiona Cullen in some exotic Oriental setting.

> *Mr Simon Sturgess and his wife have been on honeymoon on West Uist these last few days and have been keeping a close watch on the investigations.*

A picture of the young couple who had befriended Calum and who were responsible for his hangover flashed onto the screen.

Mr Sturgess actually found a smashed laptop computer believed to belong to Fiona Cullen. His literary contacts on the island, including Calum Steele, the local newspaper editor who has until now been supplying us with news bulletins, have confirmed his belief that the laptop could well contain information that could lead to the murderer.

Calum stared at the screen. 'You wee bastard! What drivel is this? Me! One of your literary contacts!'

Mr Sturgess was also able to inform us that his friend, Calum Steele, had told him that inspector Torquil McKinnon, the Inspector in charge of the case, known locally as Piper McKinnon, had a close personal relationship with the deceased, Fiona Cullen.

Calum smacked the side of his head. 'You bloody idiot, Calum Steele! What did you tell them when you were drunk in your cups?'

Mr Sturgess, who has recently begun work as a private investigator, and his wife Carol, a writer, tell us that this information was well known on the island, and that despite his conflict of interests, Inspector McKinnon continued to lead the inquiry.

Calum reached for his mobile telephone. The snakes! What would Torquil say about all this?

But Kirstie Macroon had not finished her report.

Mr Sturgess is considering reporting this to HM Inspectorate of Constabulary in Scotland, since he feels that the police inquiry on the island has been heavy-handed, citing the fact that several hundred people were effectively detained on the island against their will by Inspector McKinnon. He also believes it was —

But Calum had heard enough. He pressed the hold button on the control and typed in the Kyleshiffin police station number on his mobile phone. Torquil, I am sorry, he thought. I am so sorry! I'm just a jealous wee idiot!

* * *

Superintendent Kenneth Lumsden's gout had kept him awake half the night and the early morning news had not helped him one iota. He had listened in amazement and horror. Finally, banging his cup down and breaking the saucer, much to his wife's consternation, his daughter's embarrassment and his son-in-law's increasing irritation, he rose from the breakfast table and reached for the telephone.

'What the hell is McKinnon playing at? Why didn't he tell me that about being in a relationship with the Cullen woman? By the time I finish with him he'll be pounding a beat in Ullapool!'

* * *

Neil Ferguson hated the immediacy of the mobile telephone with its texting facility. It just leant itself as an instrument of blackmail. And that was something he was beginning to feel, for he was conscious that he was being manipulated. So far there had been no mention of money, merely threats of exposure and scandal. A man in his position could not afford either.

Who the fuck was it? And what did the evil

fuck actually want of him? Hadn't enough happened? And just what did the last text message mean? Should he ignore it? Go to the police, maybe?

He poured milk into his coffee and added a large measure of whisky. He felt he needed the alcohol, yet by mixing it with coffee he didn't feel that he was really drinking. Psychologically he still felt in control.

'Baxter can screw himself!' he muttered to himself. Just where did he think he was coming from, warning him about the funding for his chair. Bloody politicians! Always careful to hide their dirty secrets, never talking in plain English but using hyperbole and veiled threats.

He swigged his Gaelic coffee and started to feel better as it hit his stomach. He stood and looked out of the window of his room in the Commercial Hotel. It was a gloomy morning with poor visibility due to the fine drizzle or Scotch mist that had enshrouded the island overnight.

Fuck! What does he want now? he thought as the mist swirled and he saw Piper McKinnon park his Royal Enfield Bullet opposite the hotel, then stride purposively towards the front door.

He looked again at the last text message, then pocketed the phone. There was time.

The bastard said he'd text the hour and the place.

* * *

Annie Campbell, the Masonic Arms' early morning room-maid knocked on the door of room seven, fully expecting the occupant to be up and about as usual. Every morning for the past few days she had enjoyed a chat with Allegra McCall when she called to change the towels and make up the room.

A nice lady, Annie thought. A bit like herself, disciplined. An early starter.

The sound of the television meant that she was in there, of course. But why wasn't she answering? She couldn't still be in the shower, could she? She was usually up and working away on something by now.

Annie was a naturally curious girl. She reckoned that she would make a pretty good spy or one of those investigative journalists — if only she could write, she chided herself. She knelt down and squinted through the keyhole.

'Oh my God!' she gasped. 'I can see her feet! She's lying on the floor!'

She stood up and tapped again on the door.

No answer. She tapped again — louder this time.

But still no answer.

Maybe the poor thing is ill? She pulled out her master key and opened the door.

Her scream woke several of the guests and brought George MacFarlane, the manager, springing up the stairs. He found Annie rooted at the entrance, her shaking hand pointing to the body lying face down on the floor, a pool of blood surrounding her head.

⋆ ⋆ ⋆

Neil Ferguson opened the door in answer to Piper's knock.

'Morning Neil,' Piper said. 'I need to have a chat.'

'An official one? I thought you had this mess sorted out after Wattana's suicide.' He stood back and let Torquil enter.

'We don't know that he did commit suicide, Neil. We have no body.'

'But he took my boat out to sea! The whisky, the pills and the note.'

'Indicative, but not conclusive. But I want to ask you some questions on another matter. For starters, why did you tell me that cock and bull story about a monkey's grave?'

The professor shrugged. 'I wasn't aware that it wasn't true. I was following up on a curious tale, that's all.'

'Are you sure that you weren't looking for an actual grave? The grave of Flora Buchanan, for example.'

Two small pink patches appeared on Neil Ferguson's cheeks.

That's hit home all right, Piper thought.

'Flora Buchanan is buried there? Ranald's daughter?'

'Did you know her?'

'We were — close, once upon a time. A long time ago, when I first came to West Uist to do research on the crannogs for my doctoral thesis. I understand that she died?'

Piper nodded. 'She was schizophrenic, Neil. She died in a mental hospital.'

'I'm sorry to hear that, but in answer to your question — no, I wasn't looking for her grave.'

Piper nodded. 'Well would you have any idea why Ranald had the words *'Finally safe from the Selkie'* carved on her headstone?'

Piper fancied that the professor's brow had suddenly developed a patina of perspiration.

'As far as I know the Selkie is just an old myth. I'm a scientist, not a mythologist.'

'But for some reason Ranald Buchanan was obsessed with the whole Selkie story,' Piper went on. 'He wrote reams of poems about it. A seal man who seduces young women and impregnates them before returning to the sea. And then he comes back years later to reclaim his child and carry it off beneath the water.'

'What are you getting at, Piper?'

Torquil was about to reply when his mobile went off. He answered it, his face hardening as he listened. 'I'll be there in five minutes, Morag. Keep everyone away.'

'Trouble?' Professor Ferguson asked.

'Another murder!' Torquil replied. He made for the door. 'Look Neil, don't leave the island yet. We need to finish this talk later.'

'Who has been murdered?'

'I can't say yet. But we'll talk later, OK.'

When Piper had gone Neil Ferguson opened a drawer and poured more whisky into his coffee cup. 'Maybe we'll talk, Piper. And maybe we won't!'

13

Dr Ralph McLelland was kneeling beside the body by the time Piper arrived at room seven of the Masonic Arms Hotel. Morag was standing by the window, ready and waiting with her digital camera and fingerprint kit.

'She's dead all right,' Ralph McLelland said, rising to his feet as Piper came in. 'The blow to the back of the head with some sort of bludgeon looks to have been instantly fatal. Rigor mortis has set in.' He pouted thoughtfully. 'The room is warm; the television set is still on. I'd say she's been dead for at least eight hours. Maybe a couple of hours longer.'

'Any idea about the murder weapon?'

'It's in the shower, Piper,' Morag volunteered. 'It's a brass candlestick.'

'You are joking!'

'It's in there and it has been washed clean.'

Piper bashed one fist against his other palm. 'Dammit! Any idea where this candlestick was from, Morag?'

His sergeant pointed to the side table just inside the door. At one side there was a large brass candlestick beside a doily. 'It was one of a pair. Whoever did it had a weapon ready at hand.'

'Have we a motive here?' Piper asked. 'Anything stolen? Bags searched?'

Ralph McLelland nodded. 'She's had something pulled off her wrist, a bracelet or a watch, I think. You can see where she's been scratched as it was pulled off. A couple of rings also look to have been taken. You can see her hands are fairly tanned, and she's got ring marks.'

Torquil closed his eyes for a moment, picturing the watch she had been wearing when he 'interviewed her' in her four × four Mitsubishi Shogun the day before. 'It was a gold Rolex,' he volunteered. 'I bet it had to be worth at least fifteen grand, maybe more. So, we have a possible motive. Has anyone seen anything suspicious? Did she have any callers?'

'No one noticed anything. Except that she bought a new bottle of vodka and took it upstairs with her last night. She bought it from George Macfarlane at the bar.'

'Who found the body?'

'Annie Campbell, the room-maid. She's upstairs in a spare guest room,' Ralph volunteered. 'She was well nigh hysterical so I gave her a sedative.'

Piper shook his head. 'And so it goes on.

But why, for God's sake?'

Morag bit her lip. 'I think it's about to get even worse, boss. The superintendent phoned just before I called you. I'm sorry, in the heat of the moment I forgot to tell you when I rang. He's on the warpath and wants you to ring him back straight away.'

Torquil shrugged. 'He's going to really love this then.'

* * *

Back at the station an hour later Morag tapped on Torquil's office door and popped her head round. 'Well? What did he say?'

'That I'm an incompetent oaf and that I should have told him about Fiona and me. He was livid that it had been splashed across the television.' He sighed. 'And now with Allegra McCall's murder he's beside himself. He's already on his way across to take charge and could be here literally any minute. He's coming care of a Scottish TV helicopter.'

'Rushing in like the seventh cavalry, complete with the media to record the event,' Morag said sneeringly. 'I'm sorry Torquil. Can I do anything?'

Torquil shook his head. 'We'd best get all the information together. Anything useful to report about the laptop?'

Morag's face brightened. 'Actually, yes. My cousin Hughie had a good look and was able to find a few files. They're separate book chapters, but none of them are new. Hughie is a Fiona Cullen fan himself and he's pretty sure that they are all to do with her last book — *Flesh Trimmers*.'

'Dammit! So there is no clue there after all. Come on then, let's get on with it. Is everyone here?'

Ewan had put up a new pinboard and was waiting with the Drummond twins and Ralph McLelland for an initial meeting.

'I'll be doing the post-mortem as soon as you can give me the go-ahead from the Procurator Fiscal,' said the GP-cum-police surgeon. 'But as you know already, an initial external examination makes it look as if death was instantaneous from a blow to the back of the head with a blunt instrument, almost certainly the brass candlestick found in the shower.'

Torquil nodded at Morag who stood up to give her report. 'There were no fingerprints. It looks as if whoever did it only touched the candlestick and washed that immediately. I haven't even tried to do anything with it. It would probably be a job for the Forensic Department at Dundee.'

Piper stood and crossed to the whiteboard,

adding Allegra McCall's name and drawing lines between some of the names, to complicate the web even further. 'It's a tangled skein and no mistake. And all to do with writers and books.'

'Do you think she knew who killed Fiona?' Morag asked.

Torquil shrugged. 'Maybe. But if so, why was she robbed?'

Wallace Drummond clicked his teeth. 'She was an attractive lassie. Classy too I thought when I drove her back yesterday. Had she been . . . ?'

'Molested?' Ralph McLelland said, then shook his head. 'No, I'm pretty sure she wasn't. She seemed to have been bashed on the head as she sat on her bed, then fallen straight over.'

Ewan shuffled in his chair. 'Piper, can I just say — '

But precisely then there was a banging noise from the outer office, as if someone had just thumped the counter several times. It was followed by the noise of creaking metal, a heavy slapping sound and several other footfalls.

'I'll go and see,' Ewan began, crossing to the door which at that moment was hurled back and a large uniformed man on crutches appeared. He was red-faced with a crisp, unfashionable black moustache and an aggressive square chin. Behind him was a television crew consisting of a producer, a female reporter and a cameraman, who was already taking pictures.

'Why isn't there an officer on the desk?' the big man barked.

'Superintendent Lumsden,' said Torquil, advancing with his hand outstretched. 'Welcome to Kyleshiffin. We are just in the process — '

'Aren't you forgetting something, Inspector McKinnon? How do you greet a senior officer?'

Torquil eyed the superintendent dispassionately, his hackles rising. 'If you will step in, Superintendent Lumsden, out of sight of the cameras, which are not authorized in my station, then I will brief you.'

And stepping past him he put his palm over the video camera and gently, but forcefully, marched the crew backwards. 'This is a police station and the media are not permitted into the offices. One of my officers will be with you in a moment to answer your questions.' He turned and ignored the protestations of the trio.

'Ewan, can you look after the Press,' Torquil asked a moment later.

'But Piper, I wanted to tell you — '

'Later, Ewan,' Torquil said, a hand on the big constable's back urging him forward. 'And now, Superintendent Lumsden, let me fill you in.'

Lumsden was clearly seething, his moustache almost literally bristling. 'That was bloody stupid, McKinnon. Antagonizing the media like that. Don't you see that we need them right now, after this pig's ear that you've made of the investigation.'

Everyone in the room squirmed and felt for Piper. Only Ralph McLelland felt able to say anything, since his position as police surgeon was not directly under the jurisdiction of the superintendent. 'I take exception to that, Superintendent Lumsden. This investigation has been dealt with efficiently and — '

'Efficiently!' Lumsden exclaimed. 'How many people are going to die before this investigation is over? I make it four deaths so far. That's more than bloody Glasgow gets, let alone a twopenny Western Isle.'

'Steady now!' said Douglas Drummond, coming swiftly to his feet. 'This is our island. Our home.'

Throughout these exchanges Torquil had stared resolutely at his superior officer, his temper rising exponentially. Yet somehow he managed to keep the lid on it. He had developed a facility for keeping his emotions in check ever since Fiona's death. 'Do you want to know what's been happening, superintendent?' he asked calmly. 'Or do you just want to scream and behave like a prat.'

Superintendent Lumsden stared in disbelief, then his face went even more puce. 'The sergeant will brief me,' he said slowly. 'Then I'm going to take over and get a result. As for you, McKinnon, you are officially suspended forthwith. Now please leave the station.'

Once again Ralph McLelland began to protest, but Piper placed a hand on his arm. 'It's OK Ralph, I'll go. Perhaps the superintendent is right. I haven't got the result we need.' He picked up his scarf and wound it round his neck. 'I'll see you all later,' he said, walking past the superintendent and letting himself out.

Ewan was busy with the reporter, a pushy young woman who would undoubtedly prove too much of a match for the big constable. Torquil let himself out and passed Izzie Frazer as he made for his Bullet.

'Inspector McKinnon,' she said, catching his arm. 'Ewan told me about that poor woman. Did he tell you about — ?'

But Piper was in no mood to stop. He shook his head. 'I have no official position here any more, Izzie. There is a superintendent on the case now.' And he went over to his bike, pulled out his Cromwell helmet from the pannier and started the bike up.

'But it could be important,' Izzie mouthed as she watched the tail light of the Bullet disappear into the mist as he headed up the hill road out of Kyleshiffin.

* * *

After a hard morning the Padre had taken half an hour off to play the first, the third and the sixth holes, then returned to his study where he set about cleaning his irons and polishing his woods. He was surprised to hear his nephew come back so soon.

'You obviously haven't heard the news,' Torquil said when the Padre beamed a greeting at him. 'Allegra McCall has been murdered.'

'*Truaghan*! Poor creature!' he exclaimed. 'Have you any idea who did it?'

'And I'm off the case. I've been suspended by Superintendent Lumsden. He thinks I've been incompetent.' He gave a wan smile. 'And I suppose calling him a prat didn't help.'

The Padre shook his head. 'I don't know what to say, laddie.'

Torquil shrugged, then threw himself down in the chair and rubbed his temples. 'At least

I didn't deck the bugger!' He sighed, then went on. 'Nothing much seems to matter any more. I think I've been wandering around in shock since Fiona's death.'

'Are the deaths linked? It seems odd, her being Fiona's publisher.'

'Oh it's linked somehow, I'm sure. The odd thing is that she was bludgeoned to death and then robbed.'

The Padre patted his nephew on the shoulder, and then snapped his fingers. 'I almost forgot. That fax you wanted, it came through.' He handed Torquil the sheet and waited while he read it.

'So! Wattana's clinic does all sorts,' mused Torquil. 'Cosmetic surgery, gender reassignment, transplantations. And it has been under investigation by the Medical Association of Thailand and by the Bangkok Police Department. It is entirely private, with a lot of foreign money pumped into it.'

'That's no surprise.'

'You obviously didn't look at the list of sponsors, Lachlan. Top of the list is AME — Angus MacLeod Enterprises. And the concern about the clinic is that it might be acting unethically, doing operations without too many questions being asked. You know, buying kidneys from the local poor people and selling them on to rich ill folk who have no inclination to wait for a legitimate tissue typing.'

'Wow! So that could be why Wattana was here as Angus MacLeod's guest!' The Padre struck a light to his ever-ready pipe. 'And I have another interesting piece of news. It was in that heap of correspondence that I have neglected.' He reached across his desk and picked up a letter. 'It's from a solicitor in Glasgow acting on behalf of the estate of a Mrs Rosamund Armstrong of Milngavie, née *Rosamund MacLeod* of Dunshiffin Castle, West Uist. That's Angus MacLeod's sister! She died a few weeks ago and wanted her ashes to be placed in the family vault in the St Ninian's crypt.'

Torquil had sat upright on hearing this news. 'Now why on earth hasn't Angus MacLeod mentioned this? His own sister.'

'It doesn't make sense, does it?' the Padre agreed. He scanned the letter again. 'It mentions that her son may well be in contact himself.'

'Her son? Angus MacLeod's nephew. That means he would be — '

'Angus MacLeod's heir to the Dunshiffin estate, and that presumably would include AME.' Lachlan puffed on his pipe, sending billows of blue smoke ceilingwards. 'The plot thickens, laddie.'

'And gets very muddy indeed!' said Torquil. He reached for the telephone. 'I think a call to the Milngavie Registrar of Births, Deaths and Marriages is called for.'

⋆ ⋆ ⋆

Despite what many people thought, Superintendent Kenneth Lumsden had a very fine police brain. He had the ability to absorb facts fast, see links and act quickly. And in this case, this was precisely his aim.

'A swift arrest should now be on the cards,' he said into the camera, as it trained on himself and Donna Spruce, the Scottish TV reporter, as they stood in front of the whiteboard with its network of leads and connections. 'I have personally taken over the case.'

Outside, in the main office, Izzie Frazer stood leaning on the counter as Ewan talked to Morag.

'I kept trying to talk to Piper, but yon muckle superintendent arrived and I couldn't get a word in,' Ewan told his sergeant.

'Well, tell Morag now,' Izzie urged.

Ewan smiled at her, then turned to Morag. 'Izzie saw Genevieve Cooper go into the Masonic Arms Hotel last night, before she came over to my place.' He blushed. 'We didn't think anything about it until I got to work this morning and we heard.’

‘Did you spend the night together?’ Morag asked.

‘Morag!’ Ewan protested, blushing an even deeper shade of pink.

‘I stayed over, Morag, that was all,’ Izzie explained.

The sound of laughter, the bluff snort of the superintendent and a trill flirtatious peel from Donna Spruce preceded the door to the incident room opening. ‘We’ll be over at the Masonic Arms filming a piece while we wait for your call with any developments then, Kenneth.’

When the film crew had gone Morag addressed the superintendent. ‘PC McPhee has some information you should know about, sir. It’s a possible lead. A possible suspect.’

Lumsden rubbed his hands together. ‘Into the office then lad. All leads are worth looking at.’

‘What a smug git!’ said Izzie as the incident room door swung closed behind them.

‘That’s official,’ agreed Morag.

⋆ ⋆ ⋆

Genevieve had just popped into the Bonnie Prince Charlie for a swift drink before making her way along Harbour Street to catch the Macbeth ferry *Laird o' the Isles* back to the mainland, via Lochboisdale. And it couldn't be too soon now.

The bastard, calling in her debt like that. Making her do that thing. She shivered involuntarily and reached for the packet of Gauloise cigarettes on the table in front of her. Just one more cigarette and one more drink then I'll be off. She flicked her Zippo and inhaled greedily as the strong smoke seemed to calm her. Then she rose and went over to the crowded bar and signalled to Mollie McFadden for replenishment.

'Genevieve Cooper?' someone asked behind her.

She spun round, her Jack Daniels-induced smile ready to greet whoever it was. She didn't recognize the big man on crutches, but she did recognize the nice sergeant and the tall hammer-throwing constable who flanked him.

'My name is Superintendent Lumsden. We'd like to ask you a few questions about the recent death of Allegra McCall.'

Genevieve's lips quivered, then her eyes rolled upwards and she dropped to the ground in a dead faint.

* * *

Roland Baxter watched the colour drain from Angus MacLeod's face as the latter read the new text message on his mobile. He muttered and turned away to face his desk.

'Bugger! It's all going pear-shaped!'

He tossed the phone down on the desk and drew out a key to unlock a drawer. The Scottish Minister for Culture's eyes opened wide when he saw his friend reach in and draw out a Beretta Vertec handgun.

'Some personal stuff I need to sort out,' he explained tersely.

'Angus, I want no part in any shooting.'

'Then bugger off.'

'Can I use your helicopter?'

The laird just grunted and made for the door. 'Do whatever you want.'

* * *

Geneviève Cooper's confession tumbled out of her upon questioning at the station. Gambling debts, huge ones thanks to an addiction, poor judgement and foolishness beyond measure had put her into the hands of one Albert Conollan, Glaswegian money-lender and agent for one of Glasgow's oldest mobs. Her debt had been called in suddenly a few days ago, along with threats of personal violence and worse, as far as she was concerned: a promise to exterminate her dog unless a payment of ten thousand pounds was made by the following day.

Genevieve had drunk herself into a state. She had gone to Allegra McCall's room at the Masonic Arms Hotel with the intention of asking the publisher for a loan. The door was open, Allegra was sitting on the end of the bed drinking neat vodka and sobbing her eyes out, mumbling about Fiona. Then Genevieve saw the Rolex, a timepiece that would easily take care of the ten grand and save her kneecaps and her dog. It was an impulse. She had picked up the candlestick, intending only to stun the publisher, knock her out. But she had hit her too hard — and panicked.

'I never meant to do it,' she sobbed, looking up at the officious Superintendent Lumsden while Sergeant Driscoll made notes and from time to time checked the tape recorder at her side. 'You won't let them hurt Ozzie, my Labrador, will you?' she asked pleadingly.

Superintendent Lumsden eyed her dispassionately. 'I make no promises, Miss Cooper. It's the unlawful killing of Allegra McCall by your hand that concerns me.'

* * *

Half an hour later inside the public bar of the Bonnie Prince Charlie the afternoon film on the big, broad television screen was interrupted by a newsflash. Kirsty Macroon's familiar features appeared as she announced the news just received from West Uist. The picture changed to a live picture of Donna Spruce standing outside the Kyleshiffin police station.

Further tragedy hit the island of West Uist as another body was discovered this morning. Allegra McCall, the publisher of Fiona Cullen's crime novels, was discovered bludgeoned to death.

Inspector Torquil McKinnon who has been leading the investigation into the novelist's murder has apparently been suspended from duty in circumstances yet to be explained. His superior officer, Superintendent Kenneth Lumsden, flew in this morning to take over the case and — we have it on good authority — it appears that an arrest has been made, a confession received and charges are about to be made.

We believe that a serial killer may have been apprehended.

This is Donna Spruce reporting for Scottish TV from Kyleshiffin, West Uist.

Wallace and Douglas Drummond, who had popped in for a swift half pint of Heather Ale, grimaced at one another as the film continued.

'They're making a scapegoat of Piper,' said Wallace.

His brother nodded, then drained his glass. 'Aye, we'd better get back and see — '

A hand clapped him on the shoulder and made him jump. It was followed instantly by Calum Steele's indignant voice. 'Did I hear right? Have you got someone? How do the television people know and me not?'

Douglas turned to the local newshound. 'We have someone, Calum Steele. But as you know we are just a couple of lowly minions and are not at liberty to divulge — '

Calum Steele held up his hand. 'Spare me the usual excuses. I'm used to being sold down the river, just like poor Torquil. Anyway,' he went on, changing the subject, 'I looked through the window and saw you two drinking on duty as usual. I won't bother reporting you because I need to report a crime!'

'Not another one, Calum?'

'Aye, another crime has been committed. And it is seriously pissing me off almost as much as all those fancy TV news-usurpers. My Lambretta has been stolen again.'

* * *

Piper roared into the courtyard of Dunshiffin Castle and braked hard, the Bullet's wheels spraying gravel as he abruptly halted by the grand steps leading up to the main door.

Jesmond, the laird's retainer opened the door so swiftly that Piper wondered if he had been waiting for his arrival. 'The laird has gone out,' Jesmond announced in his usual haughty tone.

'Is Baxter still here?' Piper snapped.

'I'm still here,' came the Minister for Culture's smooth voice from an open door to the left of the hall. 'But only just. Tam McKenzie has gone to start the helicopter up. I'm heading back to civilization in a couple of minutes.'

Torquil brushed past the butler and entered the drawing room to find the Minister for Culture dressed in a sheepskin jacket, a brandy in one hand and a Montecristo cigar in the other.

'Where's MacLeod?' Torquil demanded.

Roland Baxter shrugged his shoulders and languidly drew on his cigar. 'Business to attend to, he said. He's graciously given me the use of his helicopter.'

Torquil stepped close to the minister. Too close for Baxter's comfort. 'Business connected with Dr Wattana's clinic in Thailand, by any chance?'

Roland Baxter coughed, and then spluttered.

That caught him off guard, Torquil noted.

'Dr Wattana's clinic? No idea, old fellow.' He took a sip of brandy, then asked, 'Cosmetic surgeon wasn't he?'

'You know very well he was,' Torquil replied. 'As well as all sorts of other surgery. Some of the operations he was carrying out were ethically questionable, so I understand. The clinic is currently under investigation by the Medical Association of Thailand and by the Bangkok Police. Apparently a lot of British businessmen are involved in financing the clinic — including Angus MacLeod.'

Roland Baxter drained his brandy. 'Really?' he looked at his watch. 'I'm afraid I'll have to go, inspector.'

'I'll find out, you know! I'll find out about every connection that Angus MacLeod has with Wattana's clinic. And I'll discover all the people who he's fronting for.'

Torquil noted the beads of perspiration forming on the Minister for Culture's brow. He stared him straight in the eye, sensing the politician's nerve beginning to buckle.

'He had a text message a short while ago and he said it was something to do with someone called Selkirk.'

'Selkirk?' Torquil repeated. 'You're sure he said Selkirk?'

Roland Baxter shrugged his shoulders helplessly, his whole demeanour becoming like a frightened rabbit. Then his eye fell on the mobile phone on the desk. 'Look, he left his phone,' he said pointing it out. 'He had to get something from that drawer and he must have forgotten to pick it up again.' He neglected to say that the something was a gun.

Torquil picked up the phone and accessed the message file. He pressed the button and the last message showed up on the screen:

THE SELKIE RETURNS.
I KNOW ABOUT THE POET.
MEET ME AT 3 OR BE EXPOSED.

Torquil looked up at the Minister for Culture. 'Baxter, you're a fool,' he said as he made quickly for the door.

The politician felt himself begin to tremble and he stood for a moment, unsure of his next course of action. He started for the door. 'But what about Wattana? You won't say anything about me will you?'

The screech of tyres on gravel indicated

that either Torquil had not heard or that he was not interested.

* * *

The Padre had felt a growing indignation ever since he watched Torquil ride off on his Bullet. Grabbing his six-iron and a bag of old balls he had gone outside with the good intention of hitting their covers off to relieve his frustration. But he had thought better of it and instead stuck the golf club and bag of balls in the pannier of the Red Hunter and headed off to Kyleshiffin. As he rode through the patchy mist, his machine splashing through puddles, he went over the tongue-lashing that he intended to give Superintendent Lumsden.

Then riding along Harbour Street he saw Professor Neil Ferguson striding along in the direction of the *Unicorn*. The Padre honked his claxon and coasted to a halt alongside the professor.

'Heading off now, Neil?'

Neil Ferguson looked distracted. He nodded assent. 'Yes Padre, but I've got some unfinished business to attend to first. Can't stop I'm afraid.' He strode on, adding over his shoulder, 'See you — sometime.'

Lachlan gunned the Red Hunter and set

off again, up the hill to the station. He had business of his own to finish.

Ewan McPhee was chatting to the Drummond twins behind the counter when he entered.

'Is that superintendent of yours in?' he asked.

'He is, Padre,' Ewan replied. 'But I'm afraid he's busy just now.'

'Well you can tell him I want — '

Sergeant Morag Driscoll appeared from the incident room at the sound of his voice. 'Tell the superintendent what, Padre?' she asked.

The Padre was about to go into his carefully rehearsed diatribe, but thought better of it. Instead he shook his head and said, 'I'm just worried about Torquil, Morag.'

Morag lifted the counter-flap and came through. 'Come outside for a minute, Lachlan,' she said, hooking his arm and guiding him towards the door. Then, with a nod to Ewan and the Drummonds, 'Look after the shop for a bit, OK.'

Outside the station she led him down the road. 'We're all concerned, you know. Torquil has been through hell these last couple of days.'

'It's not fair, Morag. The lad has done all that he reasonably could.'

'I know. But maybe he can have a rest now that Superintendent Lumsden has got Genevieve Cooper to confess.'

'Has she confessed to killing Fiona and Ranald?'

'No, but he's convinced that she did. She has huge debts you know.'

Morag's mobile beeped to indicate that she had received a text message. She accessed it, then muttered a curse. She showed it to the Padre.

I'M GOING FOR THE SELKIE
I'LL FINISH THIS CASE.
TORQUIL.

'What does he mean?' Morag mused. And before Lachlan could reply she tried calling her erstwhile inspector.

'Blast! He's turned off his mobile now. What does he mean 'finish this case'?'

'I'm not sure, lassie,' replied the Padre. 'But I just saw Neil Ferguson and he was talking about finishing some business as well.'

* * *

Torquil cut the Bullet's engine and coasted to a halt about a hundred yards from *Tigh nam Bàrd*, Ranald Buchanan's House of the Bard, which stood shrouded in mist. He advanced stealthily on foot.

To his right, through the mist, he saw the outline of a boat, undoubtedly the *Unicorn*, tied up to the jetty.

'So you are here already, are you Neil Ferguson,' he muttered to himself. As he edged forward, carefully lifting and placing his feet to avoid kicking any loose pebble, he was grateful for the cover of the mist.

He climbed the outer wall then flattened himself against the wall of the cottage and carefully peeped through the window into the front room.

Dr Viroj Wattana was sitting on the settee, a gun in his hand. Beyond him, in shadows, another figure was sitting upright in a chair, the posture distorted as if tied to the chair with the hands tied behind the back.

His eyes widened further as he saw a dim shape on the floor between them, almost certainly another body.

Inwardly cursing himself for not having his truncheon, Torquil looked for something to use as a weapon. A loose stone from the wall would have to suffice, he decided, as he edged round the side of the cottage. Somehow he would have to sneak up on the gunman.

The back door was unlocked and thankfully opened without a creak. Piper crept across the kitchen and peered through the crack of the open door where he could clearly see Dr Wattana with the gun in his hand.

Suddenly, there was a crack and he felt a searing pain in the side of his head. For a brief moment he felt himself pitching sideways, diving into a pool of blackness. And yet dimly he thought he heard Angus MacLeod's voice, followed by a laugh — a peal of hysterical laughter that accompanied him to the depths of unconsciousness.

14

Torquil was vaguely aware of motion, of being dragged along the floor by his wrists, then of being rolled over onto his belly and having his hands bound behind him and then being hauled into a sitting position and propped against a wall. He struggled against nausea and almost unbearable pain in the head as he felt himself returning to consciousness.

Angus MacLeod was still laughing. 'Welcome back to the land of the living, Piper,' he said, 'for the time being!' His laugh turned into a strange giggle that sent a shiver up Torquil's spine.

He shook his head and blinked, his eyes perceiving the body of Neil Ferguson lying face down in front of him.

'Don't worry, he isn't dead,' came MacLeod's voice. 'He just can't move. As you can see, he's effectively hog-tied — and gagged.'

Torquil saw the rise and fall of the professor's chest. He shook his head again and looked towards the settee where Dr Wattana was sitting with the gun held unwaveringly in his hand.

'But I'm afraid poor Viroj was not so lucky!'

And as Torquil's eyes began to focus in the half-light of the room with the mist swirling against the windowpanes, he saw that the surgeon's eyes were staring sightlessly ahead, like a doll's, and that his skin was mottled and his lips were almost purple. Just above the collar of his shirt a garrotte was visible, so tight as to have almost cut into the flesh. Torquil felt a threatening wave of nausea begin to rise.

Angus MacLeod laughed again, the same hysterical peal of laughter. 'And soon we'll all be dead!'

Torquil looked round at the speaker for the first time, and was surprised to see that he was sitting in the shadows, ropes binding his torso to the chair, his hands behind his back. Blood had oozed down the side of his face from a gash on his temple and soaked into the collar of his Harris tweed jacket.

The light suddenly went on and Torquil turned to see Izzie Frazer standing by the door with her hand on the switch. She was dressed in a black wetsuit, her hair tied back in a pony tail.

'Izzie?' Torquil breathed.

'That's me,' she replied with a broad feline smile. 'Welcome to my parlour.'

Torquil gave a short humourless laugh. 'But of course! It used to be your parlour didn't it — *Izzie*!'

Izzie Frazer smiled and crossed the room to remove the gun from the hand of Dr Wattana. She bent in front of his immobile face. 'Thanks for looking after Angus's gun for me,' she said, wrinkling her nose at him, then with a shove she pushed his body sidewards and he slumped to land in a grotesque heap on the floor. Izzie straightened and slipped the gun behind a belt, from which also dangled the two ends of a doubled-over bag, rather like a wheatbag.

'You're cleverer than I gave you credit for, Piper McKinnon. You surprised me by showing up here.' She waggled a finger at him. 'You almost cramped my style, you naughty boy!'

'You mean I cramped your style the same way that Dr Wattana did?'

She bent down and caught Neil Ferguson by the belt of his trousers and dragged him with surprisingly little effort towards the same wall that Torquil was propped up against. 'My word, you are astute,' she said, reaching up and pulling masking tape roughly from the professor's mouth. She grinned at his gasp of pain, then went on, 'Yes, his death was unfortunate — but necessary! And my little ruse with the note seemed to work.'

'That was clumsy,' Torquil said. 'It was too pat.'

Izzie shrugged her shoulders dismissively. 'It served its purpose.'

Neil Ferguson's voice quavered. 'Wh . . . What the hell is this all about?'

Izzie reached out and gently stroked his cheek. 'Oh don't be nervous, Professor Ferguson,' she said soothingly. 'Not here when you're with friends. No need to be nervous — yet!'

Angus MacLeod began to giggle again, but went quiet when Izzie turned her head to stare him down. 'That's better Angus,' she purred. 'Let's keep some sense of dignity, shall we?'

Again she turned to Neil Ferguson. 'But do you really not know what this is about? After all my little messages.'

'Your messages?' he gasped. 'It's been you? My God! Why? I don't even know you.'

'I think you'll find it's to do with the Selkie, Neil,' Torquil ventured. 'That's right, isn't it Izzie?'

Angus MacLeod took a sharp intake of breath and made a guttural sobbing noise.

Immediately, the smile vanished from Izzie's face to be replaced by a thin-lipped piercing glare. 'I think that you seem to know too much for your own good, Inspector McKinnon. Enough to sign your own death warrant, in fact.'

'In that case I think that I deserve to know why I'm going to die,' Torquil replied. 'And I think that we all need to know why you're planning to murder us. Just like you murdered Ranald Buchanan and Fiona Cullen.'

'Do you really think that I wasn't going to tell them?' Izzie returned. 'They need to know exactly why they're going to die, just like Ranald Buchanan did. The Selkie returned for him!'

'And by the wetsuit I see that you are the Selkie,' Torquil said.

'No I'm not,' Izzie returned with an emphatic shake of the head. 'But the wetsuit is symbolic of the Selkie coming back from the water to collect his own. I'm symbolic of the Selkie coming back to deliver retribution.'

'Y . . . You are mad!' Neil Ferguson exclaimed, tremulously.

Izzie's eyes blazed. 'Don't call me that! I'm the sanest person here.'

'There's no shame in mental illness, Izzie,' Torquil said. 'Take your mother for instance.' He watched her closely to see if there was any stirring of emotion. 'Flora Buchanan *was* your mother, wasn't she?'

'Very good, inspector! Go on!' she urged, the feline smile returning.

'Ranald Buchanan was your grandfather. And he arranged for you to disappear. Seemingly, to drown. And he fostered the rumour that the Selkie had returned to claim you.'

Angus MacLeod stifled a gasp.

'And then your mother had her breakdown and never recovered. But you never knew her properly, did you Izzie. She was committed to a mental hospital with schizophrenia and never recovered. Ranald never visited her, the only thing he ever did for her was to bury her and carve an obscure note on her headstone.'

Tears seemed to form in the corners of Izzie's eyes. She turned abruptly and pointed an accusing finger at Angus MacLeod. 'And he bought me from the bastard Buchanan and gave me to his sister!'

'Who died recently in Milngavie,' Torquil announced.

The Laird of Kyleshiffin began to sob.

Izzie Frazer sneered. 'But not before I got the whole story out of her. And out of her bastard husband, before I pushed him down the stairs. Then I gave her an overdose of insulin.' She smiled as she patted the bag hanging over her belt. 'And you're here with me, aren't you, Rosamund? You've been the instrument of retribution — several times!'

'Her ashes are in that sandbag, I assume,' Torquil queried. 'So you used her ashes to batter Ranald Buchanan?' He swallowed hard, forcing the lump out of his throat. 'And you used it to bludgeon Fiona Cullen before you strangled her and tried to make it look like a sexual crime.'

'Don't mention sex to me!' Izzie hissed. 'I hate it! I hate all you bastard men. That bastard Buchanan buggered me senseless before he sold me to that sod. I . . . I remember — '

'And that's why you wanted to become a woman, wasn't it,' Torquil continued. 'You had been abused.' He tried to make his tone sound sympathetic. 'And that's why Dr Wattana had to go, wasn't it, Izzie? He recognized you, didn't he? He had performed the sex change operation in Bangkok, hadn't he? And modified your features a fair bit as well, I guess.'

'That's right. And then the bastard showed up on West Uist, as a guest of that creature,' she almost spat, pointing at the laird. 'He saw me at the Gathering and he had to go as well.'

'And so you took the professor's boat and headed off to sea, then dived in and swam ashore.'

‘That’s right. Wattana was already dead,’ she replied, with a hint of pride. ‘He’s been sitting here all this time.’

‘But I still don’t understand,’ Neil Ferguson said. ‘Why have you been sending me those messages? I thought you were just someone trying to blackmail me.’

Her eyes turned to the professor of marine archaeology, hatred emanating from them. ‘Just blackmailing you? You bastard. Don’t you realize what you are? *You* are the fucking Selkie!’

‘I . . . I . . . don’t understand!’

She hit him ferociously with the back of her hand, sending his head crashing against the wall. ‘You’re my father! You abandoned me. You caused all this!’

Neil Ferguson looked aghast. ‘You, you are my daughter? It isn’t possible.’

‘I was your son! But you never came back, did you. I had to bring you back. But you had the luck of the devil. Like that day in the St Ninian’s cemetery, when I sent you to find that grave. *Her* grave!’

‘You did that? But I never found it. I . . . I was hit on the head.’

‘By a golf ball!’ Izzie wailed, then touched the sandbag hanging from her belt. ‘Not with this little beauty, like you should have been. I was waiting in the porch of the church.’ Her eyes blazed. 'But now I'm going to send you to hell.'

Torquil's mind went back to that day, to that moment when he, the Padre and Fiona had rushed over the crest of the fairway to see Neil Ferguson curled up by a gravestone, his hands about his head. He was speechless at the realization that it had been Fiona's miss-hit tee shot that had ironically saved him; and that Izzie had been hiding a few feet away, ready to commit cold-blooded murder — a murder that, if she had committed it, would have meant Fiona would probably still be alive today. His blood boiled.

Izzie reached behind the settee and pulled out a crate of bottles. 'The bastard Buchanan's peatreek,' she explained, pulling the cork on one bottle and casually pouring its contents over the prone body of Dr Wattana.

'It's all been about Professor Ferguson, hasn't it, Izzie?' Torquil said. 'You just botched it up.'

'I botched nothing up!' she hissed. She uncorked another bottle and poured the contents over the floor, and over Neil Ferguson's legs.

'But you did botch it up. You had left a message to him in the programme at the Gathering and didn't expect it to get switched. It was an accident actually. Ewan

McPhee bumped into the professor and Fiona, and their programmes got mixed up. Fiona found the message and thought — ' Again he forced back the rising lump in his throat — 'and thought that the message was from me. It said to meet at the crannog, didn't it?'

Izzie nodded. 'I took that newspaper idiot's scooter and rode out to the loch, then dumped it in the bracken. I swam out and was waiting inside the ruins. Then she came over in the boat. The stupid bitch! I had no choice.'

Torquil's blood was boiling. He wanted to get his hands around her neck, to choke the life from her. But it was not possible.

'Then you swam back, put on her helmet and got on her bike. And then you got clever with the laptop didn't you?'

'I had been at her lecture and I'd read her books. I knew that she wrote thinly disguised hatchet jobs. It gave me time to think again; to plan how to get the two people I hate most in the world to come here together. I was going to kill them — and you, you interfering pig, at one stroke.' She pulled another cork and let the liquid flow all over Torquil.

'And then you were going to sail away in the professor's boat?'

Neil Ferguson shook his head. 'I had no

idea,' he said in astonishment. 'If I had I would have — '

'What? What would you have done? Claimed me as your own?'

'If you hate me so much, then kill me,' Neil said. 'But don't add to your crimes. Let them go.'

Izzie sneered as she uncorked yet another bottle and went over to Angus MacLeod, who was now simpering like a baby. She poured the contents over his head and shoulders. 'What's this? Self-sacrifice? It's a bit late for all that now — *daddy*!'

She reached for a lighter on the mantelshelf and backed towards the door. 'You're all going to burn in hell. Where all men deserve to go!'

She flicked the lighter into flame. 'Good-bye!'

But suddenly through the door rushed Morag, crashing into Izzie's midriff and propelling her to the floor in a near-perfect rugby tackle. The lighter arced through the air, to fall on Dr Wattana's prone body, where it ignited the alcohol with a whump.

'No you don't, you sick bastard!' Morag cried, attempting to pin Izzie down. But in a trice Izzie head-butted the sergeant who recoiled for a moment, blood streaming from her nose. And in that instant Izzie Frazer reversed their positions. She manoeuvred herself astride Morag and began pounding her head with her fists.

Torquil seized the opportunity to struggle onto his knees. Somehow he had to do something to help his sergeant.

The flames were engulfing the dead Dr Wattana and threatening to leap across the floor to absorb Neil Ferguson and Torquil in a fireball.

Angus MacLeod was screaming and Morag was grunting in pain as she continued to take a pounding from the maniacal Izzie Frazer.

Then the Padre entered, a six-iron in his hands. With a single well-aimed swipe he connected with the side of Izzie's head and she collapsed on top of Morag. 'God forgive me!' he muttered, staring momentarily heavenwards. 'But she shouldn't have been trying to hurt my friend.' Then in a trice he had pulled a blanket from the settee and began trying to beat the flames.

'It's no use, Lachlan,' Torquil cried, 'we need to get everyone out.' He had made it to his feet and turned his back to his uncle. 'Get a knife and cut me free and I'll help.'

The Padre went into the kitchen and returned instantly with a bread knife. He sliced through Torquil's bonds and together they pushed Izzie aside and pulled Morag free. Lachlan carried the stunned Morag out while Torquil tried to help Neil Ferguson up.

The flames jumped from Wattana's body igniting the peatreek and spreading instantly across the room. They engulfed Neil Ferguson's legs and Torquil's clothes.

'Come on!' Torquil screamed, dragging the professor out the door and out through the kitchen. He threw him to the ground and followed by throwing himself down. 'Keep rolling over, Neil! Try and smother . . . '

The Padre and Morag immediately sprang to help, pulling off coats and sweaters and trying to stifle the flames. It seemed to take forever, but finally the flames were out, leaving clothes and flesh badly burnt.

Looking back, the cottage was already blazing furiously, the doorway now an impassable wall of flames.

Angus MacLeod was screaming his head off, in fear and in pain.

'We must be able to reach him — them!' gasped Torquil.

And then suddenly there was the noise of breaking glass and a nerve-jangling screaming. They ran round the side of the house in time to see a fireball running from a window and racing towards the *Unicorn*.

'There he goes! I'll get him!' cried Torquil, setting off at a sprint. The smell of burning rubber and flesh was awful. Yet screaming in agony, Izzie Frazer made it to the boat.

'Get in the water! It's your only chance!' Torquil screamed.

But the fireball that was Izzie Frazer ignored him. Probably past all sentient thought, it stood teetering on the boat, the rubber wetsuit burning brightly and bubbling, sending out billowing black clouds.

The explosion as the flames ignited a petrol drum was deafening. Torquil was thrown to the ground where he lay with his hands over his head as the debris from the boat cascaded around the area.

A few moments later, once the detritus settled, he rolled over onto his knees. Just in time to see the roof of the House of the Bard collapse. Angus MacLeod had stopped screaming.

* * *

Superintendent Lumsden had been furious upon hearing that Sergeant Morag Driscoll had gone without leaving any message. But when he received the telephone call and the brief report about the events at Ranald Buchanan's house he mobilized the necessary help. He was enough of a policeman to realize that a result was a result. Apart from which, he had quickly understood that Genevieve Cooper was no serial killer.

The sight of the burning ruin of *Tigh nam Bàrd* sickened everyone. The fact that it had been impossible to save Angus MacLeod left everyone with a heavy heart. PC Ewan McPhee felt particularly unwell when he heard of how he had been duped by the killer.

'She — she used me, Piper. I am so sorry.'

Torquil had patted his friend and constable on the arm. 'We'll talk about it all later, Ewan. Right now I think that the professor and I need a bit of medical attention.'

'And don't forget your sergeant,' Lachlan added.

Torquil put an arm round Morag's shoulder. 'How could I ever forget the woman who saved my life?'

'It was the Padre,' Morag said as Ewan phoned for Dr McLelland. 'He brought me on that evil old Red Hunter of his. He almost did for us both on some of those bends.'

A whirling noise sounded from a distance away and a few moments later a Bell 429 helicopter, emblazoned with the Scottish TV logo, broke through the mist, hovered overhead, then landed in the pathway behind the West Uist police Ford Escort. The doors opened and Donna Spruce and her camera crew climbed out and advanced towards them, bending low under the gyrating helicopter blades.

Superintendent Lumsden broke away and hobbled over on his crutches to meet them. He talked with her for a few moments then turned and came over to Torquil, Morag and the Padre.

'A word with you, Inspector McKinnon,' he said, a half smile playing across his lips. And drawing Torquil aside he went on in hushed tones. 'I have explained that we have solved the whole affair, but I have not told them all the details. I said that we need to complete our investigations first.'

'Our investigations, Superintendent Lumsden?' Torquil queried. 'I understood that I was suspended.'

Lumsden snorted dismissively. 'You have been reinstated, inspector, with a clean copy-book. Clearly you've got information that I don't know about yet, so I look forward to reading your report ASAP. But for now I want you to come and give an impromptu interview with me. I'll lead, but you back me up. The Division can come out of this pretty well, I think, all things considered.'

'Apart from the fatalities.'

Lumsden bit his lip. 'McKinnon, you're a maverick, but I think you might have the makings of a good officer inside you. Play ball with me and I'll play ball with you. Now come on, let's do this TV thing.'

'Was that an apology, sir?'

'I suppose so. But just one other thing. Never call me a prat again!'

Torquil shrugged. 'As long as you don't behave like one.'

Purple patches formed on the superintendent's cheeks and he seemed to consider his words for a moment. He nodded his head slowly, then whispered, 'I think we understand each other, McKinnon.'

'I think we do, superintendent.'

* * *

Later that evening, after a simple meal of cold roast pheasant and a bottle of good claret, the Padre and Torquil sat on either side of the fireplace in the sitting room of the manse.

'It's been a hell of a day, laddie,' the Padre remarked as he stuffed tobacco into his briar. 'But at least we know the truth now.' He shook his head in disbelief. 'I always thought of Ranald Buchanan as a bit of a rogue, but I would never have thought him capable of what he did.'

'Which do you mean, Lachlan? Of child abuse or of selling his own daughter's child, his grandson?'

'All of it. He screwed up their lives, didn't he?'

Torquil sipped his wine. 'I think that young Archie Buchanan must have had a hell of a life. My guess is that he was so traumatized by his abuse as a child that he had developed a disgust of being a male himself. And that was why he had gone off to Thailand and had a sex change and cosmetic surgery by Dr Wattana. It was ironic that Angus MacLeod had been pumping money into Wattana's clinic.

'And later, when he wheedled the truth out of his stepmother, Angus MacLeod's sister, he must have snapped. And worked out a plan to kill all the people he felt were responsible for his real mother's fate.'

The Padre had puffed his pipe into life. 'Those people being Ranald Buchanan, Angus MacLeod and his father — Neil Ferguson.'

'And all because of a mix-up with the programmes at the Gathering, Fiona ended up in the wrong place at the wrong time. Neil Ferguson was supposed to meet Izzie on the crannog. And after she had disposed of him I expect that Angus MacLeod would have been next.'

'And poor Wattana also happened to be in the wrong place — on West Uist that is.'

Torquil nodded. 'The fall-out from all this will be considerable. There's bound to be an exposè of Wattana's clinic and an investigation of all the investors and the clients that were treated. The blackmarket in organ transplantation needs to be brought out into the open.'

'And you think Roland Baxter and Angus MacLeod knew about it?'

'I have little doubt, Uncle.'

The Padre nodded. 'I am sorry that Angus MacLeod lost his life, but I have little sympathy with Roland Baxter. A politician needs to be squeaky clean.' He puffed on his pipe for a moment, then asked, 'But what about Genevieve Cooper? There is no doubt, I suppose, she killed Allegra McCall?'

Torquil bit his lip. 'I'm afraid not. She was a desperate woman and she'd drunk too much. Apparently she'd gone to ask Allegra for help, but saw the watch and on the spur of the moment had the idea of stunning and robbing her. It seems completely out of character. She didn't mean to kill her. I'm guessing she'll go down for manslaughter.'

'And Izzie — or Archie Buchanan has gone, too. A dreadful way to go. Burning to death and then being blown to bits.'

Torquil unconsciously laid a hand on his own heavily bandaged leg, which Dr Ralph

McLelland had treated that afternoon. 'I don't know how it will affect Neil Ferguson. Apparently he'd been receiving letters from Izzie for some time. He'd thought they were the work of a crank, yet there was enough in them to have him both intrigued and a bit wary.'

'So he knew nothing about Izzie?' Lachlan queried.

'Nothing until she told him that he was her — or his — father. And that she was going to kill him. I think he's going to need pretty intensive counselling.'

The Padre looked concernedly at his nephew. 'And how about you, laddie? How can I help you?'

Torquil pushed himself to his feet and pointed to the two Silver Quaichs at either end of the mantelpiece. 'By having a drink with me. Shall we put them to their true purpose, Lachlan? A dram for Fiona.'

And a few moments later, with their quaichs charged, they saluted each other and drank to the memory of Fiona Cullen and what might have been.

Other titles published by
The House of Ulverscroft:

THE GLASS WALL

Clare Curzon

When Ramón witnesses someone plunging to their death from seven storeys up, instead of phoning the emergency services, he heads straight for the apartment from which the woman has fallen. Superintendent Mike Yeadings and his Thames Valley team investigate the death, and the complexity of their enquiries deepens when they discover further mysteries behind the glass wall of the luxury penthouse. Meanwhile, Dr Keith Stanford gazes up from the street below, the glass wall framing the woman he must love in silence whilst his sick wife plays her suicidal games to keep him beside her.

THE LYING GAME

Maxine Barry

After serving thirteen years for a murder she didn't commit, Oriana Foster returns to her home village with only one purpose in mind — to find the real killer of Rollo Seton. With her, she brings Connor O'Dell, a good-looking bodyguard for when things get rough. But it is Lowell Seton, younger brother of Rollo and the love of Oriana's life, who quickly becomes the greatest danger — to her heart. And when Connor falls for Mercedes Seton, Oriana's former best friend, things are in danger of totally falling apart. For the killer now has other victims in mind . . .

DEATH CALLED TO THE BAR

David Dickinson

In 1902, Queen's Inn is the most fashionable of London's Inns of Court. On 28th February, at a Queen's feast, senior barrister Alexander Dauntsey collapses into his soup and dies of poisoning. Soon afterwards, his friend Woodford Stewart is shot dead, and Lord Francis Powerscourt is summoned to resolve the matter of the murdered barristers. His investigation takes him to Calne: a mysterious country house where the past is boarded up and treasures lie hidden beneath dustsheets. Powerscourt, with a list of suspects, pursues the murderer through an increasingly dangerous spiral of events.